Hiding Away

3rd in the Beachside Romance Series

Carrie Thorne

Also by Carrie Thorne

A Demon Hunter Romance

Six

Wildest

Changed

Echo

Fury (TBD)

Foothills

All the Days After

The Next Day

A Day Late

A New Day

About Yesterday

280 Days (2025)

Day Dreaming (2026)

Again Tomorrow (TBD)

Days of Summer (TBD)

A Beachside Romance Series

Chasing Forever

Running Home

Hiding Away

Standalones

The Christmas Bet: A Double Feature Christmas Standalone.

Enjoy free books, first looks,

review team access,

and occasional hellos from Carrie?

Let's do this: carriethorne.com/newsletter

For Grummy. I miss her every day. She always finds the language in my books a bit more graphic than she's comfortable with, the print a bit small, but she is and has always been my fiercest supporter in all things. Not to mention, she's a diehard romance novel fan, since the early days of the original boddice-rippers (I still have a few of her old favorite paperbacks on my bookshelf).

1

In. Out.

Inhale. Exhale.

One. Two. Three. Natalya lowered her gaze, slowly raising her lids as the headlights faded down the dark lane of uppity suburbia.

Now. Four strides and a leap, her heart pounded in rhythm with each step. Like a coiled hinge, she rappelled off the tree, fluid as she caught the branch and swung over. Weightless until the moment of impact.

Feet turned out, the wobble threatening to shake her off like a dead leaf, her arms spread as she rose to stand. One foot in front of the other, she advanced along the branch, legs vibrating in rhythm with its rebellion of her presence.

Knees bent, she vaulted and laced her hands around its elder above. Hand over hand, her gloves sticking like a lizard with each movement, she eased over the top of the fence.

Breath held, she dropped in a silent freefall; knees bent, body shifting as she absorbed the impact. Twelve meters to the house. Scanning the manicured back yard, Natalya froze behind the nearest topiary and ensured the area was clear.

With precise strides, she sprinted over the squishy lawn. Nearing the building, she released off the last step and clung to the wide iron downspout. Climbing swiftly, hand over hand, foot over foot, she reached the third floor.

Shuffling steps below shattered the still of the night, thunderous to her ears although truly nothing more than a murmur within the empty property. She glued her body to the wall. The guard sauntered across the shadowy lawn. He turned left, then right, pulled out his flashlight and spun it like a cowboy practicing his quickdraw. With a peppy twist of his knee and a rhythmic head tilt back and forth, the boogying guard spun and continued his patrol.

Smirking, Natalya waited until he rounded the far corner of the mansion.

Okay, focus. Two meters to the window; too far. The wall was smooth as glass, no way to scale it. Above, the overhang was solid stone. Fueled with the adrenaline of uncertainty, she drew in a long breath as she recalculated her route.

Climbing to the top of the downspout, well above her target, she moved her sticky-gloved grip to the ledge and shuffled her hands until she hung above the window.

Closing her eyes for another count of three, she let out a careful breath. Loosening her fingers, she dropped.

With one hand, she caught the window overhang, her feet just touching the window ledge. Heart leaping into her throat, she swallowed the panic of the close call.

Okay. Made it. That wasn't so bad.

Leaning down, she peered in the window and scanned the room. Empty. The owner was out for the night at a charitable event. Ha. As if. Either siphoning the funds or finagling a selfish tax write-off.

Or so she suspected. Not her job to care.

Okay, so she wasn't exactly Robin Hood herself. She was just here for the data. Correction, she was here for the fat paycheck.

While her peers were muddling through their freshman year at college or earning pennies interning for their parents' companies or gaining life experience through volunteer programs, Natalya was making hand over fist. A few more jobs, and she would be set up for the next few decades. For life, really, if she invested well. She wasn't one for extravagance anyway, not like her parents. Give her a beach house, a camera, and some privacy. Maybe a fast car. Otherwise, that's it. No fancy parties or expensive dogs or... topiaries.

Pulling out her phone, she punched in a series of codes and held the device up to the locked window and initiated the program she lovingly called, *Open Sesame*. Not very clever, but it was better than her second choice of *B&E*. And... click. Okay, so the electronic lock didn't actually click, but the light did flash green.

Sliding her fingers into the crack, she pulled. Tugged. Ground her teeth and heaved.

Argh. The stupid window was jammed; she was not going in through the ductwork again. She may be petite, but the resulting claustrophobia still ate at her. Carefully squatting down on the narrow ledge, she squinted... and the window had been painted shut. Who did that, anyway? Slackers.

With her pink pocketknife, she sliced through the dried paint, closed it, and slipped it back into her pocket. Bingo. The window slid open without further argument.

In the midnight blackness of the room, she crossed to the computer. With her gloved fingers, she fired up the slick PC. Connecting her device, she ran her program. She was tempted to tap her foot and hum while she hacked the system, but that would be too droll.

Finally.

On the home screen of the asshole's PC, she dug for the files she was looking for. Huh, this must be it. What kind of idiot names their illegal deeds folder *Eyes Only*?

Encrypted, but retrieval was all her employers were paying her for. If they wanted a full hack, they'd have to dish out a hell of a lot more. Not that she even wanted to know what tripe these politicians were trying to dig up on each other.

With a few quick keystrokes, she loaded the file onto her data card. They'd wanted her to start sending everything to the cloud immediately, but she knew better.

It was almost too easy. Natalya loved her job. And she was damn good at it. Ought to be after all the uppity private academies her parents had shoved down her throat since she was in preschool, the years of gymnastics. Joke was on them when she didn't make the Olympic team, when she used all those advanced programming classes for theft rather than getting on at a high-profile tech company like her instructors had dreamed.

Quickly shutting off the computer, not leaving a trace, she climbed back out the window. No sign of the guard below. Perfect.

Shit, how was she going to get down? Well, a few hundred thousand was worth risking a fracture or two.

Lowering so she dangled from the ledge by her fingertips, she let go to slide down the wall to the second-story window below. Slipping with the full force of gravity, the slick wall not providing a scrap of friction, she swallowed a squeal and scraped her gloved hands in a fruitless attempt to slow the freefall.

Landing on the overhang with a thud, balancing precariously on her toes that screamed from the impact, she held her breath and quickly crept to the side. Okay, that was a terrible idea. Pulse pounding through her limbs, her stomach roiling at her stupidity, she clung to the wall as she calmed down enough to figure out how the hell she was getting down the last two stories.

Louder than the ringing in her ears, resonating through the window, she heard a blood-curdling scream.

Still running on the adrenaline of the near fall to her death, the terror in the next room sent her heartrate through the roof. Sealing her eyes shut, she couldn't look. Blinded by fear the unknown threat, she held tight, hoping she was concealed enough to not attract the sort of attention that could trigger such a terrified sound.

Grinding her teeth, she kicked herself for being the spoiled brat. Dammit, someone was in danger.

Easing over, ignoring her trembling lower lip, she peeked in the room. Lights illuminated the opulent guest bedroom.

Dressed in a formal tuxedo, the owner of the house shoved a woman inside. He slipped off his jacket and laid it neatly on a chair, then rolled up his sleeves without a care for the woman stumbling backwards, catching herself on the bed.

Bracing herself against the fluff of the bedding, the woman snarled, "You're a monster."

"Sometimes." He strolled toward her, cracking his neck and rolling his shoulders like he was settling in for a casual chat.

"Please." Nowhere to go, the woman scanned the room like a mouse surrounded by traps. His indolent approach might almost seem seductive, but the menace in his eyes told a different story. Head held high, the woman took a deep breath and wrapped her hands around her middle. "I worked for you for ten years, but I can't do this anymore. I'll leave quietly. You'll never hear from me again."

"You're right. I won't." He drew a handgun from his back waistband and shot the woman so fast, so carelessly. The woman's head wrenched back, her body following from the sheer force of the blow, blood trickling from her skull as she instantly lay lifeless on the bed.

Natalya's vision darkened as she so violently comprehended the true meaning of the phrase, *in cold blood*. Nausea clenched her stomach into a jagged knot. Panic rocked through her; she shook her hands to wake them back up, the numbness coating into her bones.

Inhaling one, two, three. Out four, three, two, one.

Carefully pinning herself to the wall, she ensured she wouldn't be seen.

Scanning the area, she searched for a quick exit. If not for her own safety, she needed to do what she could for the dead woman.

The guard was nowhere in sight. The bedroom light flicked off.

Two floors up, garden mulch below. Lowering herself so she dangled from the window ledge, she dropped to the ground.

Razorblades spiked through her feet, her knees as she hit the ground. Steadying herself, checking the sightlines, she took off across the yard. Sprinting along the fence, she aimed for a boulder, the highest point along the fence line. She rocketed atop a boulder and used the momentum to vault over the fence.

Landing on the other side, she rolled when she hit the loose gravel over asphalt. Ignoring the ache in her hip that would be black and blue, the limp as she shook off the impact, she eased to her feet and took off down the street. Rocks imprinted into her hands, she brushed them against her pants with each stride.

Holding it all in, not the time to collapse, she kept up the agonizing pace until she reached her concealed car. Sweat beaded on her forehead, breath refusing to slow in the safety of her car, she edged out of the shadows and hauled her ass home without breaking a single traffic law.

Her adrenaline plummeted, hollowing out her gut as she finally turned up the final hill toward home. She rolled into her usual spot in the alley carport behind the house, then quickly changed into innocent looking jeans and a t-shirt, tucking her black gear under the seat.

Forcing a cheerful smile, just in case, she strolled across the backyard. Lifting and sliding, she jimmied open the glass door.

Holding back the terror, the tears; just a few more seconds and she could crash on her bed and let it all out. If her parents wondered at the red eyes in the morning, she'd claim it was a boy. Not the mangled skull of the woman she'd seen murdered, her blood seeping into the blankets.

How could she call the police? What would she say, *While I was burgling this asshole, I saw him murder someone?*

"Welcome home, darling." Her dad's voice dripped with sarcasm. He sat at the foot of the stairs, his broad shoulders taking up the path, his stern expression sending all the adrenaline that had detoxed from her blood straight back into her veins.

"Dad. Hey." She forced the angsty teen head flip she'd rehearsed so many times when her parents would ask about her future or her friends. It had come pretty naturally since blowing it at the Olympic trials, but tonight... she wanted to curl up in a ball and wish it all away, but getting past her dad was no easy hurdle.

"Have fun?"

"Yeah. I know, I shouldn't sneak out." She bobbed her head up and down as she struggled to keep her shit together.

"No, you shouldn't. Where were you?" His dark eyes drilled into hers. Lucky thing he'd taught her well, smooth talking bigshot that he was.

"With friends."

"What friends? From what your mom tells me, you haven't talked to any of your friends since graduation."

"You're right. I talked to Nel earlier, and a few of them were in town for the weekend." Couldn't he just give her a break? She'd been the perfect daughter, the perfect student, the perfect athlete... until it had all come crashing down.

"When are you going to realize how important your future is? I can get you an entry level clerical position if you truly need to put off college. It's not too late; I can make a few calls and get you into any Ivy League you want." His eyes softened.

"I know. It's been a weird night and I'd like to sleep on it. How about I think it over and we can talk more tomorrow? I was considering going overseas, you know, travelling a bit before college?" The night was crashing down around her, and she needed to get out of there before she lost it.

"Sure darling, let's talk more tomorrow." He rose from the stairs and pulled her in for a bear hug like when she was a little girl.

What the hell? Heart thundering in her chest, she feared he could tell that "weird" was a massive understatement. For a man that hugged so rarely, the overdue affection worried her more than getting caught. Like he was planning a full interrogation tomorrow, or he was buttering her up for something big. The manipulative warmth certainly worked on her mother, who never seemed to anticipate, or maybe not care about, the inevitable duplicity.

She bit her lips together to block the waterworks from starting. The hug worked; she wanted to tell him everything, only holding back because she knew he'd flip if he found out about how much trouble she'd gotten herself into, probably even more than her career choice.

A jarring chime bellowed from the doorbell. Stiffening, she struggled to catch her breath as her heart leapt out of her chest.

Deep creases formed in her father's brow as he scowled at the door. He moved to open it.

"No, wait—" She grabbed his arm to stop him, unsure if it was the cops or the psycho murderous asshole that had found her. Shaking her off, he swung open the door.

Two men in bullet-proof vests and dark blue jackets with FBI printed in big yellow letters stood outside, holding up their badges. "Special Agents Huong and Dawson."

Natalya shrunk back. Agent Dawson looked barely a few years older than she was; not intimidating like she would have imagined as his eyes landed on her. He flashed her a mournful smile. "We need to talk." Must be the good cop.

Her father's head whipped around, and his eyes grew wide as he assessed her petrified expression. "Weird night, huh?"

"Alone," the agent clarified. His partner, Agent Huong, quite the opposite with silver hair, eyes creased from seeing too much, yet equally *safe*, not the bad cop so far, held back in silent observation.

"She's my daughter."

From just outside the doorway, Agent Huong leaned to make eye contact around her father and raised an eyebrow. "How old are you?"

Exhaling heavily, crossing her arms so they couldn't see how bad she was shaking, she said, "Nineteen."

He shrugged casually. "I'm going to need you to come with us."

Shit. She flashed back to the woman bleeding out on the bed, her brains splattered across the damn blankets. Natalya should be relieved; she was doomed to spend the rest of the night worrying over whether to do the right thing for the woman murdered in front of her eyes, risking prison herself, or keep quiet and think about the stupid Ivy League her father promised... without anyone ever knowing the dark secret she carried. At least now the decision was made for her. "Okay." She nodded, swallowing the bile that burned her throat, envisioning her orange jumpsuit.

No. She righted her posture and faced the FBI guys. Whatever her crimes, this woman deserved vengeance.

Shoving her hands in her pockets, she thought about the data. She was willing to bet whatever she'd stolen would incriminate Peterson, but if he was already going to be arrested for murder? Okay, so maybe she could be a little selfish and *not* add to her prison sentence. Or, better yet, she'd have an ace up her sleeve if it came down to it. No one needed to know. "Can I go grab a jacket first?"

Pushing past her father, Agent Huong gestured for her to lead the way. He nodded, an apologetic smile breaking through his poker face. "Of course, let's go."

The FBI agents followed her up the stairs, her father nipping close at their heels. He growled, fists balled at his sides as he spewed threats. "I'm calling my attorney. You are not taking my daughter from her home in the middle of the night."

Her mother came tearing out of the bedroom, clinging to her bathrobe as she wrapped it around her silk pajamas, her voice weak as she demanded, "What? No." She shook her head back and forth, her sleepy curls swishing over her face as she struggled to catch up, the waterworks already flooding down her face as she stood stupefied in the hallway.

While they were distracted, heart thundering in her throat, Natalya slipped into her bedroom and into the closet. Reaching up on her tiptoes, she slid the data card into a crevice between the sheets of drywall over the inside of the closet door. Quickly lowering and turning, she grabbed the nearest coat from its hanger.

Dawson appeared a moment later. "Better grab a few changes of clothes while you're at it."

She nodded softly as she calmed her breathing. "Okay." Without a word, she stuffed some basics into her old school backpack, holding back the searing hot tears that welled behind her eyes.

Maybe they weren't arresting her after all? She'd be well clothed in that orange jumpsuit if they were here to drag her to prison.

She didn't dare ask. Not in front of her father. Roaring across the house, his voice shook the walls with increasing threats of legal action, adding how he would personally destroy their careers.

She followed Dawson back out of her room while Huong was attempting to calm her parents. "We just need to ask her a few questions. She'll be safe with us."

At the end of the hall, she saw her brother's door crack open, his little face peek out. She waved gently and mouthed, *Be good okay? Love you.* Her heart broke at his big eyes, his lips turned down with a pitiful quiver. Xander was such a good kid, his nose always in a book or in front of the computer or playing in the street with the neighbor kids.

Slinking behind Huong to keep a safe distance from her parents, knowing either of them would latch on and make it worse, she followed Dawson down the stairs. Part of her wanted to throw herself in her parent's arms and never let go. Let them stand up for her and hire an attorney so they couldn't take her away.

But that would only make things worse. For everyone.

Especially the woman who was probably being buried under one of those topiaries right now, the sheets being washed or burned or buried along with her.

Enough of her recognized she'd been a selfish idiot. Crashing around her like shattered crystal, her invincibility was gone. She'd never lacked for self-esteem. Maybe she should have, just a little, and she wouldn't have dug herself in so deep in shit.

As she reached the bottom of the stairs, her father scowled past Huong, adding a disappointed head shake for her. Was it because she'd gotten herself in legal trouble, or because she was taking the high road and going with the agents?

Never showing his back to her father, Huong followed her down the stairs. Filing behind Dawson out the front door, Natalya held her head high as she accepted her fate, refusing to let her parents see her fear, her guilt, her regret. Huong reassured her parents one last time as he backed out the door, her father's expletives threatening the foundation beneath him.

Still, her parents didn't look half as crestfallen as they had when she'd blown the Olympic trials. That had been a lifetime of their investment in her, and in one failed landing, she'd proven she wasn't the gifted athlete she'd been raised to be. Her last hope at representing her country as an Olympic gymnast shattered. Disappointment. Wordless head shaking.

There was nothing she could do about fixing that day, about changing the outcome.

But she could make amends in this.

Dawson slid into the driver's seat while Huong climbed in the back next to her. Huong spoke directly to her for the first time. "We followed you from Peterson's. Natalya Haldon?"

She nodded, trying to find her voice through the frog lodged in her throat. "Yeah. That's me." She bit her lips together to hide the tremble.

"What were you doing there?"

Inhaling deeply, watching her neighborhood fade in the distance, she gritted her teeth and laid it all out, finding that attitude she'd flipped her father. "Trying to rob him."

From the front seat, she heard Dawson chuckling, shaking his head. Huong let the corner of his mouth turn up, but otherwise maintained a straight face. "I appreciate your honesty. You're not under arrest at this time."

"I'm not?"

"Look." He sighed, crossing his arms over his chest. He exuded the calm confidence of an experienced agent. "We've been tracking Peterson for a while now. Tonight, a woman went home with him, hours before he was to have left a fundraiser."

She blinked desperately but could no longer clear the watery grief from her eyes. Couldn't shake the image from flashing in her mind over and over again.

"Imagine our surprise when we watched you bailing over the fence, minutes after his arrival."

She shrugged, wiping away the tears that streamed down her cheeks.

Huong continued, "We thought you might be her at first, but she's built quite differently than you are. Tell me, do you know anything about her whereabouts?"

Swallowing the hot lump in her throat, Natalya nodded. The agents fell silent, waiting for her answer. Clearing her throat, she answered, "He shot her."

Huong's eyebrows drew together as he took in the information, but he held his calm. She glanced ahead and saw Dawson's knuckles turning white on the steering wheel. "You're sure? It was Peterson himself?"

"Yeah, it was him alright. I was climbing up the building to get to his office, but I stopped when I heard the scream at the second story window." She described the scene as precisely as she could. Of course, she mentioned she'd been on her way *up to* his office, not on her way down with stolen data. If she wasn't under arrest, she may as well not give them any reason to consider it.

"Dawson?" Huong asked his partner.

"Yeah, I know. We're not going back to the office tonight."

The drive was interminable. Where were they taking her? She didn't dare ask. Asking might give her an answer she didn't want to hear.

As they drove further into the night, her eyes grew heavy. She should be terrified. After what she'd seen, she was grateful to be in safe hands. Even if just for the night.

Boston

Scowling at the three microscopic blank lines, Aiden grimaced. Resigned, he raised his hand and caught the professor's attention. "It says to provide an explanation on the attached page if you need more room, but there is no attached page." Oh boy. Off to a great start.

"Mr. McAllister, right?"

"That's right." And now he would permanently be known as the guy who had a record. A few of his fellow law students looked his way and snickered, already done with their perfectly above-board background checks. Across the room, Ev, his ex-girlfriend, and only friend in the program, rolled her eyes and winked.

Clearing her throat, his professor sauntered toward him with a ream of white paper. "And how many pages do you require?"

"Just one, thank you, Professor."

She cleared her throat again as she slid a blank page onto his desk and strolled back down the aisle. Maybe she needed a lozenge. Or she just enjoyed passing not-quite-silent judgment.

While his classmates all handed in their paperwork and left, he scrawled the last of his *additional information*. Nothing serious, he just... come on, you couldn't tell him that every lawyer out there hadn't experimented a bit. That every one of them hadn't found themselves on the wrong side of the law a few times. He'd be willing to bet half the damn med students across campus had some condition that had turned them onto medicine from an early age. Why would it be different for law students?

Ignoring another throat-clearing from his ancient professor, he set the completed form on her desk. Slinging his backpack over his shoulder, he steadied his pace so it wasn't obvious how terrified he was that that ridiculous sheet would get him kicked out before he even started. A dirtier record than his own, maybe his buddy Chase would get him a job deep-sea diving. No way was he working on the boats at his dad's fisheries company.

As he neared the door, she cleared her throat with a finality that drilled into the last of his confidence. "Mr. McAllister?"

Cringing as he turned back, he nodded, "Yes, ma'am?"

"Nobody wants a lawyer that makes them feel judged."

He angled his head in question.

"If you've got a good head on your shoulders, a decent heart, and a window into what it's like on the client's side of the bench, you're already miles ahead of your peers." The corner of her wrinkled mouth twitched as if she was considering smiling.

"Yes, ma'am."

"And watch you're not saying *yes* all the time. Can't win them all."

He flashed her a self-effacing smile. "Yes, ma'am."

She shook her head and actually completed the smile. "Keep your nose clean."

Not a problem, there. Those days were done.

As he stepped into the hall, he found Ev with a group from the class, already making friends as he knew she would. "Hey, Aiden. If you're done brown-nosing, we thought we'd head out for drinks."

Nodding, he followed them into the sunny afternoon. Still wound up from the fucking bizarre interaction with his professor, he begged off to drop off his backpack first. In his shoebox apartment, he dumped his bag, and splashed cold water over his face.

His phone buzzed as Ev hurried him along. Rolling his shoulders, he locked up and strolled down the block to the bar. A local favorite watering hole from the looks of things; it was doggy enough to be unimposing with its dim lighting and weathered wooden tables, yet was clean and packed with familiar faces from campus.

Glancing down, he double checked that his white t-shirt was un-rumpled, the fly on his jeans was up, and he smoothed down his walnut-brown hair that he'd had trimmed a few days ago. All good. He passed through the chattering crowd and waved to Ev and her new friends. Stepping up to the bar, he ordered a pint.

A juicy-lipped blond in a lacy black top and tiny skirt that barely covered her ass sidled up next to him. "Buy me a drink?" she asked, eyes wandering along his arms like she wanted to lick him, then hanging on his lips.

Inhaling cautiously, he shook his head. "Sorry, but I'm meeting some friends."

Tucking that plump lower lip into her teeth, he couldn't tell if she was pouting or purring. "Maybe next time, then. You seem really sweet."

For all the five seconds she'd been around him? She must be an excellent judge of character. The bartender slid his beer over. Aiden replaced the frothy glass with cash and backed away. "Have a good night." He nodded to both.

Parking on the stool at the high-top table Ev had saved for him, Aiden took a welcome sip of the fizzy brew.

She raised an eyebrow. "Not your type, huh?"

He groaned. "Hell no. Hot, but looking to pull the old 'I got you through law school' divorce in a few years."

On his other side, one of the guys, Stan? Yeah, that was it. He couldn't keep track of everyone's names yet. Anyway, Stan air-saluted before downing his gin and tonic by half, "You can tell that from one come-on? Be my wingman?"

Chuckling, Aiden shrugged, "I can show you the ropes."

From across the table, he felt high heels link around his leg from another classmate. Not a word, just a wink.

Goddammit.

At his side, Ev laughed out loud and slapped him on the back. "Looks like you're the one that needs a wingman."

2

"You wanted me to come out more? I'm out. I don't know why you seem to think I was hiding. I've been working eighty-hour weeks to get my practice off the ground," Aiden snorted as he followed his sister into Winter's Tavern.

Spring was still chill on the air, but the tavern was toasty inside. Not that he would call the ambience warm; well, it was, but not in a homey way. It was more due to the relaxed atmosphere, full without being crowded, by people who were here to burn off the edge from the work week and chill with friends. Most were laughing over a beer at billiards or cozied up in cracked-leather-seated booths with surprisingly tasty comfort food.

Waving from the far side of the tavern, Maddy's friend Payson flagged them down. She was munching on a plate of nachos that must have just arrived; steam wafted from the cheesy mass. At his side, Maddy, his sister and tormentor... and, well, his best friend, waved wildly back and met him halfway. "Hey, you're normally the one dragging my ass out of the house. My turn to make sure you engage in the world of the living."

"Sure. Or, you're trying to set me up with your friend." He waved politely to Payson. She was gorgeous; silky straight auburn hair, green eyes that knew your next move before you did.

Shrugging, Maddy smiled. "Of course not, Mr. Hotshot attorney can find his own dates. Go grab us a pitcher?"

Rolling his eyes, he headed for the bar. Aiden came in with his folks on his many visits home over the years, and was always amazed how Winter, the seemingly immortal white-haired, owner-operator, seemed to know everything about everyone.

Winter waved with one hand while his other rested on the tap and filled a frosty glass with an amber brew. "I heard you were back in town. On this side of the law now." He chuckled and slid the beer to a young fisherman at the end of the bar.

Aiden didn't recognize most of the crowd, but there were definitely a few older fishermen that had worked for his dad over the years, a few others from high school. Still a tight-knit town, but Seaview had grown up in his absence. "Damn right." He parked on one of the few open stools.

Winter grabbed the next check and began to pour a pair of rum and cokes. Keeping his mind on the conversation, Aiden tried to ignore the petite blond next to him that was absorbed in a book. A whiff of coconut, and, was that lime? Something refreshing and tropical cast a compelling air around her.

Passing the next two drinks, Winter worked the queue. "Your partner in crime coming back, too? Your sister's back, you're back, maybe we'll even see the mysterious Ronan McAllister one of these days, and we'll have the whole McAllister clan."

Aiden smiled at the reference, an easiness settling over him, as clearly, anyone that knew the McAllisters considered Chase to be one of them. Hell, he'd spent more time at the McAllister home than his own, and Aiden thought of him as more of a brother than Ronan. "Chase will be back soon, actually. Not a chance in hell that Ronan will grace us with his presence anytime in the next decade, if ever."

Winter chuckled and moved to the back of the bar.

Inhaling the yumminess of the woman next to him, Aiden felt the stress of the long week fade away. His forearms settled on the bar, his feet rested on the ring at the base of the stool, his body melting, eyes struggling to stay open, and his knee accidentally bumped into her.

Like shoving his fingers in a light socket, he was electrified.

Glancing down in genuine surprise, he lost all train of thought at the view. Distressed jeans with more holes than denim, her toned, tanned leg held against his for a whisper of a moment, enough to singe his skin, the heat radiating through his veins and setting his heart into an erratic rhythm... only to pull away and leave him cold.

"Sorry," he apologized, his voice no more than a whisper, as the ability to speak had flown away with his brain.

"No worries," she muttered, her eyes not veering from her book. Clearly, she was underwhelmed by the connection that had rocked the fuck out of him.

"Good book?" Okay, so he was rusty at pick-up lines, but he was curious what could draw her in, leading her to ignore him so fully. Even if she wasn't interested, well, that was fine, but... she smelled so damn good he wanted to sit and breathe a little longer.

Exhaling sharply, he mentally smacked his forehead against the table, avoiding the exaggerated idiot gesture for real. Okay, so he hadn't been with anyone in way too fucking long... after the bar exam, grinding to get some experience with a big-city firm, and now starting his own one-man-practice and building a client base... she was way more than he could handle right now, and she didn't even care that he existed.

"Uh-huh," she murmured. Her teeth clenched tight, a wisp of blond wave fell from her messy bun and curled around the curve of her jaw. Okay, so she wasn't interested. He was good with that.

At his other side, he felt a leg press up against his left leg, not a trace of zing like he'd gotten from the woman on his right. Glancing down, a long, slender, excessively uncovered leg didn't shy away from his. Following from ankle to thigh, astonished at the vision that had parked on the stool next to him, he choked on his own tongue as he realized those weren't panties that her short skirt failed to cover. Eyes wide, his gaze shot straight up to the ceiling. Holy shit. He really, really, really... really shouldn't know that she had endured a thorough wax job a few hours ago.

"Hey." Skimpy-skirt laughed, taking her plump lower lip between her lip, pricelessly amused as if their meeting right here and now was the best, most fortuitous coincidence of her life.

"Hey." He nodded, keeping his eyes no lower than her nose.

"I was going to ask if you were new in town, but I'd know those ice blue eyes anywhere. Aiden McAllister. How are you?" Expression brightening, she seemed to relax. No longer on the prowl, but equally interested.

He stared for a moment. Lightbulb. "Kelli? Wow, how long has it been? How are you?" She'd certainly... developed since he'd seen her last.

"Great, now that you're here."

The mysterious woman on his right slid a neat pile of cash across the bar, then rose from her barstool, her shoulder brushing against his as she scooped up her backpack. Lightning bolts jolted through his arm at the light contact; she whispered a polite apology. Then without even a glance back at him, she stalked out of the tavern. Mourning the loss of the mouth-watering scent, the simple warmth of her presence, he watched her saunter out the door without a care in the world.

Clearing her throat at his side, Kelli was smiling when he turned back toward her. They politely caught up for a bit, before Winter finally passed his pitcher across the bar.

Scooping it up, he muttered, "Bye, Kelli," and escaped to join Maddy and Payson.

He slid in next to Payson. "Make a new friend at the bar?" she asked. No fire there. Pity; Payson was hot.

"Not exactly. The title *dog meat* comes to mind."

Maddy swallowed a hefty bite of gooey nachos, her voice still muffled when she said, "Are you kidding? I'll be surprised if she doesn't find her way into your bed tonight. Remember when you woke up with Lori Donner wrapped around you on your first trip home from college?"

He set the pitcher back down before pouring, afraid to spill at the memory. "Don't remind me. She cried when I told her to go home." Shaking it off, he grabbed Payson's glass first and started pouring. "I think this woman was more interested in her book than me."

Payson looked back to the bar, then back to Aiden, her brow scrunched. "Oh, you mean Natalie. No, you don't stand a chance with Natalie."

He cringed. "Oh, you meant Kelli. Yeah, been there, done that. Not interested."

"That's harsh." Payson pulled the glass from his hand and finished pouring the rest before the foam completely took over. Admittedly, he had been a bit distracted.

"Not interested in a woman that once tried to convince me she was allergic to all condoms."

"Aw. The woes of Aiden McAllister," Maddy teased with the sarcasm only a little sister by the nominal eighteen-months could produce, brushing her wild chestnut hair out of her eyes. "Do you radiate something that says, *'Jump me and I'll rock your world'* or something? Or do they see Mr. One-Night-Maximum as some sort of invitation to flash you?"

He groaned. "You know I have terrible luck with dating. Even avoiding those with fabricated condom allergies and clever come-ons, I still end up getting trapped and cheated on and... I'm just done with it all."

"Now we're speaking the same language. Why bother?" Maddy air toasted.

Green eyes flashing, Payson scowled. "Listen to you two. You sound like a bunch of whiny ninnies who had a few bad relationships and are convinced it's all a bunch of bullshit. You can't blame all your woes on partners you haven't even passed more than a few words with. Would you stop going out to eat because you'd found a hair on your food once? Or stop travelling because you hit some turbulence? The right person will change your minds in a heartbeat."

Aiden shoveled in a bite of nachos to avoid answering that one.

3

CHEERS BOUNCED OFF THE waves as the volleyball game concluded with a spike. As the shadows grew long across the shore, the Seaview Annual Beach Party shifted from toddling kids, lathered in sand-encrusted sunscreen, to grown-ups with beers and bonfires. Across the beach, Maddy and Chase were engrossed in each other, the frothy ocean waves dancing over their feet. With the heat emanating off of them, still honeymooning, Natalie was surprised the bonfire Aiden and she were sitting in front of didn't blast up to the dusky sky.

"Not in this lifetime. Not in the next. Not in the last." Aiden McAllister scowled into the heart of the flames as he sat shoulder to shoulder at her side in the sand. Natalie reached behind her and a grasped an ice-coated beer from the cooler, popping the top off before passing it over to Aiden. With an easy, "Thanks," he took a swig.

She snagged another for herself and stared at the brown bottle, scowling as she tried to recall what they were talking about. The bonfire was toasty, but his bare arm pressed against her sleeveless shoulder rose concern for her sunscreen melting off. Maybe even her toenail polish if his foot accidentally met hers again in their bare-footsy match. "Hang on. Take someone like Payson. She's tall without being taller than you, gorgeous, intelligent, successful, has good taste, and you click with her socially... but despite all that, and her perfectly perky breasts, you still never slept with her? Why not?"

Digging his beer bottle into the sand, Aiden shrugged. "I actually did go out with her once."

"What? When?"

"Maddy made us. Thought we were a match made in heaven. Undeniably, Payson is empirically attractive, and irrefutably stirring on an intellectual level, but first and foremost, we didn't connect on *that* level. We could have pushed it I'm sure, but it would have felt forced. Second, and admittedly a major factor in determining the outcome of the first conclusion, she was looking for forever. Turns out, great decision, as she and Ronan are perfect for each other. It would have been really weird if he lapped up my leftovers."

"No wonder your reputation is, well... I'll just say scandalous. Disgusting might be more apt." The corner of her mouth turned up in smirky amusement. It hadn't been easy, but she usually managed to keep her attraction to him tamped down, so neither he nor anyone else knew that stupid torch burned bright.

Seriously, Natalie hadn't wanted a police officer for a friend in the first place, but, like Payson, Maddy was a tenacious friend. Adding a lawyer to that list pushed her past her social comfort level. Criminals did not befriend those who upheld the law. Not wise.

Yet here they were, playing footsy and shoulder-snuggles by the fire, right on track to rekindle what they'd started at the town beach party last year.

"Yours isn't any better, you know that, right?"

"You're a walking thirty-something-male-commitment-phobe stereotype. How is that better than my introversion?" Natalie frowned, then turned to dig through the picnic basket for the bottle opener. Where had she put it in the last sixty seconds?

"Hey, it's not about commitment-phobia, but about the fact that I'm content with what I have. Work, friends, family, hometown. All good." He reached around her and snagged the bottle opener from under her leg and popped the top off her beer.

She took it from his hand and offered an easy, "Thanks," then added, "You forgot about sex."

"I didn't *forget*, I just didn't want to sound like an ass."

Under a blanket of sand, his foot submarined under hers and rescued her from the gritty grave she'd dug herself into. In the chaos of the playful movement, somehow their legs intertwined. Melting was no longer a worry; full ignition was far riskier as her slick-shaved leg looped over the course hair of his.

Wow, that man had amazing legs. Had she ever thought of a guy's legs that way? She certainly would *now*. Nice calves; that line that declared he knew how to *run* was well defined, and even his feet were actually appealing. And she hated feet.

Dammit, nice moves, too. His reputation was warranted, as she well knew. When did footsy become equivalent to foreplay? "Sex is an important part of life, but it doesn't make you sound like an ass. Stating your disinterest in a woman on the primary reason that she is only interested in pursuing a serious relationship? That comment dug the hole deep enough on its own." She didn't move her leg from his.

She should. Instead, she found the inner side of their ankles linking and teasing, their feet necking where their mouths shouldn't.

How often did she get to indulge? Once as the aspiring athlete, regrettably with a naïve teammate, then rarely as the criminal mastermind. Occasionally, as the mysterious woman without a past, finding a partner for the night was a well-deserved reward.

Then there was that night she'd relived in her dreams every night for the last year.

Where Aiden suffered from commitment-phobia, Natalie might actually enjoy committing to *something*, but safety came first; for her and those she let into her bubble, unwittingly or not. The lease on her apartment was daunting enough.

Taking a slow swig of her beer, she savored one long gulp. As the suds coated her mouth, her throat, she felt Aiden's eyes on her. Gliding her tongue over the crease of her lips, she licked away a stray drip. Turning her head, she found his icy blue eyes fixated on her mouth.

Okay, so he wasn't the only one with moves. Not that she'd tried them out on many guys besides Aiden, but he was an appreciative target. His gulp was more audible than hers, somehow music to her ears that set her pulse dancing a chipper tune, wanting that open mouth pressed against her throat, his tongue grazing until he found her ear and pulling, nipping… Flirting was far from her strong suit, but as a constant student of life, she was willing to practice. And Aiden was, well… Aiden made it too easy.

Ice water splattered over the bare skin of her tank-topped back, the chill rushing over her spine. Turning her head, she laid eyes on the guilty culprit.

"Sorry," Chase winced, pulling out a pair of beers from the cooler, brushing off the remaining ice particles that had followed.

"No worries." She smiled up at him, ignoring the chill drips skating down her skin. "It's too damn hot around here anyway."

He dropped to the sand at Aiden's other side. "Where's Ronan? Thought he and Payson were bringing the dogs?"

The cooldown was well timed. Probably for the best. She'd played with more than her share of fire, and Aiden was trouble she didn't need. Sliding her foot out from their entanglement, she defiantly, subtly informed him it wasn't happening, no matter how good his moves were tonight.

She turned and looked up the beach. Strolling toward them, Payson wore a blue summer midi dress that looked delicate on her pregnant body. Not that Payson could ever look anything but pretty. The six-month belly made her curves that much more romantic. Grinning at her side, their hands linked in an affectionate declaration of partnership, Ronan carried an ice chest like it didn't weigh a thing.

He dumped the cooler and grabbed a pair of drinks from behind Natalie. Maddy walked up the beach after chatting with a group of women Natalie had begrudgingly met last year. She shouldn't say *begrudging*, that wasn't exactly true. She didn't like meeting new people, hence moving to the hidden coastal town of Seaview. The quiet was nice, but she hadn't predicted how grossly the anonymity would be lacking.

While Payson laid out a picnic blanket next to Natalie, Maddy dropped to the sand next to Chase. Handing Payson a La Croix and joining her on the blanket, Ronan nodded across the fire to his twin. "I thought you were on patrol tonight?"

Running a hand through her hair, Maddy took a disgusted whiff of her own skin and scowled. "You didn't hear? I figured Chase had texted you all pictures of how ridiculous I looked when I stumbled home this morning. I got called in on a B&E last night."

Chuckling, Chase pulled his phone out. "Damn, I got so distracted cleaning you up, I forgot to send it."

Maddy grumbled, "Might as well get it over with."

A buzzing chorus of incoming texts echoed around the fire. Aiden checked his and found the incoming pic of his sister covered in chocolate syrup, topped with rainbow colored sprinkles, standing pitifully in the middle of their driveway, with her head down and her lower lip turned out in a pathetic pout.

Pure enjoyment of his sister's predicament rumbled through his chest until he burst out in uncontrollable laughter.

She huffed, "Sometimes, I miss the drug deals from Seattle. Small town policework is not for the faint of heart. That stuff got everywhere. I'm still sticky."

Chase wrapped his arm around her middle, nibbling along her neck. "But you taste so damn good."

"Come on guys," Aiden cringed. "I'm still weirded out that you two had the hots for each other for forever, all the while, I thought we were Han, Luke, and Leia. Shit, we were. Except you two were Han and Leia and I was oblivious C-3PO."

Maddy nudged him. "Okay, fine, we were Harry, Ron, and Hermione... wait, same deal." She feigned a scowl of concentration. "Okay, wait—"

Aiden flipped her off. He slid his phone back in his cargo pocket.

Musing, Chase pulled Maddy even closer. "I always wanted to be Kirk, Spock, and McCoy, but you two made us Larry, Moe, and

Curly." Subtly, but obvious for anyone paying attention, Chase drifted his hand under Maddy's shirt and traced his fingertips over her skin.

Aiden managed to mask his... wait, jealousy? *That can't be right.* Dammit, not for the married shit, but that they were getting some on a regular basis. *Sure, whatever.*

He masked whatever was going through his head with sarcastic humor. "Come on, at least the *Three Amigos.*"

From out of absolutely nowhere, Nat was scrolling through his phone. When had she snagged it from his pocket? Seriously, he was fused to her side from when he'd nudged her earlier and was still stuck to her like a high-powered magnet.

And he was very, very aware of her every movement. Of her unique, summery scent. Somehow, she always smelled like a romantic getaway on an isolated Caribbean island. Not that he'd imagined her there with him on a nearly nightly basis for... longer than he cared to admit.

"Nah. *The Good, the Bad, and the Ugly.*" Nat looked up at him and didn't bother to hide the shit-eating grin.

"Chase is an ugly son of a bitch," he countered.

"Nice try." She raised her eyebrows in amusement, then opened to the picture Chase had texted him. Wait, how did she know his passcode? "I'd heard about the break-in at the ice cream shop. Did you catch them?" she asked, holding back her chuckle more successfully than Aiden had. He couldn't miss her biting her lip as she masked her mirth with a sympathetic nod.

Her amusement renewed his, and he nearly lost it again. Nudging her in the side, he was still shaking with humor and silently dared her to lose her calm.

As she swallowed a choking sound, her hand reached behind him and bit a tiny pinch into his side like a bee sting.

Maddy glared at him and turned her attention to Natalie, who maintained the straight face remarkably well. "I think I'll be able to laugh about it someday. Not yet. I'm never, ever eating chocolate syrup again." Glancing behind her, Chase nodded to the chocolate syrup poking out of the cooler.

Maybe they could still be the *Three Amigos*. How had he ever doubted how awesome it would be to have his best friend marry his sister? No annoying new addition to the family, both were happy, and he and Chase got to see each other way more often. Just had to put up with the PDAs, which, admittedly, tended to be sweet rather than excessive.

Maddy flashed him a glare as she continued her story. "And, yes, we caught them. As expected, we found a group of fifteen-year-old kids a few blocks away, high as kites on sugar. The bellyaches hampered their escape. Guess I'm glad they're not doing drugs or harder crimes." She shook her head helplessly. Before Aiden could crack another taunt, she added, "Not to worry, I told them about a great lawyer that would absolutely take their case."

Cringing, he guzzled the last of his beer before his sister could rail him any further. "You know I can't say no." Their parents would have been thrilled if all he and Chase had been doing at fifteen were bingeing on stolen ice cream. Well, at least they didn't know the worst of the shit he'd pulled, or not even his honorable mother would have been able to protect him from prison.

Which was why he'd worked his ass off through law school and took every sucker case that came his way. Could have been him. Maybe should have been.

He felt Natalie stiffen at his side, and he turned to see what was up. As expected, her expression was bright, as if she hadn't reacted at all.

Her wide, hazel eyes told another story. He let her get away with it. This time.

Going on well over a year, and he was about done pretending he didn't notice she was hiding from something. Whenever he, or anyone else, ever tried to discern what bothered her, she either laughed it off or made some excuse to rush home. Something ate at her, and she wasn't sharing what.

As they dined on cheese-stuffed hot dogs, despite the brief lock-up, Natalie looked relaxed. Like just for a moment, she was choosing the moment over the past.

A deep sinking sensation lingered in Natalie's belly as she glared at the phone. Her mother hadn't mastered the advanced technology of texting. Her father only called on the first Sunday of each month for their structured five-minute-no-more-no-less conversation. And her brother stuck to email.

That only left one person that would be texting.

Another buzz.

Opening the text, angling her body so no one could read over her shoulder, she bit the bullet and read the damn messages.

How's my favorite witness?

Okay, maybe nothing bad. Every time Dawson texted, she feared the worst. Even though he checked in at least once a month and hadn't delivered bad news in years, she knew the day would come again. *Just another day in paradise.*

Good to hear. Be safe.

She'd been in Seaview longer than she'd planned. Grown close to these friends she didn't deserve. Who knew too much. Inside jokes. Intimate knowledge of her habits. Natalya Haldon may be off the grid, but Natalie Smith was in deep with good people.

It was a miracle she'd made it this long without anyone finding her. Every night, she told herself Peterson was locked away for a long, long time. He'd forget about her.

And it seemed he had. But that look when he'd killed that woman. He liked it.

And she had been the last witness on his list, the one with the most immediate knowledge of his crime... and the only one that had lived long enough to testify.

At her first attempt at hiding, she'd been found in Tallahassee within a week of her arrival. Even from prison, Peterson had a few loyal friends and a whole lot of fury. Learning from her mistakes, she lasted longer in Virginia Beach. Nearly a year in Newport. Blending in had been a challenge at first, but she'd learned she was actually pretty adept at accents.

Always. You too. She smiled as she looked at the time, so late on a Friday night. *And get a life.*

Long pause. *I will when you do.*

Ha. She tucked her phone back into her back pocket. While the others laughed and bantered over the course of the evening, Natalie dreamily savored in the easiness of the night, thinking how great it would be to get to keep all this. Leaning forward, she wrapped her hands around her bent legs and watched as they joked and chatted and savored the hard-earned sense of normal.

She knew it hadn't come easily for some in this group. But together... they were free and easygoing. Made her feel safe. Like her past wasn't the worst secret among them.

Lost in the roaring flames, she thought about Dawson's message. *A life*. Had she ever had one of those? Even before Peterson had both wrecked everything and saved her from prison in one dreadful act?

She'd lucked out with Dawson and Huong. Stupid kid on the radar of a globally powerful man. They'd offered witness protection, but they'd known it was more of a death trap than her disappearance.

With Huong retired, only Dawson knew her whereabouts. It had ultimately been her decision, but they'd agreed with her paranoia. Slowly but surely, they had chipped away at Peterson's contacts, but had a long way to go to cut his ties to the outside world.

A beer appeared in front of her face. Glancing to the bearer of the bottle, she found Aiden smiling at her, a mischievous twinkle in those intensely glacier-blue eyes, always warm with humor despite the subzero color.

"Thanks." She took the offered beer and gulped down the first half before stopping for a breath. Liquid courage. "Trying to get me drunk?"

"Never," he scoffed. Eyes twinkling like a movie star from the first addition of color to the silver screen, he raised his eyebrows and grinned with devious mischief. "Reduces orgasmic potential."

She shook her head, her breath caught in her throat and her ovaries poking at her in a plea rebellious to her brain.

He sipped his own beer and shifted his gaze to the glowing cinders where the flames were starting to recede. "What's up? You shut off. Missed Payson admitting she wasn't good at something."

Natalie found herself melting into Aiden's side, absorbing some of his warmth as the chill of the night blew in with the evening breeze. She sighed, eyes glued to the curious flames that licked the last of the uncharred wood. "Must be a record. Bummed I missed it."

"You ok?" His voice was soft, with a hint of gravel from an evening of laughing around the campfire smoke.

"Yeah," she responded quietly.

What was it about Aiden? He was like a truth serum or something. When she was around him, she couldn't hide. Or maybe she just didn't want to. While he was gorgeous and articulate and confident, he was also gentle and self-effacing and genuinely cared. No wonder his clients sung his praises, whether they won or lost.

As if reading her broody mood, he sat quietly at her side, following her lead. His breathing slowed and matched her contemplative rhythm. Looking up, he seemed to find something intriguing in the sky.

Natalie followed his gaze but couldn't see what he was looking at. Turning toward him to see what had captured his attention, he looked at her and she nearly ran into him for how close he was. Inches away, his eyes rested on her lips, his own slightly parted.

"Sorry," he whispered unapologetically, his heated expression morphing into that damn panty-melting grin he was so adept at.

Her eyes rolled, but the traitorous corners of her mouth curved up at his flirting. Foolishly, she didn't pull away. "Another of your infamous moves?"

"Is it working?"

Remembering herself, she grabbed her beer and took a sip to separate them. To distract herself. To do anything but let herself get lost in those eyes; being another Aiden-groupie-cliché? No thank you.

She kept her voice quiet enough the others wouldn't hear, flipping attitude. "Footsy, stargazing, discrete skin-to-skin connection. If I didn't know better, I'd say you were hitting on me."

"Only if you want me to."

Avoiding eye contact, Natalie double checked the others were well distracted before responding. "Coming back for seconds is neither of our style." She blushed, picturing his mouth joined with hers, his body pressed up against her, her legs wrapped around his hips.

"Then we'll get creative. Appetizers. Better yet, I'll bet you'd make a tasty dessert." The heat in his voice shot an electric thrill through every nerve in her body.

Chase and Maddy had been whispering across the fire, absorbed in each other as usual. Suddenly, both hopped to their feet and started their goodbyes.

Aiden looked at them like they were totally nuts. "In a hurry?"

Winking, Chase took Maddy's hand and started backing away. "Hell yeah. It's our sexiversary. As much as we'd love to stay and chat…"

Natalie bit her lip, staring off across the beach, masking her fiery blush, right as Aiden said meaningfully, "Sexiversary, huh?"

Tossing a handful of sand at him, Payson laughed, "You can't tell me the eternally horny Aiden McAllister has never heard of a sexiversary?"

He nudged Natalie's shoulder, his voice a little too familiar as he said—in front of everyone, "Did you know that was a thing?"

She shook her head, too tied up in knots to say anything.

"I guess I haven't hung around long enough to celebrate any sort of annum, but, I suppose returning for seconds on the annum would count. That's a thing I would be willing to try." He grinned, throwing back the last of his beer and tossing it behind him into the trash bag. "Nat," he announced, "Have you ever considered anything like that?"

Maddy shook her head, ignoring Chase trying to pull her away. "You know, you never did fess up to the lucky lady that brought you to suffer the walk of shame this time last year. Maybe look her up and see if she's open to celebrating a sexiversary."

Natalie tipped her head back as she chugged the last of her beer, dumped the bottle in their garbage bag and popped up to her feet. "You guys go celebrate. We'll clean this up. One of us will return your cooler later."

Maddy and Chase didn't hesitate, dashing down the beach.

Ronan nodded, "We're going to hang out under the stars a bit longer. Aiden, if you don't mind grabbing their cooler, we can get the rest."

Natalie shook her head. "Thanks. I'll grab as much as I can carry so you guys can head home and relax soon." She waved goodnight and headed up the beach toward her studio.

As she neared the sidewalk, the sound of sandy steps pounding the beach approached her from behind.

Blushing well beyond her control, Natalie let herself make eye contact this time. Those dang ethereal blue eyes twinkled with merriment... and irresistible flirtation.

"I'm not sleeping with you," she immediately clarified. She shouldn't have flirted so shamelessly tonight, but it felt so damn good. She veered away, toward the nearest trashcan.

"I didn't ask." He wasn't smiling when she turned back to him.

"But you were hoping."

"Maybe," he relented, relaxing to a smile. "Always." He adjusted the soft-sided cooler over his shoulder. "I mean, this sexiversary thing might be a worthwhile exception..."

"Aiden, I—"

"Nat, I know. I'm *mostly* kidding. Really, I don't ever want to be *that* guy, who can't take no for an answer. Despite the damn irresistible sparks that fly when you look at me like you did a few moments ago."

He walked backward a few steps ahead of her, daring her to challenge him.

Rolling her eyes, she wanted to declare that she didn't fall asleep imagining herself entangled in his arms each night. That his humor and humanity didn't make her feel so *normal* and wish for more than she could have.

Stepping off of the beach, they walked synchronously toward her apartment. Just after ten o'clock, and Beachside Avenue was still packed with revelers that had moved from the beach to the bars.

Pausing before crossing the street, she stopped in front of him. Rising to her toes, she gripped the back of his neck and pulled close until they were a breath away. "If I were to invite you up, I have no doubt we'd have a good time." She nipped his bottom lip before grazing the tip of her tongue along where she'd bit.

Groaning, he leaned in for more.

"Aren't you afraid I'll want another night? Then another? Like you said, you can't say *no*. Eventually, you'll realize we're in a *relationship*." Stepping back, she moved just out of his reach.

His cheek parked between his teeth as he chewed on that one. A drunk, arguing couple brushed between them. Aiden crossed his arms and said, "A relationship scares you even more than it does me."

A dark figure caught her attention in the distance. Aiden followed her gaze.

With a glimpse at the busy Beachside Avenue, Natalie slipped across.

She knew the dark figure was probably nothing, as it usually turned out to be nothing. But a handful of times, it hadn't been nothing. If they'd been seen looking intimate, she'd have put Aiden right in the crosshairs she lived in.

Peterson might be locked up, but he still had friends. Friends that had found her before.

And she was at the top of his shit list.

Aiden squinted, realizing something was up. Turning, he searched for the cause of her spook. By the time he looked back, she was already across the street.

Maybe he was a glutton for punishment. Maybe he was a sucker for a damsel—not that she was anything close to helpless and would sock him for implying it. But he knew she wasn't the lost cause she seemed to think she was.

Dashing across the street, he caught her just before she went inside her apartment building. "Nat, wait."

She glanced down the street again. He followed her gaze and saw nothing more than locals chatting on the sidewalks.

"I want to apologize. I'm an asshole." He shoved his hands in his pockets to avoid reaching for her. If he tried, he knew she'd run and never look back.

She didn't run. Her unnervingly mysterious green and tan eyes, like standing in the middle of a tropical forest at night, were heavy with what he hoped was regret. Yep, he really was an asshole.

"All foreplay aside, please, whatever you're hiding from... let me help."

Surprising him again, Nat scanned the streets, bit her lip on a slow inhale, then narrowed the distance between them and wrapped her hand around the back of his neck again. She pulled him down as she raised up to her toes. Before he knew it, her soft lips were pressed against his, her tongue gently teasing entry.

Dropping the cooler, he wrapped his arms around her. Heat spread through his limbs, his knees melting to mush as her tongue grazed along his, sliding deeper when she didn't pull away.

Groaning hungrily, he relished in the warmth of her mouth, sweet as the summer sun and twice as scorching.

Stars flashed across his vision as he was lost in the sensation of being *taken*. Of being wanted by Nat... without hesitation.

Like it had been the one time she'd let him in.

Well before he was ready, she pulled away. Her lips pink and plump, cheeks flushed from the kiss, her chest rose and fell as she caught her breath.

Miles behind, he tried to remember which way was up.

"My life's too complicated to celebrate things like sexiversaries," she said. As she backed away, he watched helplessly, his feet rooted to the sidewalk as she disappeared into the darkness.

Heart thundering in her chest, Natalie's feet pounded up the stairs at a fraction of the pace of her racing pulse. What was it about that man that set everything on edge? She was both completely relaxed and rigid with tension when he got close.

The man did something to her, and not just the way one hungry look turned her into a dripping puddle of melted snow. Nor the way his mouth moved over hers, sending liquid fire rushing to the tips of her extremities.

Natalie had never been one to crush lightly. A pretty face, some good abs, and a tireless wit. Aiden had those, and then some. But the way he looked at her, the way he dove in to help someone in need, his dry humor... she was crushing hard.

Aiden said he *couldn't* say no. That was a total lie. He didn't *want* to refuse anyone. Maybe it was the do-gooder lawyer in him, or the guy who had danced around which side of the law he preferred through much of his beginning that was making up for it in spades now. Another reason to not let him in.

Dashing up to her apartment, she unlocked the door and heard the familiar squeak of the hinges as she entered. She dropped her backpack onto a dining chair.

The stars shone down through her picture window. Sadly closing the blinds, just in case, she flipped on the bedside-slash-couch-side-lamp. Her apartment even smelled like home. Sea air, sand, wind, this morning's summer drizzle, and her own favorite coconut and lime scents created a hominess in a life that could so easily be dark.

Pulling off her tank, sliding her jeans over her hips, she tossed her clothes into the closet laundry bin and dragged herself in the bathroom. Twisting on the hot water, balancing it with cold from the other squeaky knob at precisely measured angles, she found the almost intolerable steaming temperature she craved. Tossing aside her lace-trimmed panties and barely-a-B-cup bra, she stepped into the narrow shower.

As the hot water rushed over her shoulders, soaking her wavy blond hair, she lathered the shampoo. Nearly reaching her clavicle, her hair was longer than she'd ever let it grow.

Leaning into the soothing spray, she let the hot water wash away the long day of... longing. What was wrong with her? For some stupid, stupid, foolishly hormone-driven reason, despite her knowledge that the yes-man was all wrong as she was entirely a no-woman, all she could think about was Aiden McAllister.

Aiden's hands on her.

Everywhere.

His lips trailing along her shoulder.

His tongue gliding over her skin, settling at her core.

His tongue flicking over her clit and tasting, drinking until she couldn't stand the heaviness of the sensation.

She dropped her head against the cold tile of the shower wall, the impact not even close to masking the sexual frustration. Dammit, not again. She really, really needed to get out of here. Before she let herself say: *yes, yes, again and again, YES.*

4

"Case dismissed." Judge Meyers pounded the gavel with a decisive crack. Rather than the expected whoops of joy beside him, Aiden heard a heavy sniffle. The pathetically empty courtroom, at least on their side, was silent as a graveyard.

Turning to his client, Aiden discovered that she was frozen, a river of tears flowing down her wrinkled cheeks. "You ok, LuAnn? It's over. You get to go home."

Pursing her lips tight, she tilted her gaze in his direction, looking down at him, despite his six-foot frame. "I guess I just didn't believe it, when you told me I had a chance."

Poor thing had called him on a last-ditch whim. From a few towns west of Seaview, she'd asked him to take her case. Because no one else would. Ever the sucker, he had been unable to turn her down. Not when she'd been arrested for, as her husband described it, *"Sending my boys into my belly with a baseball bat."*

With the sonorous resonance of a foghorn, LuAnn blew her nose with gusto, coming back to reality. Yeah, there wasn't any great mystery why no one would take her case. At six foot three inches tall, packing farmer's biceps, and as foul-mouthed as a ranch hand... well, she was intimidating. A few helpful interviews with the neighbors, coupled with the plaintiff's complete lack of medical evidence supporting his assault claim, the prosecutor's case was blasted out of the water.

Once the courtroom had cleared, dear LuAnn lumbered out alone. He knew she had friends, as he'd interviewed several, but she hadn't wanted anyone to see her humiliation firsthand. One of the stranger parts of his job, not knowing the aftermath of what he had accomplished.

As luck would have it, LuAnn was a highly successful farmer. Not that he was in it for the money, but he had just hired on a partner to his previously one-man law firm and could use a little extra cash. Sliding his papers back into his briefcase, Aiden was more than ready for the weekend.

Judge Meyers caught him as he was pulling out his phone.

Tucking the phone back into his pocket, he shook the offered hand.

"Nice work today, Aiden. When are you going to follow in your mother's footsteps and join us behind the bench?"

Chuckling, Aiden shook his head. "Give me a few decades on that one." *Or, more like, never.* Independence was awesome. Why would he want to work for, well, anyone?

Striding out to the street, he tugged off his tie and hopped in his silver Audi. Pulling his phone back out, Aiden glared at his contact list. Furious as he kept scrolling past the number he shouldn't be so drawn to, he considered calling Olivia instead, see if she was game to hang out tonight. Nah. She'd slipped him her number at the grocery store a few days ago, and she was curvy and independent and fucking gorgeous.

But he just wasn't feeling it. Like a sexy-blond-with-a badass-attitude of a thorn in his side, thoughts of Nat blocked out anyone else. That face, that body, that mysterious grin of hers had been a go-to on lonely nights for a while now, but after that kiss again last weekend, knowing she thought about that night too... yeah, he needed to find a way to get her out of his head. Just not tonight.

Glaring at his phone that was blindingly devoid of messages, he scrolled to Chase's number. Maybe Maddy would be working tonight and his best friend would be game to go out for a drink. Shooting off a quick text, he tried not to sound needy or lonely. *Maddy working tonight? Bored?*

Giving the engine an extra rev before shifting into gear, he grinned to himself. Officer Maddy McAllister—correction, Maddy Anderson—would have his hide if he floored it out of here, maybe leave a creative skid mark. His sister hadn't caught him yet but had threatened many a speeding ticket.

Resisting the urge, he headed for home. His phone chirped just as he was pulling into the narrow driveway. Trying to not respond immediately, again—sounding desperate really wasn't his thing—he slid the phone into his pocket and grabbed his briefcase to head inside. Crunching on dry gravel on his way to the side door, he took in a deep breath of the baked sand that penetrated the July breeze.

After unlocking the side door to his office, he took the stairs two at a time until he reached the door to his apartment. When he'd moved home to Seaview, a local accountant had rather conveniently been closing up shop to retire to Florida, so Aiden had jumped on the deal for the converted house just up from Beachside. The downstairs had been made into a cozy office space, and upstairs was all mancave.

He hated the term mancave. His apartment wasn't at all cave-like. Yeah, the furniture was a durable espresso leather and decorations were sparse, but he thought the picture windows, white pine floors, and cashmere throw blankets were damn classy.

Tossing his suit jacket on his bed, he gratefully changed into his weekend uniform of crisp white tee that was just fitted enough to look badass, paired with his favorite Seven for All Mankind jeans. His sister teased him for being a bit of a brand snob; 'metro' was the term she favored, but come on, he was thirty, single, and didn't answer to anyone. And he liked nice things.

Settled and having allowed a reasonable amount of I'm-not-lonely time lapse, he let himself read the text. Dammit, he couldn't lie to himself, he hadn't been playing it cool. Who wanted to admit to themselves, a *happy* single guy, that he dreaded spending another evening alone and bored? Mentally kicking himself in the ass for being such a pansy, he read the message from Chase.

A flip-off emoji.

What?

Gravel crunched under tires outside. Moving to the window, he watched as Chase's truck pulled in behind his car in the narrow driveway.

Chase and Ronan piled out of the truck simultaneously, glancing up to the window as they were clearly enjoying some joke at Aiden's expense.

Not bothering to unlock the door, Aiden knew Ronan, his younger brother by a eighteen months, would be disappointed if he did. As much as he seemed to be enjoying the quiet life, Ronan jumped on the little opportunities to keep up his CIA-acquired skills. In fact, both of his visitors could break into his apartment with little difficulty and would have been disappointed if he'd left the door unlocked. He even changed out his alarm now and again, just to keep them guessing.

He could hear them taking the steps two at a time. A few more seconds, and Ronan had Aiden's apartment door unlocked.

Both came in wearing shit-eating grins.

"Dude, we already had plans for the night." Chase raised his eyebrows as he strolled in the door.

Oh yeah. Maddy and Payson were both working tonight, miracle of miracles. Tough being the only single guy in their three-man trio. He ran a hand over his face, trying to not rub his eyes and let on how wiped out he was. "Long week."

"When you declared you wanted to set your own hours, did you really mean seventy-hour weeks?" Chase ragged him.

"Used to be eighty." Dropping onto the couch, Aiden sprawled his legs out in front of him and he melted into the soft leather. "My new partner starts on Monday. That'll take some of the load off."

Ronan shoved his hands in his pockets and wandered around the apartment before settling in. Aiden couldn't imagine how exhausting it would be, to be unable to relax and assume no one was hiding in the next room, waiting to shoot you in the head. From the kitchen, he asked, "Friend of yours from college, right? You said she was looking to slow things down by transitioning to small town law?"

"Yeah. Hell of an attorney. She'll hit the ground running. Slowing her down will a bigger problem."

Chase parked on the facing sofa across from him, his boots thunking on the wooden coffee table as he put his feet up. "Or you could just say 'no,' now and again, and not take on so many cases."

Ronan returned from Aiden's bedroom and tossed a pair of shoes to him.

Chase didn't bother whispering as he said to Ronan, "Maybe that's why he's been haranguing us to go out with him. Too tired for a booty call and can't get it up."

Rolling his eyes, Aiden didn't bother to interrupt. Knowing they weren't entirely wrong, he pulled on his Adidas as directed and stayed quiet.

Ronan motioned for the door, impatient to be on the move. "Or, maybe he's slept with them all and none will have him back again."

"Shut it," he said as he tightened his laces and dragged himself to his feet. Some lawyer he made; by the end of the week, he could hardly remember his own name.

No way he was going to tell them why he needed a friendly night out and wasn't interested in romantic company. They probably wondered if he was depressed. He preferred that over the truth, at least there were treatments for that. He pulled on his light Patagonia jacket in a nod to the cooling wind tonight and followed them out the door.

Increase the contrast a smidge. Nope, too much. Decrease the lowlights. There. Perfect.

Natalie leaned back in the booth and admired her latest masterpiece. Sometimes, she missed real photography like she'd learned in school. Dark room chemical experiments, the thrill of waiting to find out if she'd timed the exposure right. Other times, like now, she enjoyed getting to tweak her photos on the laptop until it was exactly what she wanted.

Satisfied, she took a drink of her oaky porter and savored another gooey bite of a jalapeno popper from Winter's off-the-menu snack platter he'd invented for her, after seeing her consistently leave the mozzarella sticks and pickled carrots untouched but devour the poppers, pickles, and mini quesadillas. She should head home soon, as the Friday night crowds were starting to filter in. Stuck enough in her own head, she actually found the noisy chaos soothing, but the constant comings and goings of who-knows-who were too much. Winter was awesome and didn't mind her spending a few hours working at the tavern for a change in scenery.

Not that anyone other than locals ever came in, which was why she liked the place, but she still couldn't help but watch the door and ensure the emergency exit remained clear. Lately, she'd felt edgy. Restless. As if her favorite routines, like this afternoon's editing at Winter's, were breaking the rules. Ex-criminals on the run from powerful-psycho-murderous assholes didn't get to settle into normal routines.

As the music flipped from an airy concerto to Chris Isaac's *Wicked Game*, the door swung open with a blast of evening breeze. Sensing him before she even saw him, Natalie's heart pounded erratically before plunging into the pit of her stomach with a nauseating splash. Aiden McAllister strode in like he owned the place, exuding confidence, as always. His seemingly ordinary white t-shirt clung to his flat tummy, those corded arms showing off their definition as he slid off his jacket.

Behind him came Ronan and Chase. The energy of the place seemed to hum as the tall, dark, and dangerous trio crossed the room to find a billiard table. As much as she wanted to say that the wives of two of the three that caught her eye were her reason for stalling her exit... she refused to admit that it was her blindingly unreasonable crush on the man crossing the crowded tavern toward her now.

Sinking into the booth, suddenly unable to get comfortable, Natalie wished she owned a bigger laptop so she could hide behind it. No such luck.

Traitorously, her cheeks flushed red and heated, and her pulse thundered perilously fast as he swaggered toward her.

Trouble with small towns, it was impossible to avoid anyone. Definitely impossible to hide from your most foolish crush since puberty. She'd hoped the little itch-scratch last year would take care of that, but now she *knew* what made him so appealing, and it wasn't just the glacial blues and irresistible smile.

Idiot that she was, her subconscious must have held her at Winter's later than planned, hoping he'd make an appearance tonight. Stupid subconscious.

Sliding into the booth across from her in all his prowess, Aiden made himself right at home and stole a jalapeno popper. Plopping it into his mouth, he wiped the stray cheese from the corner of his mouth with his thumb and licked off the tasty morsel, flashing her a ridiculously sexy wink. Dammit, she was not going to let her blush heat further as she pictured *everything* that mouth was capable of.

"Hey, Nat. Don't see you hanging out at Winter's much."

"I'm here at least once a week, while you and the rest of the nine-to-five riff raff are still toiling away at your offices." Expression bland, she hid the blush behind her feigned disinterest. After eight years in hiding, and a year of dodging Aiden McAllister, it was becoming remarkably easy to pretend she didn't care. Despite the inability to sleep as she imagined what might have happened on that sexiversary.

Running his tongue over his teeth to wipe away any lingering cream cheese, he paused to consider what she'd said. "You should take a break and join us. Two on two," he nodded his head toward Ronan and Chase, who were setting up a round at billiards.

Wistfully, she wanted to say yes. Like she had once. She'd come so close to inviting him up last weekend, but in the nick of time, a shadow had spooked her and reminded her why she couldn't. "Thanks, but I should get going."

Running a hand through his never-overgrown hair, he leaned back in the booth. "Hot date tonight?"

Natalie couldn't help but roll her eyes. And they were back to this conversation. "Not everything is about sex."

The corner of his mouth quirked up in a devious grin. "You're the one that keeps coming back to the sex thing." He leaned in on his elbows and linked his feet around hers under the table. Dammit, not another titillating game of footsy.

Natalie inhaled cautiously, grateful he couldn't see how quickly her pulse was racing under her skin at the intimate connection. Her poor brain scanned the ether for something clever to say, but was completely distracted.

"How about tomorrow night? We could do something fun without those two yokels." He nodded toward his brother and friend before flashing her another infamous panty-melting grin.

Oh boy. "Sorry, but I don't do... Well, I don't indulge on seconds with guys like you." What had her life become? She hadn't been on a real date in... ever? And Aiden was about as safe as they came. He was less motivated to stick around than she was.

Snapping her laptop closed, she focused on packing up her stuff. *Stop justifying things. You're just horny.*

Aiden winced, biting his cheek and looking away. He almost looked like he was suffering from hurt feelings. As if.

Sliding back out of the booth, he turned abruptly, stilling her hand as she zipped up her backpack. "I'm really sorry. I didn't mean anything by it. Whatever you may think of *guys like me*, or me in general, I'm not the kind of guy to bark up an uninterested tree."

"I'm not sure that metaphor made sense."

He cracked a half smile. "It didn't. I just... I like you. Sometimes, like last year, like last weekend, we get along like we've known each other forever. Other times, it's like you go into your shell and push everyone away."

"Again with the mixed metaphors," she teased, unable to stop herself. Finding her stern again, she corrected, "You're right. I do like to flirt with you. But that doesn't make celebrating that sexiversary a good idea." She pasted on a phony look of easiness to combat the heartache that was throbbing under her chest like a stubbed toe.

"Dammit, Nat. We had a great time that night, yeah, but if you'd let those walls down for a few hours, we might even enjoy each other platonically."

"Probably."

"Who are you? You've lived in Seaview for well over a year, but no one knows a damn thing about you. You never say anything about yourself. Hell, Payson and Maddy are the best friends you have, and they don't even know where you're from. If you've got a family. What brought you to this corner of the globe."

Ouch. He was in a feisty mood all of a sudden. "Nice deflection," she teased, easing up on him a bit and coating the moment with levity in the only way she could think of to let him know things were okay between them.

He sighed, gave her that ridiculously sexy half smile and snagged another jalapeno popper.

"I'm sorry too. I know you're not the type to push when a woman's not interested. You're a good guy and I like you."

He slowly unlinked their intertwined feet under the table, releasing her, but the curiosity didn't leave his gaze. Not a heated, sultry look like she'd expected, but a slow burn that simmered deliciously from the ends of her hair to the tips of her toes.

She swallowed the lump in her throat as she pictured what it might be like to let him in. To tell anyone, Aiden in particular, about her history, the real her, from her random thoughts to her heaviest wishes. To find out what made the playboy-next-door tick, as she knew it wasn't the superficiality he wore on the outside.

"Just give us all a chance to get to know you. To let me get to know you better." He grinned mischievously. "And I'm not talking about sex this time, I promise. Seriously, you're one of the best fair-weather friends I've ever had."

Man, she'd like to surrender. Her heart would smush flatter than the peanut shells on the ground, and a big-ass target would paste on his back. Okay, so the bullseye excuse was growing old. Peterson had another few decades of prison ahead of him, and despite her occasional scares, Dawson would let her know if she was being threatened. The heartbreak... *that* was growing more likely by the minute. Especially when those pale blue eyes looked at her like a sponge ready to drink her up.

Natalie grabbed her backpack and rose from the table. She flipped on the flippant again. "I'm not a scratching post you can use to soothe your itch whenever you'd like."

Aiden moved in front of her, standing a breath away. Nearly a foot taller than her five-foot-two-inch frame, she felt enveloped by his warmth without even touching him. Her traitorous nipples stood fully erect, like magnets pulling her closer to him. "Wait. Hear me out."

She tilted her head up and looked him right in the eye, a fierce challenge burning behind her eyes.

"Just, think about it." He paused, sky blue eyes swimming with sincerity. "Come out with me sometime. Just platonically. Have a few laughs. Be carefree, just for a few hours. No pressure. No expectations."

Keeping her expression flat, she repelled him with everything she had, refusing to let herself melt into his arms tonight, to be who and what she wanted tomorrow. It would be way, way too easy.

"Who's the real Natalie Smith? I don't buy that she's the recluse you claim to be."

Grinding her teeth, she forced sad into angry, for her more than him. "And you're not the goofy playboy you want everyone to think."

It was all she could do not to look back and watch him rejoin his friends. She waved to Winter as she strolled out into the misty evening.

Aiden stared at the door as she disappeared. What was it about her? She worked so hard to repel anyone that dared get close, but somehow his pole had flipped, and he was irretrievably stuck to her. Okay, so she had a point about his terrible metaphors, but he couldn't explain her, nor his reaction to her, through any logical analogies.

As the door creaked to a close behind Nat, a stalky guy in a shiny new pro-football fan jersey scanned the tavern, a bitter scowl on his face, then sifted back out the door.

Goosebumps prickled over Aiden's skin. Maybe Nat's jumpiness was getting to him too.

He leaned against the billiard table and nodded to Ronan. "Have you see that guy before?"

Winter's wasn't exactly welcoming to tourists. Most didn't know about it, or at least knew to stay out of the fisherman's bar.

Ronan crossed his arms over his chest, standing at his brother's side. "Nope."

Setting his chalked cue on the table, Chase shook his head. "Me neither."

"We might lose our table." He looked to the others.

Chase and Ronan shrugged and started toward the door, no answer required.

Aiden felt the panic bubbling up in his chest, his pace quickening as he worried his hesitation had taken too long.

Dashing ahead of the others, Aiden halted and eased his hand onto the door, gently opening against the wind.

The stranger was gone. Vanished into the dusky evening. Relief washed over Aiden that he hadn't walked out to screams or to see the asshole shoving Nat into the back of his van or something.

Running a hand through his hair, Aiden let out a stiff exhale. He glanced to his friends, about to apologize for his paranoia.

Ronan was staring down the sidewalk.

Aiden nodded. "What's up?"

Shaking his head, Ronan silenced them.

Listening, Aiden heard what he had missed in his panic. Voices around the corner of the building.

An engine coughed and sputtered and failed. Then again.

He creeped down the sidewalk, Ronan and Chase following right behind.

"Don't need any help, thanks though," Nat responded dryly to an unwelcome invitation.

A slurred voice pathetically argued, "Your engine says different. Come on, Natalie. I'll give you a ride. I saw you inside with McAllister. You should ditch that asshole and come out with me instead."

An inebriated gruff chortle joined in. "A ride," more guffaws. "You give her a ride and I'll give her a jump."

Shit. Aiden shook his head to himself.

Strolling around the corner, he stumbled upon exactly what it had sounded like. Nat sat in the driver's seat of her angular ancient sedan, trying the engine again, Roy blocking her door from closing, and Mr. Brand-New Shirt from out of town stood in front of the open hood.

Aiden muttered to Chase, "These your guys?" McAllister Fisheries had a reputation for hiring a decent crew—not that they didn't get in their share of friendly bar fights, but Chase would fire their asses so damn fast if he ever caught them doing shit like this.

Chase scoffed, loud enough for the jackasses to hear, "Hell no." Feet planted on the sidewalk, brawny arms crossed over his chest, Chase said, "Roy, I didn't realize you knew how to fix cars. Thought your gorilla brain was too witless to figure out anything but beer and crab pots. And I've never met your little friend here, but from the looks of him, I'm not sure either of you are getting the date you're hoping for."

Stepping away from the door, Roy stalked closer, a sloppy sneer on his face. "Oh I can fix her engine no problem. My brother here, he's in town visiting and I'm just trying to show him a good time. Now if Natalie would give me a chance, I'm sure we'd get along—"

A low growl rose from deep in Aiden's chest. "Your drunken powers of flirtation are sure to win her over." He stalked closer, fists balled at his side, hoping he got to use them.

"Oh excuse me. I know the ladies all dive into the sack with you, with your pretty clothes and snooty attitude."

Aiden was done with this conversation already. Teeth gritting together, he silently willed one of them to make a damn move already.

Roy puffed out his chest, egging Aiden on as he strolled around the front of the car. His buddy turned so he stood at his brother's side, equally interested in a decent fight to cap off the week.

Ten feet away, Aiden got a nice view as the drunken duo cracked their knuckles. His lips quirking up in a satisfied grin, Aiden tried to make his face as punchable looking as possible. No way was he racking up an assault charge by swinging first. But he'd be more than happy to defend himself.

Chase snickered behind him. "Aiden? You won't need any help with this one, will you? My beer's getting flat inside."

"I got this. You guys can head back in."

Ronan kept his feet planted. "And miss the show? When's the last time I got to watch you get your ass kicked? Dear old Roy is twice your size. I think his brother is even bigger than that."

Nat grabbed her backpack and slid out of the car. The obnoxious brothers' backs to her, Nat slammed the car door.

Roy jumped, quickly calming his expression and looking around to be sure everyone knew he hadn't really been startled.

Her mouth quirked up at his denial. She stepped onto the sidewalk and came to a stop at Roy's side. What the hell was she doing? "Hey boys, I'm sorry to interrupt. Aiden? I could use a ride home."

Aiden nodded to Nat. "Hang on a minute honey, I'm trying to defend your honor." He flashed her a baiting wink.

She clenched her jaw and fired him nasty eye daggers at the moniker he hadn't earned, then theatrically rolled her eyes and muttered to Roy at her side, "If you can get one good hit on Aiden, I'll happily let you give me a ride. McAllister here isn't good for anything more than a fly-by anyway, and he's certainly not my honey."

Shaking his head, Aiden added, "But it was a hell of a fly-by. These assholes are probably too drunk to get it up anyway." Biting his tongue, he held back on adding that he was game for another fly-by. What was wrong with him? Some stupid piece of his brain, or something further south, had claimed her and wasn't letting go. Possessive today, then what, was it going to be pining for her call tomorrow? Pleading down on one knee the next?

About damn time. Roy growled and seemed to actually scuff his feet on the ground like a steam-snorting bull, rescuing Aiden from the mind-numbing feud between his dick and his brain, each with very different ideas about Nat. And smashing his fist into this asshole's face would at least satisfy something tonight.

Huffing, Roy lifted his foot one last time to take off. Nat laced her ankle around his. Reflexes too dulled, he face-planted onto the concrete, his body thudding on impact. She winced comically. "Oh, ouch. You may want to watch where you're going. That stick came out of nowhere."

Roy's brother growled and stalked toward Aiden, his meaty fists swinging wildly. With an easy bob, Aiden dodged the blow, the dumb-ass knocking himself over from the force of his own attempted punch.

And another one on the concrete.

Aiden scowled. "Dammit, that was anticlimactic. I can't even re-member the last time I got to indulge in a good fight."

Nat stood and grinned. "Less dramatic, but subtlety can be so much more effective."

She stepped over Roy's grumbling lump of sidewalk litter and closed the hood of her car.

Aiden nodded toward the opposite end of the parking lot. "Still need a ride home?"

"That would be great, thanks." She nodded to Chase and Ronan, "Not to worry, he'll be back in ten minutes."

Scoffing, Aiden started toward his car. "I think I've got a little more staying power than that."

Rolling her eyes, Nat walked alongside him, "You're cute. But just the transportation please."

He nearly linked his hand with hers as they walked, but caught himself and jammed his hands in his pockets instead. Dammit, even the rest of his appendages were betraying the commands from his brain, set on the woman that wouldn't have him.

5

Sliding into Aiden's convertible, Natalie stretched her legs and sank into the leather seat. "I like your car." It still even smelled new, not even a trace of dust on the dash.

He fired up the engine and eased out of the parking lot. "Thanks. Me too."

They didn't chat much on the ride home. Probably a good thing. She was enjoying his company a little too much lately.

As they neared her building, Aiden offered, "Unlike your new friends, I actually do know a thing or two about cars. Want me to take a look at it?"

"I would really appreciate it, but I think it's time to invest in something a bit more reliable." She knew the car had been a terrible idea. She'd been going for inconspicuous and minimal documentation with the piece-of-shit car, but... she sighed as she realized how awful it would have been if those had been Peterson's goons, and she'd actually needed a dependable car.

As he pulled the car in front of her building, she leaned over and gave him a friendly kiss on the cheek, hopping out without another word.

She'd probably stayed in Seaview too long. She'd rearrange some money and pick up a new car. Something fast like Aiden's car, so she could easily run at a moment's notice.

Not that she wasn't always one hundred percent mobile. Even her backpack contained her laptop, camera, cash, spare phone, and some basic changes of clothes. As a quirky photographer, people generally didn't question the upcycled canvas backpack going everywhere with her.

Dashing up the three flights of stairs, she unlocked her door and it squeaked its welcoming chirp of ancient hinges. Flipping on the lights, she dropped her backpack on the chair. Flopping onto the futon, she rubbed her hands through her unruly blond hair.

The apartment wasn't anything impressive by her parent's standards. Roughly the size of her bedroom in the house she'd grown up in, it was tiny, but it was her domain. She'd dressed it up with stormy blue-gray walls, adding her own black-and-whites. The picture window overlooking the beach was her favorite part, with the sounds of Seaview's small-town nightlife below. To top it off, she had found a driftwood coffee table at the farmer's market that she often topped with a couch pillow, rested her feet, and sipped her morning coffee as the sun rose over the horizon.

Rather than enjoying the view tonight, she glared at her phone. She took a steadying breath and lifted the irritating contraption.

Nearly a month since her last call home. She should check in with her mother before she started to worry. Clicking open her secure app, she dialed using the untraceable connector. Handy thing; her first few years in hiding, she'd been so careful with rotating burner phones, never connecting to Wi-Fi or using data or even charging with the power on. She'd found the app preferred by criminals and hideaways worldwide, then tweaked it to suit her needs better.

As expected, the phone rang for several minutes before her mother was able to find the burner phone. "Hi Sweetie." The soothing voice of her mother radiated through the receiver, a bit out of breath as she'd clearly just run to find the phone.

"Hey Mom," she said, relaxing into the pillows.

"It's been so long. You know I worry when I don't hear from you. I know you say I shouldn't call you—"

"I know. I'm really sorry Mom. I've just been busy." She hated the 'busy' excuse. Helene Haldon had always been 'so busy' through Natalie's childhood. They would run into friends at the grocery store, the theatre, gymnastics competitions, and Helene would always apologize for not getting together, as she had been 'so busy.' For a stay-at-home mom with a hired cleaning service, premade meals, and independent children, her reasons for being 'so busy' were always beyond Natalie's comprehension.

Yet, here she was, using her mother's hated excuse right back at her.

"I'm sure. It's not easy to become such a successful photographer, with only limited access to marketing."

Resting her feet on the bench, she beamed at the praise. Whatever her mother's faults, she had always been her fiercest supporter. And, quite likely where her historically overgrown ego had stemmed from.

Along with excuses of being 'so busy,' her mother had dumped braggery on anyone who risked mention of her bright, athletic child. The compliments meant so much more today than when she'd assumed that she was great at everything.

"I just wish I could see your work and tell others about what a wonder you are." Her mother's regretful sigh gutted into her chest.

If Helene fell into an old boasting habit, things could get a bit more stressful. It was risky enough sharing so much of her life with her mother, but despite their odd relationship, she loved the woman.

"I just wish I knew where you were. That anyone knew where you were. What if you disappeared? How would I know something had happened to you or where to send help?"

"Mom—"

"I'm sorry honey. Have you at least gotten yourself out there and started dating yet? I worry about you, being so alone."

Oh boy. *Nice segue, Mom.* Of course, Helene assumed having a man around equated to safety. She had dodged the relentless hounding for the last several months, by sheer luck and clever segues of her own, as opposed to a lack of persistence on her mother's part.

Sniffling on the other end.

Shit. If she wasn't careful, the 'who will take care of you' would start. Then the baby conversation. Then the 'dying miserable and alone' punctuation to her dire threats about the desolation of life as a hermit. Which Helene had never experienced, so how would she know?

Natalie liked being alone. Admittedly, she was sexually frustrated, but survival and the ability to be happy were entirely her own responsibility. Even if she was married.

May as well throw her a bone, even if it was a bone that she ought to bury rather than fantasize about. "Uh, yeah. I've sort of been seeing someone." Okay, so her nightly fantasies about a 'fair-weather friend' and one-nighter over a year ago really didn't count, but her mother's sad sniffle swiftly morphing into a watery happy chuckle was worth the fib.

"Really? What's his name? Tell me everything about him."

"No names, so please don't ask."

"At least tell me what he does for a living."

"He's a lawyer. A good one."

"A hard worker, educated. I like him already. Your father will be impressed. Does this young man know about *you*?"

"Let's just say I told him more than I should have." *Quick, subject change.* Too detailed for comfort. "How's Xander doing? Is he staying for summer school like he wanted? I haven't heard from him in a while."

"Yes, and he's loving it. You were right. MIT has changed his life. Where did you find that scholarship? Your father was so furious that Xander wanted to major in physics rather than economics or business, that he refused to pay for his education. I'm sure he'll come around eventually, but until he does, this scholarship has made Xander so happy. I was bragging to Vivian about it, but she thought I was nuts."

"It wasn't easy to find," she said lightly. It had taken some creative wiring to send the funds in the name of a scholarship. Rarely did she touch her savings. Not that it was traceable, she'd seen to that, but as none of it was obtained legally, and it was her life savings, she used it judiciously.

Her brother deserved that money more than anyone else. Certainly more than she did. He'd been so scared when the FBI had shown up that awful night. Their childhood hadn't been the pearliest, and she hated that he'd had to live half of it alone. At least he was a good email buddy the last few years.

She hated that her family was so torn apart because of her. Because she'd been too caught up in her own amazingness to realize that burgling might lead to something other than fortune and secret success. That her family would suffer because of her.

Ouch. She hated even thinking it. What happened to the little girl who wanted to rock the world with her Olympic glory?

Wow, she'd had a *massive* ego.

Snorting, she remembered exactly what had happened to that girl. Disappointed in her second-rate gymnastics performance, the spoiled, overly competitive girl she'd been had blown it at trials and capped it off with a humiliating, public temper tantrum.

Waiting in the wings had been the opportunity of a lifetime.

One that she should have refused.

They'd known her dreams and had offered her a fortune for her skills. The challenge of the century that only *she* could handle.

They had fed off her overconfidence like the piranhas she hadn't recognized them as.

One job, one tiny gymnast that could scale her way up the mansion wall, tech-savvy enough to pull data files direct from the source, and then sneak out with untraceable financial reports, completely unde-tected.

One job had turned into two, then three. Before she knew it, she was spending every weekend making buckets of money.

Well, whatever she'd been at gymnastics, academia, anything... she was amazing at burgling. Most of her friends got their first jobs work-ing at their parent's businesses through school, then internships at tech companies. Her parents had wondered why she'd chosen to delay college.

Enjoying her own wealth, learning about money laundering from a ripe age, she had invested well. More, the thrill of it, being the *best* at something, Natalie was gifted at *something*. She had worked for... well, she still didn't know exactly what they were. Her employers, R and L as they were known, dealt in information. Not all data could be hacked without leaving a massive trail. Well, just send in this agile teenager to go straight to the datapoint.

If she were to be caught, no trail would lead back to them.

They enjoyed the risk-free investment in her. Natalie had loved the adventure of it. The silent glory. By the time she was eighteen, she was writing her own programs to extract the data efficiently and inconspicuously.

A stupid kid, but not so stupid. Yeah, stupid enough to not see that last job for what it was: too big for her, and so far above R and L it wasn't even funny.

Dawson strolled down the steps of 26 Federal Plaza, letting the last of the evening sun warm his face. Long damn week. His new partner, Rogers, was a straight shooter. Sometimes a bit too straight.

She was brilliant, but too new to realize life couldn't revolve around the bureau. Okay, so he knew he wasn't one to talk. His mother, his father, his sisters… and even Natalya, badgered him to find a life outside of work.

And he did. It wasn't even dark yet. The last of the sun glinted off the mirrored windows as he walked toward Lafayette. His stomach rumbled, but he ignored the call of the restaurants along the way, anxious to get away from the rest of the Feds out to celebrate a Friday night.

Okay, so his version of a life was not taking work home with him. He'd learned that lesson on one of his first investigations. He didn't need another witness to look after, entirely off the record. At least she was independent, but maybe to a fault.

He cut across the park and headed down to catch his train. As the doors closed, the stragglers, all eager to get home for the weekend, pushed in at the last second. Glancing around, as was his habit, he checked that his fellow passengers were staying chill.

No worries, just a bunch of suits that were dead on their feet.

As the train pulled up to his stop, he beat the last-second mad-dash out the door. The crowds thinned as he rose back to the street and aimed for his apartment. His phone buzzed in his pocket, and he answered the incoming call. "Hey, Ma."

"Hi, Honey. Have you decided if you're coming home this week-end?"

"Probably not. It's been a long week."

"I get it. But if you need a break to put your feet up, well, retirement is kicking my butt, and your dad and I would love some company. So if you change your mind, hop on the first train in the morning, shoot one of us a text and we'll pick you up and take you out for brunch."

His stomach growled at the thought. Mother's Day. That's the last time he'd been home.

As he reached his building, he pulled out his keys and let himself in. His voice echoed as he dashed up the wide staircase, "Know what? That actually sounds amazing. I'll get to bed early tonight and see you at the station in the morning."

"Oh, before I forget, I bumped into Skylar last week when I took the car in to be serviced, and she asked about you."

Shit. "What did you tell her?"

"That you love your job and New York and it's hard to pull you away, so I don't know when you'll be home next."

His pulse was racing and his legs burned as he reached his floor. "One of these times I'll swing by her place when I visit."

"I know it's a lot, that's why I didn't make any plans."

"Thanks."

Dawson unlocked his door and headed inside, locking up behind himself. He tossed his jacket on the entry table and rubbed his hands over his face. Stalking to the fridge, he pulled out a leftover steak.

Snatching the remote while the microwave nuked his dinner, he took a swig of beer and blindly looked for something to bore him into sleep.

Click.

Jerking his head up, he was met by the barrel of a .22. Dressed in a dark sweater and jeans, the bearer of the weapon sauntered closer. "Hands where I can see them."

Dammit. He'd been meaning to upgrade the damn alarm. Too late now.

"I have no intention of shooting you until I know why the fuck you're in my home." Dawson shrugged and held his hands up.

The intruder stepped closer, her dark eyebrows coming together. "Where is she?"

"She? I live alone." *Come on, Natalya, what trouble are you in now?* Huong was so going to pay for retiring to Hawaii and ditching him with their little witness.

"I need that data." The New York accent was thick, but as unfamiliar as the woman.

"You're going to have to be more specific." The microwave beeped behind him. Damn, that smelled so good, he could kill the woman just for interrupting his dinner. That apple for lunch just wasn't cutting it.

"Natalya. Where is she?"

"Who?"

"Don't play dumb. Your little star witness that eluded Peterson."

"How the hell would I know? She ought to be hell and gone from anywhere assholes like you can find her, and she's not stupid enough to let a Fed know how to find her. I'm sure you know what happened to the rest that tried witness protection. Or maybe you're the reason."

He stepped closer. The gun aimed higher, resting dead center in his forehead.

Ha, maybe not the best time to think about 'dead.' The corner of Dawson's mouth quirked up as he amused himself. Long-ass week getting longer by the minute, at least he could have a sense of humor about it.

Now if only this creep would get the fuck out and leave him alone.

"She must have handed it over to you, or she'd have her own cell a few blocks down from Peterson. I'm going to need that data."

"Why now?"

"Peterson's going to want it back."

"What's it to him? He's not getting out anytime soon." Something wasn't right. Not that having someone hold a gun to your head in your own home was right.

"Stop dicking around." She pressed the barrel into his skull.

Fluttering his eyelashes in irritation, he sighed. "Look. We can talk in circles all damn night. I'm tired. Yes, I protected Natalya until she testified. No, I don't know where she is. No, she never said a damn thing about data, and she certainly wouldn't have given something like that to a Fed like me. Now get that gun out of my face, and I'll give you a five second head start."

The woman bit her lip, her nostrils flaring as she decided whether or not to believe him.

He took a half a step back. "One. Two. Shit, who is—"

Something out the window caught his eye.

Not really, but worked every damn time.

Almost.

She followed his gaze to the window. As her eyes bounced back to his, knowing she'd been had, he ripped the gun from her hand and slammed his fist into her nose.

Blood gushed out both nostrils. Nice. That should cost her a pretty penny to fix.

As he swung to take her out, she ducked and took off, grabbing a rope he hadn't seen and leapt over the deck.

Sprinting after her, he halted and looked down for any sign of her. The rope swung back and forth, its rider having released it moments before. No squished red blob on the concrete. There were at least ten apartments she could have dropped into.

Gone.

Dammit, Huong. This is why this was a terrible idea. He couldn't exactly report the situation, without drawing attention to Natalya.

He stormed out the door and locked up, leaving his leftover steak uneaten in the microwave.

6

STARING AT THE BLANK—ALTHOUGH cheery—blue wall, Aiden frowned. It didn't look *that* bad.

Ev stood at his side, her head tilted sideways in deep ponderance. "So, when you said the office was fully furnished, you meant with minimalist taste."

He shrugged. "I've been busy."

"I thought you said small town law was a pleasant change of pace?"

"It is. But there aren't enough of us to go around, hence my request for a partner." He plopped onto the edge of the desk next to her.

"'Request' is an understatement. I would describe it more as manipulative tactics to convince me to leave Boston to ease your workload, to save you from your overzealous caseload."

"Hey, all I said was that you're going to run yourself into the ground, your entire life passing by in a worthless blink if you kept on your greedy path." He nudged his shoulder into hers.

"You promised me the quiet life." She scowled at him before turning her eyes back to the blank blue wall.

"It will be. I currently work seventy-hour weeks. Divide that in half, and we both will be so bored we might just remember what hobbies feel like."

She crossed her arms and sat on the edge of her desk. "I used to knit."

"I used to date."

"That's not a hobby. Besides, I have a hard time believing you don't date anymore."

Against his will, the corner of his mouth tugged up in amusement. "Okay, so I've never really had a hobby. But I've been thinking about developing one."

"Have you been out with a woman on more than one date in the last decade?" She leaned her head on his shoulder.

Grinning impishly, he shrugged. "Sure."

"You're such an ass. You still refuse to come back for seconds, claiming you're just trying to ward off talk of babies and marriage and growing old together, don't you?"

"Maybe."

"I suppose that's why we lasted so long. Neither of us were interested in all that back then."

"Nah, it was the sex. Want to give it another go?" He winked at her playfully, flashing a charming grin.

She raised an eyebrow at him. "Oh boy. You must be desperate. The sex was decent, I'll give you that, but it was a long time ago, and we didn't exactly incite long-lasting feelings from each other then and I don't think we will now."

"Which is why you left me for 'Trust-Me' Terry."

"Hey, Terry was a sensible guy." She bit her lip, clearly hiding the laugh, as she knew he was the inept know-it-all Aiden had pinned him as from the first moment.

"With a ridiculous catch-phrase."

"Hey, I was still experimenting with what I wanted in a partner."

He nudged her shoulder with his. "You were right about us all along. It's amazing how you can like someone's personality and find them attractive, but the chemistry is just, well, anticlimactic."

"Truer words were never spoken. No offense, but I'm not getting even a zing from you." Of course, she'd been firmly in the friend-zone for over a decade now.

"Ditto."

She stood and paced into the lobby. Staring at the front desk, the surrounding walls, she frowned again, poked her head into Aiden's office, then back to hers where she crossed her arms and scowled.

He followed along and scanned the blank walls.

"It looks like there's great shopping down Beachside Avenue. I can head out and look for some wall art. Maybe swing into that antique shop you told me about and get some cool wall art to match the classy furniture she set you up with."

"Payson has some great stuff, but I have a better idea. Why don't you head home and finish unpacking your new place?" Not exactly his plan, but Laura McAllister, his meddling mother, had been telling him how drab his office was. How much he needed some classy photographs on his walls.

Thinking herself a sly cupid, his mother thought she was quite the subtle matchmaker. Okay, so he'd been blissfully ignorant of her ploy to fix up Payson and Ronan. And, he'd been the last to notice her blatant efforts to put Maddy and Chase together. But he wasn't missing this one. His mother's efforts to match him with Nat were getting exceedingly blatant.

Aiden, why don't you see if Natalie needs help fixing that rattle in her car? Hey, do you think you could drop this off at Natalie's on your way home? Your office looks awfully bleak, head on over to the gallery and have Natalie fix you up.

Ha. Aiden McAllister was no fool.

Well, maybe a little.

But he'd been the target of fixups from all parties on too many occasions. What his mother didn't realize, is that he was perfectly happy to do all of these things and get closer to Nat.

Not that Natalie was on board. She'd kissed his brains out, then pushed him away again. And she thought he was the player here? She may be worried about getting her hopes up, but he was so damn confused about her. His dick wasn't sure which way it was pointing when it came to her. *Yes, no, yes, no.*

He got it, he really did. She was as attracted as he was, but he was pretty damn low on her list of priorities.

No, that platonic relationship looked to be about as far as he and Nat were going to get, and she was hot and cold with even that.

Ev eyed him suspiciously as he backed out of her office. "I don't trust you. You might come home with pictures of cars and naked women."

"Hey, my dorm room looked amazing with those posters. What would you say to black and whites of the coast?"

Crossing her arms again, she raised an eyebrow. "I'd say that sounds perfect."

"Then just *trust me.*"

"Sure thing, *Terry.*"

He flashed her a devious wink, rolled up his sleeves, and headed out into the warming morning. As much as he loved his job, well, liked it anyway, he was done with it being his entire life. It had made sense when he was starting out and building his clientele, but he hadn't had the common sense to slow down.

Not to mention, it felt good to have Ev back in his life. Yeah, they'd dated in college, but that fizzled quickly, and they had remained good friends. He'd actually asked her to come to Seaview on a whim, and he suspected her acceptance had been equally spontaneous. So far, it was looking like a damn good impulse for them both.

Quenched with a fresh dose of optimism, he sauntered down Beachside Avenue. Blissfully quiet this morning, Seaview's main drag provided a pleasant walk. Mood in the clouds, he stopped into Moe's Morning Mug.

"Hey, Aiden. The usual?" Gilly tucked her towel into her apron and tossed her fluorescent pink hair into a high bun on top of her head.

Damn, did he come here that often? He hated spending money on coffee when he had a perfectly good espresso maker at home, but sometimes he needed an excuse to get out of the house.

"Yeah, thanks. Plus, whatever Natalie's usual is." He strolled up to the counter and absolutely did not drool over the freshly baked croissants.

"Natalie from the gallery? Black drip with a whisper of a splash of cream." Gilly was the manager and primary operator of Moe's, as her father, Moe, was opening a chain of Moe's down the coast.

"A whisper of a splash, huh? She can't even commit to cream in her coffee. Okay, I'll take my cappuccino and her paltrily-creamed black drip."

While Gilly steamed his milk, he wandered the empty coffeeshop and perused the local art for sale on the wall. One of Natalie's famous coastal shots dominated one wall.

"Here ya go," she offered as she slid the coffees over the pick-up counter.

"Hey, Gilly? Why didn't he call the place Moe's Joe?" He chuckled at his own antics as he picked up the drinks.

"You know, I've asked him that since the day I started working here." Her grin widened, "He claims he prefers alliteration to rhymes."

Aiden chuckled as he backed into the front door to let himself out. "Have a good one."

"Later," she waved, the dense collection of bangles chiming with the cheerful movement.

He stepped into the coastal air, the morning breeze battling with the sidewalks newly heated by the sun. Squinting in the brightness, he adjusted his eyes to the bright light. He raised a coffee in a casual wave to Ian, Maddy's partner, across the street. One of the McAllister Fisheries boats was making its return to the harbor, the familiar rumbling of its engine bouncing off the waves.

As he passed Flotsam Antiques, he hoped he wasn't caught walking by without saying hello to his sister-in-law. Payson would torture him until he told her who he was bringing coffee to and why. Small towns. No surprises.

But a nice pace. Nothing but known evils. How had he ever even considered big-city law?

Using his fingertips as he balanced the coffees, he pulled open the door to the gallery. The old remodeled chapel was a brilliant idea. The whole town had chipped in to save the landmark. A work of art itself, the building boasted high ceilings, weathered floors, and the scent of time. Anyone that enjoyed historical architecture would stop in just because they could, and leave with a piece of local art.

Nat had worked there for nearly six months, both as a contributing artist and to pay the bills more immediately as a clerk. She'd scored with the arrangement, as she could work all day on processing, but was still able to maintain a flexible enough schedule to get out and shoot photographs of the coast on her days off. Parked at the glass counter, a clever twist by one of the featured artists, in which they had repurposed antique windowpanes into a checkout counter, Nat bit her lower lip in concentration over her laptop.

He knew she'd seen him enter but was too focused on her work to acknowledge him. Or she chose not to. Too often, she ignored him just like this. She probably did it just to torment him.

It worked.

Her blond hair was tied back in a messy knot with a pen sticking out. Not a trace of make-up, yet she was stunning. Her eyes were vibrantly hazel today. Through the counter, he saw her legs crossed, ankle boots accenting her toned calves, legs bare, and her ripped-up denim skirt scooted up just enough to pique his interest, but tastefully so. Donning a pink cotton top, she softened the boots and denim skirt look with a hint of responsibility.

Strolling to the counter like he had dropped by out of sheer boredom, he set her coffee next to her laptop.

Glancing at the Moe's to-go cup, she smiled curiously, and her eyes rose to meet his. "Thanks."

"It's purely self-centered. I'm hoping for over-and-above customer service."

She shifted in her seat, a challenge in her look. "I don't need bribery for customer service."

"Call it an advanced tip."

Cautiously, she sipped the mystery brew. "Gilly?"

"Of course. Why just a whisper of a splash?"

"I'm lactose intolerant." She scoffed as if he was the confusing one, then blew gently over the mouth of the cup before taking a testing sip.

"So order it with almond or soy."

"Gross. I'd rather risk the bellyache." Savoring another sip, she closed her eyes and moaned as the hot liquid flowed down her throat.

Did she do it on purpose? That faraway look that would blossom on her face when no one was looking, the quiet savoring of the little things—like her odd coffee order. Take the air of mystery and add the fucking sexy moan on top, and his blood flowed straight south so he couldn't even remember how to breathe.

Cool it, McAllister. Air in, air out. He didn't look through the glass at her curvy thighs. Ignored how the tip of her tongue slid over her lip after the satisfying sip. Clearing his throat, he tried to remember what they were talking about. "I've seen you eat cheese."

"I love cheese. If I behave myself most of the time, I can indulge on cheese and cream when it strikes my fancy." She grinned, her eyebrow lifting deviously. "You can't seem to stay away, huh? I've seen more of you in the last two weeks than the prior three months combined."

"What can I say? You're irresistible."

Her eyebrows dropped, the hazel of her eyes darkening to the heart of the forest. "Aiden. I don't celebrate sexiversaries, or come back for seconds, and I absolutely don't make a habit of fooling around with charming playboys."

So it was going to be one of those conversations. Pasting on a casual expression, he set down his own coffee and stuffed his hands into his pockets. "Seriously. It's not intentional that we keep running into each other. And maybe, just maybe, I enjoy your company."

She scowled, her eyebrows drawing together in adorable frustration. "Huh. What interests you, art-wise?"

"My new partner at work, Evelyn, thinks we need wall art to warm up the office."

Natalie's eyes flashed with something... something. So damn fast, he couldn't place it. Jealousy? Why was he so hopeful that was it?

Jealousy was not an attractive trait; it was pure trouble and not in a good way.

"Evelyn?"

"My new partner."

"Oh yeah. I can't believe I had nearly forgotten your admission that you needed help."

"Like someone else in this room?"

Neatly dodging the accusation, she adjusted her posture. "What do you two have in mind?"

Yeah, she was totally jealous. Why did that get to him? That was definitely a first, and he really didn't care for it. "*I* was thinking some of your black and whites of the area."

"Do you have a particular image in mind?"

You wearing nothing but those heeled boots. "Anything that will make my clients feel relaxed and honest and, well, trusting."

"I can help you and your completely platonic female partner."

"Jealous?"

"Why would I be?"

"No reason."

"So, your old and unattractive female partner and you are in need of black and white photographs for the office?"

"She's attractive." He shrugged.

"Ah, I see. You've already tapped that, huh?" Raising an eyebrow in challenge, she slid back from her chair and adjusted her skirt.

Sighing heavily, he tried to not stare as she walked around the counter. Scowling, eyes bright with amusement, she was so obviously hiding enjoyment of his interest despite her desire to be irritated. Okay, maybe he was reading too much into this. But she never looked irritated with anyone else. She was a wonderfully positive person. Except around him. Yeah, she totally wanted him.

And he was officially a pathetically sex-deprived egomaniac.

"When did you sleep with her?"

"Sleeping isn't exactly the right word." He guffawed, suddenly finding an overly modern sculpture made of bottle caps incredibly interesting.

"Of course, that's too much for you. At what point in your shared history did you and she have intercourse?"

"Before law school," he answered nonchalantly. "So, this one?" He pointed to an emotional print of the ocean.

"No."

"It's nice."

"It's lovely, but it's of waves crashing violently in a storm. Not exactly reassuring."

"Fair point. What do you think? *We* need a big wide one for behind the front desk, and more for our offices."

"Hmm." She wandered over to a massive wall of photographs and paintings that highlighted the character of the area. "Lighthouse for Evelyn's office, these three tall-narrows of Beachside Avenue for behind the front desk, and the old docks for your office."

Wow. She was good. "Perfect." He scanned the photographs and saw a smaller, unframed print in the stack of inexpensive options. A cozy cabin set just off the beach like it was part of the terrain. "And that one for my bedroom."

Her cheeks flushed. Ha. He did get to her now and again. "That one?" She clarified, knowing exactly which one he had been pointing to.

"Yeah. There's something about it that I want to fall into every night."

Cheeks fire-engine red, she bit her cheek and nodded. "Me too."

Arms folded over her chest, brow furrowed in the deepest of concentrations, holding back the ornery grin that teased at her cheeks, Natalie shook her head. "Left about three inches."

Aiden held both arms wide to support the huge black and white framed print of the decommissioned Seaview docks on the wall of his office behind his desk. Glancing over his shoulder, he raised an accusatory eyebrow. While his hair was meticulously trimmed at all times, his eyebrows rebelled with a sleepy scruffiness that wouldn't be tamed. "I just moved right three inches."

"I know. I changed my mind." She grinned, baiting him to argue. Apparently, cranky Aiden was way more fun to taunt than flirty Aiden.

Growling, he moved the picture as directed.

"Almost there. Up two and left one."

"Better?" His voice was getting hoarse, his arms started to show a sheen of sweat as he struggled to hold up the weathered-wood frame.

They'd efficiently hung the print in Evelyn's office, then the trio behind the front desk, and by the time they'd reached his office, he seemed a bit impatient with her precision, especially after he'd carried the heavy load all the way back from the gallery. The office had closed long ago, and she'd heard his stomach growling as dinnertime approached.

Yeah, maybe she was messing with him. He was way too easy of a target. And she really enjoyed seeing him flustered. It didn't happen very often. Yet he powered on.

"Perfect. Now hold it there while I mark the spot." Standing on her tiptoes to mark the top of the picture, she was still a good eight inches from reaching her target. Laughing out loud, she strained to reach the tippy top of her toes.

Chuckling with her, his voice pure gravel, he said, "Here, you hold it. I'll mark it."

Sliding under him, she stretched to hold the frame in place, her arm span just barely wide enough. Wiggling to steady her grip, she found her ass pressed right up against his groin.

Stilling at the intimate contact, she waited for the flirty remark. Nothing. In the half a second before he pulled away, the intensity of the position, his breath warm against her neck, his body taut with unspoken yearning as hers was, she flashed back to the many imaginings of him wrapping his arms around her middle, holding her like this, whispering anything, everything in her ear.

Without a word, he stepped back and slid the pencil from her hand, his fingers neither lingering nor rushing, the light touch burning. He marked the corners on the deep blue wall, keeping her pinned between his arms, he lowered the framed photo back to the floor.

Turning in his arms, only inches separating them, his scent, the heat of his body so close to hers, sent an electric chill through her veins as she remembered the feel of his bare skin against hers.

She glanced up, and his glacier-blue eyes were melty sweet. Unable to look away, she held her breath, waiting for him to make the move.

His eyes searched hers, waiting for the okay.

When his gaze dropped to her lips, she reached up and gripped the back of his neck and pulled him to her.

As their lips met, softly at first, testing before her pulse accelerated beyond control, her need becoming insatiable, she gripped him close and traced her tongue over the crease of his lips. Heat curled deep within her, radiating down to her toes and into her fingertips.

Shifting, his hand splayed across the small of her back, tugging her closer. Angling, closer, he deepened the kiss.

Freezing in place, she held her breath, pulling back as she realized she'd done it again. She retreated out from between him and the wall. This saying *yes* thing was becoming a little too easy. "Sorry, I shouldn't have."

Subtly, he ran his tongue over his lips before clamping them shut. With a controlled exhale, he blinked long and heavy before speaking. "This thing that keeps happening, as much as you seem averse to the idea of it, it's not just me."

"I know. I just... I don't have room in my life for dating."

"I don't recall mentioning dating."

"Of course. Aiden McAllister doesn't 'date,' he certainly doesn't come back for seconds, but he may consider indulging on a sexiversary, but we just missed ours so it's too late for that."

"Look, I can't keep doing this. You tie me up in knots, spin me so I don't know which way is up. Tell me to fuck off, and I'll give you space. But if you're game, even for nothing more than a little dessert now and again, say the word and I'm all in." He gripped his fingers in his short hair and tipped his head back, finally turning back toward the toolbox.

The air grew thin as she tried to make sense of everything. Drawing in a long, measured breath, she opened her mouth to tell him she was done with him. That nothing could happen between them. Instead, she heard herself say, "I guess that depends on what you mean by dessert. I don't have much of a sweet tooth. Appetizers are more to my taste." Biting her lip, she masked how bad she really wanted to lap him up like a hungry kitten. Like that kitten, the cream was really, really bad for her digestion.

Freezing with his hand on the hammer, he said, "Remember last year at the beach party? You accidentally relaxed and had fun?"

Heat licked through her as she let herself remember. "How could I forget? I turned to find my shoes, and somehow bumped into your lips instead."

"Hey, I was just bringing you your shoes. And you jumped me." Rising back to his feet, he hesitated a few feet away.

"I wouldn't say *jumped*."

"You only took your tongue out of my mouth long enough to invite me back to your place."

She felt her cheeks heat, remembering how she'd run on adrenaline from the thrill of the night. How he'd held her, skin against skin, already exploring as they crossed to her apartment across the street. How she'd peeled off both of their wet clothes, showing him this daring part of herself she'd so rarely revealed.

She'd tasted every inch of his salty skin.

They hadn't paced themselves. Nothing sweet or calm about it.

"Nat?" he asked, interrupting her imaginings as she was already panting in anticipation, reliving the night.

"Yeah?" Breathless like they'd just done it again, her vision was blurred as she tried to focus on what he'd said.

He stepped closer and grazed his hands down her arms, her waist, resting on her hips. "You were thinking about last year, weren't you?"

He'd had been with other people since they'd last been together. He had probably forgotten most of the night. Her brow furrowed as she imagined how their lives had diverged over the last year in so many ways. Had he thought about her, as she had him? Wondering what could happen if either could or would say yes to more?

She nodded.

Pressing his lips to hers, he tasted, like sipping pink champagne. He whispered, his lips a breath away from hers, "I haven't had a decent night's sleep in the last year, remembering your scent, your taste, the way you move against me."

Warm and floaty and tingly all over, she felt like she'd downed a whole bottle as he swept his tongue over hers, pulling her into the moment.

Hands looping over his taut forearms, sliding around his triceps, she gripped him tight against her, rising to meet him.

Urgency fueled between them. Faster, deeper, she gulped until her judgment crumbled. Just as she thought she could handle no more sensation as he kissed her with unmatched hunger, his fingers teased at her top, sliding under the light cotton.

Shifting his hand subtly under her bra, he cupped her breast gently at first, building, until she sighed against his mouth, unable to concentrate on anything but the exquisite zing of his fingers on her sensitive skin. As if under a spell, forgetting her worries, liberated from fear, she stripped off her shirt and traced her fingers along his upper arms, needing to feel his skin, the athlete in her fascinated, wondering how he was built so magnificently despite the desk job.

Unsnapping her bra, he slid the straps over her shoulders and tossed it aside. Taking both breasts in his hands, he pressed his mouth to her sternum. Hot against her skin, his tongue trailed over the curve of her breast before taking her deep into his mouth. Arching her back to get closer, she let herself *feel*.

Breathless, he stepped back and looked her up and down, biting his lip with pure satisfaction.

Mind completely blank, she was shocked at their urgent make-out. Smug, satisfied, she rested her hands on her hips, glancing down at her naked torso and shrugged, "Thanks for the dessert." She moved to grab her top off his desk. "'Night McAllister."

Equally out of breath, Aiden shook his head. "Five more minutes?" He linked his hands into the waistband of her denim skirt, flicked open the button and slid her skirt and panties down over her hips. Breath leaching from her lungs as she steadied herself, fire burned everywhere he touched, leaving an indefinite imprint she'd never erase from her memory.

Standing in the middle of his tidy office in nothing but her heeled summer boots, she felt completely exposed. The ravenous look on his face erased any consideration for self-consciousness.

"Well, McAllister? Is this what you had in mind?" She raised a daring eyebrow at him.

Mouth quirked up in a hungry grin, he bit his lower lip and sighed. "I wonder if you taste as good as I remember, or if I've dreamed about you so much I blew things out of proportion."

He clutched his hands around her hips and guided her back a step until she was pressed against the cool wood of his desk. Dropping to his knees in front of her, he wrapped his hands around her bare thighs and pressed his mouth to her core.

Electricity shot straight through her at the heat of his mouth on her, his tongue sweeping over her. At the pressure, circling, the ecstasy of his satisfied groan as he tasted, she held tight to the edge of the desk. An echoing moan vibrated up her throat and passed her parted lips.

Accelerating his motions, heat licking through her body, radiating from her core, he drove her higher and faster. Crying out as her breaths became desperate pants, she struggled to stay standing.

Sucking, squeezing, licking in erotic torment, his mouth, his hands sent her sailing out of the atmosphere. His pace intensified with her rapid breaths, increasingly uncontrolled until her vision darkened and stars flashed in her eyes. Easing her down from the pinnacle, he shifted his hands on her thighs and softly kissed her belly before resting his head against her low abdomen.

As her brain remembered how to function again, Natalie looked down at this new predicament. Wearing nothing but her boots, spinning from orgasm... yet Aiden remained fully clothed, catching his breath as he rested against her body.

Moments passed, almost long enough for her brain to reboot, before he stood and grabbed her skirt from the floor, setting it on the desk with her top. Wordlessly, he rubbed his hands over his face, blinked with shock, then stalked out of the room as she slid her panties back on. She quickly pulled on the rest of her clothes and headed for the door.

Aiden was flipping off the lights and shutting the office down for the night. As she reached the front door, he cleared his throat. "Nat? That was dessert." His voice was laced with an edge she hadn't heard before. "If you decide to indulge in seconds, just say the word."

Dozens of comebacks would have been perfect. Something snarky, perhaps.

But, no. She was completely dumbfounded. "'Night." And she walked right out the front door into the salty summer night.

Steal a few hundred thousand dollars from a high-rise office computer? Sure.

Take Aiden McAllister up on an offer of follow-up sex? Way scarier.

7

Slow down, Ace. What was he thinking? Fricking moth to a flame, that's what.

Blatantly put the ball in her court. Not that he was open anyway. But if he was to make any exceptions on the dating rules, Nat would be worth it.

Admittedly, it might have something to do with the fact that she wanted less from him than he wanted from her. And, well, they'd had an epic time last year. Last night, yeah, that had been pretty fucking fantastic. What was one more night?

Holy shit, McAllister, get your head out of the horny clouds.

Aiden strolled along Beachside Ave, pushing through the crowds that popped in and out of the shops like it was going out of style. Nearing dinnertime on a Friday evening, low tide, high sun, the weekend vacationers were out in full force. Thanks to his new partner, he was actually done working before dark.

A little Friday-night, I-kicked-ass-this-week swagger in his step, Aiden breezed into the gallery.

Speak of the devil. Ringing up a white-haired couple with a friendly Australian accent, she tried to pretend she didn't notice him come in. But the pink blush of her cheeks gave her away. As the couple left with their cloth bags of goodies, the shop emptying out, she came around the checkout.

Her blush flamed redder, her mouth quirked up in amusement. Did she always look so damn hot, without even trying? Nothing more than mascara, her hair pulled back in a messy pony, and snug-as-sin black jeans with strappy heels and an off-white spaghetti strap tank that begged for him to slide down the thin scrap of lace...

Down boy, he argued with himself.

Took him a minute to figure out why she was grinning at him. Then he realized his blazing hot cheeks were blushing redder than hers.

Tsking, Nat strode closer, but didn't get nearly close enough. "Yikes, McAllister, and I thought I was the one left speechless after last night."

Biting his tongue, he shrugged. "I do have a sweet tooth."

"Is that why you're here? Because I'm not hungry." She folded her arms over her chest and glared at her feet.

And they were back to hot and cold. His stomach turned as if he'd swallowed a gallon of sea water. "Of course not. I'm on my way to Payson and Ronan's. Thought I'd stop by and let you know Ev loved the office."

"I actually met her an hour ago. She picked up a few pieces for her house."

"Good. Great." And he stood there like an awkward imbecile, no idea what to say. "I'll, uh, just head on out then."

"Night, McAllister." She turned and strode back to the register, not looking back. Why did he keep coming back for more? What moronic part of his brain thought coming here wouldn't be the ass-kicking, dick-softening face-slap it was turning out to be?

Because he knew she was hiding something. That she could use a friend, some help, and because one of these days she might let him try. But she wasn't ready yet. And he wasn't going to push, but he wanted her to know he was here.

He flashed her a wink and strolled out the door. He hadn't quite reached Payson and Ronan's before he reconsidered. Turning on his heel, he strode back for the gallery. Then back again. Then turned again.

Dammit, McAllister, don't be an indecisive fuck-head. Something about her was that little boy yelling at Lassie to run away. Not that he'd seen the movie, but he got the idea.

A guy in all black with a slick backpack looked up and down the sidewalk, eyes darting like a mouse thinking he was oh-so-clever.

Well that's not normal. Decision made. Aiden started back toward the gallery.

Glancing in the glass door, he saw exactly what he was expecting. Met enough dumbshits like this over the years. Nat sat on her chair, practically filing her nails for all the disinterest she showed the guy as he casually strolled by the jewelry counter, nipping a pair of earrings, and sliding them into his pocket.

Aiden stood stunned as the idiot moved further back into the gallery, seemingly out of sight. Didn't he consider a gallery would have security cameras? Or that someone would be watching from the window?

Wow, smooth move asshole. The guy heaved a twelve-inch bronze mermaid statue into his backpack, moved a few paces deeper, then added a few more odds and ends. May as well take the four-foot sandcastle sculpture while he was at it.

Once the guy closed up his bag and turned to make his escape, Aiden swung open the door, letting the bell jingle, then rattled the door a little extra to add to the drama of his entrance.

He nodded to Nat, the corner of her mouth turned up in a smug grin.

"Hey, McAllister. Looking for clients? Didn't think you did much criminal law."

Still standing in the doorway, he shrugged. "I don't defend morons that get caught on camera."

The dumbass stilled, his mousy eyes wide as an owl.

Nat hopped off her chair and strolled toward Aiden. "What if the thief was a stupid kid?"

"Maybe if they regretted it."

"And if they didn't regret the crime, just getting caught?"

"Depends on what they plan to do next." He crossed his arms over his chest, an obvious barricade in front of the door. The amateur still hadn't moved, but his cheeks drew up in bewilderment at the direction the conversation had gone.

Nat glanced back at the idiot. "How much do you think you've got in there?"

His eyebrows raised halfway to the ceiling. "A few grand?"

Aiden cringed. "Ouch. Keep it under a grand next time if you're going to try this shit in broad daylight."

Scooping up the backpack, his face darkened, finding the serious badass attitude that must have driven him in here to begin with. "Look, I'd love to stay and chat, but I've got better places to be."

Aiden stepped aside. "Sure. I'm not at liberty to provide free advice, but I'll throw in a quick tip. Don't cross state lines with that."

Nat added, "It's okay. He won't make it that far. We put GPS trackers in the higher priced items."

Before reaching the door again, the idiot turned to Nat. "Take the fucking thing out or I'll blow a hole in your head." The guy reached into his pocket, putting his hand on something that could be a gun.

She stepped an inch closer, hands on her hips, expression almost flippant. "Leave the bag, and I let you go. Shoot me, and you're wanted for murder and armed robbery. For what, a few trinkets? Next time come at night, come alone, and bring some fancier tools than a backpack and a gun."

As much as he wanted to tackle the asshole, he didn't dare risk either of their lives for some pretty bobbles. What was she thinking? Aiden stepped further from the door to leave the exit wide open, motioning his arms for the guy to get the hell gone. "Neither of us wants to get shot. The gallery is insured."

Nat walked a few steps back to the register and got out a handheld tool, stepping closer again. "Fine. I'll take out the tracker." She nodded at the backpack. As she dug through and picked up the statue, she added, "He'll never learn, you know."

Shaking his head, Aiden shrugged. "Sometimes you just need someone to give you a chance."

She rolled her eyes, fiddled with the bottom of the statue, then re-stuffed the backpack. "Alright. Get the hell out of here."

The guy snagged the backpack, heaving it over his shoulder and stalked toward the front door. He caught a glimpse of Maddy's partner, Ian, crossing toward them. "Did you call the cops?" He fired a glare back at Nat.

Aiden stepped back a few paces and waited behind the guy.

Nat shrugged in frank disappointment. "The moment you nipped those earrings. Be casual, but pop in, pop out, be gone."

Shifting on his foot, the obnoxious robber turned toward the back door. Panic had set in, and he brushed past Aiden in his mindless hurry to escape.

Balling up his fist, not bothering to hide his smug grin as the shit-head tried to pass him, Aiden plowed his knuckles into the guy's face.

His head ricocheted back. Dazed, he wobbled on his feet. Shaking away the impact, the moron reached for his pocket again.

"Damn, getting rusty," Aiden muttered, then blasted him with a left hook.

Eyes fluttering back, the moron crashed backwards onto the floor.

"Geez McAllister, Maddy's waiting at the back door," Natalie said as she strolled over.

Shaking the impact from his fist, Aiden rolled his eyes. "Hey, I was all excited about a decent fight the other night, but you and your subtlety took the fun out of it."

"You're no dummy. Don't you know brains get your further than brawn?"

He snorted, thinking about her cleverness just now. "GPS locators? A little fancy for an independent gallery in Seaview."

She shrugged. "He believed it."

Ian burst through the door a moment later, his eyes scanning the room, landing on the crumpled robber on the ground. "Thirty seconds. You couldn't wait?"

"Aiden doesn't have enough excitement in his life." She flashed him a wink. "I'll go let Maddy know we're good."

Normally he would agree with her. But her very presence seemed to attract trouble. Maybe she had a point, pushing everyone away.

Aiden stood close to Nat while Ian and Maddy took care of the failed robber. He nudged her, muttering out of the side of his mouth, "Did you ever get caught?" He raised an eyebrow at her.

"What?" She looked totally puzzled, like he was the crazy one.

"Alone, at night? No regrets?"

"Common sense. And if they made a fortune and enjoyed doing it, why would a burglar regret it?"

"Do you know who she really is? Where she came from?" Aiden parked on a stool at his sister's kitchen island. Angling away from the bright windows as the sun rose just high enough over the ocean to blind anyone foolish enough to look outside, he squinted to watch Maddy fumbling around the kitchen.

She was grouchy after truncated sleep from an early morning call. She rolled her eyes as she slipped her damp mass of hair into a knot. Measuring the coffee, she set the fancy pot to brew. Chase was obsessive about his coffee, hence the obscenely expensive machine. "I don't run background checks on my friends."

Chase ignored them both and slapped thick-sliced bacon onto the pan. The sizzling scent wafted through the kitchen.

Parking next to Aiden on another stool, Ronan rested his elbows on the counter. "If she wanted to, she'd talk about it."

"So says the former spy. Come on, she was a little too easygoing about that armed robber at the gallery. I think she's a thief."

Maddy snorted. "No way. She doesn't even run the stop sign at Fifth and Oak that everyone else seems to think is invisible."

Aiden shrugged. "Fine. What if she's in trouble for something else then? Like she's wanted by Interpol or Russian intelligence or something?"

Ok, so he knew that was far-fetched, but Aiden couldn't stop trying to guess why Nat was so secretive. He'd considered far worse on nights he couldn't sleep.

Hell, he couldn't stop thinking about her, period. That little dessert had seemed clever at the time, but he'd been rock hard since, craving her that much more intensely. "Seriously, when is trouble not following that woman around? In the last week, she's been at the epicenter of a bar fight and an armed robbery. Before that? Jumpy at the slightest sound or shadow."

Nothing that special about her. She wasn't even his type. Yeah, she was pretty. She was more of that handful breasted, strawberry-pink-nippled sorts of pretty that matched the blush in her cheeks. Although she worked her ass off at hiding that blush from him. Nor was it the badass muscle tees she favored, or the ripped-up jeans.

Hell no, he normally went for sleek styled, long-legged sorts. Not short athletic builds with badass attitudes. She was sexy as hell, and there was something intriguing that set her apart from the rest. Clenching his eyes shut, he tried to force the thoughts from his mind before he drifted to that pathetic pining that he'd caught himself falling into more and more lately.

Ronan gratefully accepted a piping hot mug from their sister. "Not Russian intelligence. Trust me," the former spy said simply. Well, he'd know better than most. "But I agree. She is hiding something. I couldn't guess what side of the law she's on."

Belly preceding her, Payson returned from the bathroom and dropped onto the stool between brothers. "Guys. Give it a break. She's just shy—" She didn't let Aiden interrupt, "I know, I know. Still, she's my friend. If she has something to hide, then let's respect her privacy. Even if she is wanted for robbing the Smithsonian, would you guys turn in your friend?"

Aiden winced. "Shit, Pace. You're asking a cop and a lawyer if they would be willing to be accessories? Even for Nat, even if it wasn't her fault... nope, my brain is not in the mood to tackle that one."

Another coffee ready, Maddy added a whopping dollop of cream and passed it across the island, holding the mug just out of Aiden's reach. "What's it to you? You've been making some pretty obvious moves lately."

"Have not," he scoffed, a bit too quickly. His sister's all-knowing ice blue gaze froze him solid. Shit, she was as scary as their mother, who redefined the phrase *eyes in the back of her head*.

"Don't add her to your discard pile," she lectured.

Awkwardly, he coughed to hide his guilt. "Not sure she'd have me anyway."

From behind Maddy, Chase—his traitorous, *former* best friend—was convulsing with mirth as he struggled to contain his laughter over Aiden's fib. Shooting discrete nukes from his eyes, Aiden hoped Maddy didn't notice.

Shit. She was psychic when it came to Chase, apparently. Sensing her husband's muffled giggles behind her, she blasted Aiden with furious eye-daggers, "You already did, didn't you?"

Aiden snatched his coffee from her fierce grip. "She's... dammit." Yikes, he'd really stepped in it this time. "She started it." Terrible argument. He was a crappy lawyer when it came to his family.

Hands on her hips, Maddy didn't seem to care about his plight. Room full of silence; no one rose to his defense.

May as well be honest at this point. "Okay, yeah, we may have had a thing."

Ronan snorted, shaking his head and staring into his coffee. "Had? How many times? And are you including the last week as past tense?"

Aiden huffed and gritted his teeth. "Okay, an occasional thing, but I only slept with her once." Multiple eyebrows raised around the room. "Nothing serious. Regardless of any... extracurricular activities, she's my friend, and I want to help. I know she's hiding something. How do I have a cop and a spy for siblings, yet neither of you cares that one of your friends has something potentially terrible she's covering up?"

A dark pall washed over Ronan. "We all have something to hide."

8

We need to talk.

Natalie read the screen on her phone. Leaping into her throat, her heart blocked off her airway.

Drying off her hair enough to make the call, she wrapped up in the towel and stalked out of the bathroom. She stared at the phone before connecting through her secure app.

Dawson fired away the moment they connected, "What data?"

"I'm sorry?" She cringed. How had he found out?

"Come on. Don't mess around. I had a gun trained on my head. In my own apartment. Some woman wondering what I did with the data you'd given to me. Tell me she was wrong. You said you witnessed the murder on your way in. Not out."

"I, uh... it wasn't relevant, and trust me, it was better that you didn't know."

"Where is it? Can you send me the file?" She didn't blame the pissed-off edge in his voice.

"It's a hard copy that I don't have access to at this time."

"Fucking..." He silently cussed and she could feel the fury radiating off him, his controlled pace as he kept calm. "Where is it?"

"In a safe place." She cringed. She bit her lip, wishing she'd just handed the damn thing over the day they'd met. But she hadn't trusted him yet. "I can get it."

"No, you stay put. I'll go get it. Where is it?"

"Really, even if I tell you, you won't be able to get to it without drawing a lot of undue attention. Give me a week."

"Done. I'll need time to figure out how the hell to tell my boss about our little arrangement anyway, so I can get a fix on the woman who tried to kill me."

She buried her head in her hands. "I'm really sorry. I should have given it to you back then."

"Damn right you should have. I'm stuck hiding out. I was supposed to go away for the weekend. Guess that's out until we get this wrapped up."

"Dammit, no. You've sacrificed enough on my behalf. Go wherever it was you were supposed to go and relax and I'll get the data."

He chuckled, a hint of humor almost rising to the surface. "Are you ever not going to be a pain in my side? Look, you stay safe. Let me know anything I can do to help get that data, and don't do anything dangerous."

"Never."

"Liar."

"Seriously. I'm done with dangerous."

"Good. You call me when you've got the data and we'll figure out how to make the exchange."

"Then I'll talk to you in a week."

She clicked off, tossing the phone onto the coffee table. Leaning back onto the couch, she gripped her fingers in her hair and closed her eyes, struggling to keep her lip from quivering. One stupid fucking mistake, and she was going to lose everything she'd found in Seaview.

For what? Peterson was behind bars. She hadn't found herself in the crosshair in years.

Dammit. She was done hiding. She was going to find a way out of this bullshit once and for all.

Natalie stormed into the bathroom to get dressed and get started on planning the toughest break-in of her career. She pulled on jeans and a sleeveless t-shirt and got to work.

Roaring to life hours later, her stomach growled to let her know she'd skipped lunch. She knew her way in, it was getting past security that would be the challenge. After all, not many security programs were designed intentionally for her.

After years away, she was rusty at programming. Back in the day, it would have taken a few hours, not days. And technology changed so quickly. No doubt the system would be updated. It would take time to work out any glitches, test out the program.

But not tonight. She'd hardly gotten a wink of sleep last night, then was right back at it again at dawn. Time for a break.

She closed up her laptop and stuffed it and her phone back into her backpack. Strolling into the bathroom, her bladder ached, belatedly warning her she was near the point of exploding.

Indulging in a steamy shower, she cleared her mind so she could start fresh tomorrow with a clear head. As she dried off, the reflection staring back wasn't what she had expected. Brushing her hair out of her face, she glared into the rusty edged medicine cabinet. Natalie cringed at her appearance in the foggy mirror. Blond, indecisive waves rested on her shoulders, tired and limp and sopping from her shower.

Eight years in hiding. Even more than that of suppressing who and what she was for so many reasons. Hell, when had she ever been allowed to be free?

Front tuck into the round-off, half turn then back handspring times two. Arms up, feet firmly planted into the mat, body tense, filled with the release of a perfect landing. Wait for it... Yeah, nailed it. Pumping her arms in the air, she whooped and dashed to bask in her victory. The reader board flashed her perfect scores.

Done with another rock-solid competition, she high fived the team and grabbed her gear, heading for the locker room, cheeks taut as her grin from the success wasn't easing anytime soon.

"Your angle was off on the pike-jump." Startling at the interruption, her chest constricted and her head whipped back to live another of her father's lectures. Don appeared in the doorway, his lip curled up in disgust.

"No more than a few degrees. My landing was flawless."

No wonder she'd jumped at the opportunity presented by R and L. For a while, she'd debated if she had even enjoyed gymnastics.

No... yeah, she did. She'd loved it. In part, she had enjoyed being the best at something. Most of all, she enjoyed the thrill of it, pushing herself to the limits. That feeling when her body spun in the air, movements precise, muscle memory mating with skill and adaptability.

Until one disheartening moment. Hell, that had sucked, but she'd been ready to keep going. Maybe teach or keep up the hobby now that there would be no pressure to win.

And then one really, really bad day.

And she became Natalie Smith. The shy recluse. Mysterious artist. Transient.

She squinted at her reflection. Picking up the scissors, she started snipping.

Slicing lock by lock, each strand floated weightlessly to the floor in an irrevocable exodus.

Tight along the back and sides, she left the top longer and unruly, just enough to tuck behind her ears. No pixie cut, or she'd be mistaken for cute. Teasing her fingers through the unruly waves, she grinned at her reflection.

Splashing on a bit of dusty eyeliner and mascara, she dropped her towel and headed to her dresser. Pulling out a lace-trimmed black satin camisole, she forewent the bra and slipped the top over her head. Tugging on her snuggest distressed jeans, more loose threads than denim, she slipped on her sneakers and fastened the laces tight.

Teasing her hand through her hair, she inhaled slowly to calm the adrenaline bubbling through her veins, knowing exactly what she wanted tonight, and headed for the front door. Halting in her tracks, she skidded to a stop as her hand covered the knob. Her backpack rested on its usual chair next to the door.

Hiking the backpack over her shoulder, its weight a bit heavier today as she anticipated her next move, she turned the knob.

Beachside Avenue was fragrant with burgers on the grill across the street, salty breeze wafting down the street, thickly caked sunscreen from the tourists... and home. Her phone buzzed in her back pocket.

Not again. Suppressing the dread that bubbled up in her throat, she slipped the phone out and punched in her passcode to read the text.

Get over here, your book is in! :)

Washing over her like a tropical wave, the words danced a happy jig in her brain. Floating across Beachside Avenue, she reached the gallery in half a heartbeat.

"You opened it already?" She felt a disappointed lurch flutter as she found the open box on the counter.

Harlen, one of the owners, smiled and said, "I thought it was my paintbrush order. If it's as beautiful as it looks from the cover, I'm ordering two dozen more to stock in the gallery."

A giggle bubbled in her throat as she ditched the backpack at her feet. A broody lighthouse dominated the cover, a simple title, *Found*, and her current name written in fine white script at the bottom, *Natalie Smith*. Running her hand over the satiny-smooth cover, she nearly felt the sand under her fingertips, the damp stone wall of the isolated lighthouse.

She couldn't even open it. This needed a little more ceremony. "I'm going to go savor it. Show you tomorrow?"

"You better. As soon as you approve it, let me know and I'll put in the order."

Slinging her backpack over her shoulder, she wrapped her arms around the book and glided out the door. Best night ever... and looking to be one of her last free nights until she took care of all this. Why not go out with a bang?

Chuckling at her own loopy elation, she tousled her fingers through the short locks and pushed through the crowded Beachside Ave, letting a hint of swagger spread through her hips.

Great. His phone was painfully devoid of messages, no cheerful light flashing to let him know someone wanted to hang out. Chase and Maddy were already out to dinner. Ronan and Payson were working together at Flotsam Antiques tonight, as town was crazy hectic with summer tourists this weekend. His parents were in Scotland for their second European tour since his mother had retired.

Netflix it is. Hunched over the fridge door, his eyes blurred at the lack of anything appealing. Bleak. Spinach with no dressing, burger with no bun, or... nope, that was it. Pathetic.

Goldie's Grill had reliable comfort food, the idea rumbling a whisper of hope into his empty stomach. Hell, maybe he'd find some comfort company while he was there.

Shit. He flicked the fridge door closed, shoved his hands into his hair, clutching his last bit of sanity, as he epically failed to convince himself to move the fuck on. There was a word to what was happening to him.

Perseverating.

Obsessing.

A whole damn dictionary of terms. He needed to get out of town, maybe find a few new partners to jostle his imagination so he could flood his fantasy life with some other woman to... well, dammit, what, to jerk off to? He'd seen plenty of exceptionally hot women naked, tasted them, been tasted by them... why couldn't he close his eyes and shuffle through his normal collection of fantasy women without flaccidity?

Now... his subconscious was so full of her, that she was overflowing into his waketime now, and his brain was mush after too many nights of vivid, epic dreams of what he and Nat ought to be doing. The ball was entirely in her court now. Not that he'd checked his phone hourly to see if she'd called or texted...

Wow, his fridge had nothing on his social life these days. At least the fridge was due to poor planning on his part, the social life... his sex drive was broken and wouldn't aim anywhere except the woman that seemed set on *not* being with him in any fashion. Goddammit, he was drowning in the age-old curse of wanting what you can't have.

Inhaling the salty air, he walked the few blocks to Beachside and popped into Goldie's. The tables were packed with families, couples, and friends all taking advantage of the gorgeous weekend. The harbor was so filled with boats, you wouldn't need a dingy to get to shore.

Not a seat to be had, either. Sliding along the navy-blue wall, trimmed with unfinished wood, he brushed passed a rowdy bunch blocking the entrance to the bar.

Must be his lucky day. A couple was just leaving a small high-top overlooking the water. Jumping in before anyone else saw it, he hopped on the stool as soon as the guy's ass was clear of it. He flashed the couple a wink, knowing they thought he was nuts for nearly tackling them to get the table.

He piled up their baskets and slid their beers to the corner. Apron filled with checks, cheeks flushed and hair a bit wild, Rena appeared with her empty tray. Seeing it was him, she smiled. "Hey, Aiden. Nice claim on the table. It's an hour wait on the restaurant side."

"No shit? Must be my lucky night." While she piled up the prior patrons' dishes, he nodded for the dishrag. She flopped it on the table and he wiped it down.

"Thanks." She was still out of breath. "I'll holler to Luke that you're ready. IPA?"

"Appreciate it."

Resting his elbows on the table, he watched out the window. Even the beach was packed, the long shadows cutting into the amber sunset glow.

A throat cleared next to him. Glancing over, he noted a barely-twenty-one nodding to the spare stool, "You using this?"

Aiden was about to say no, but a gorgeous blond scanning the crowd changed his mind. "Yeah, sorry man."

What was it about her? That *je ne sais quoi*. Fingers dancing through a new cut, super short on the sides, the top playfully long enough to cover her eyes for a moody rock ballad, if she sang, she blew slowly out pursed lips as she scanned the crowded bar.

Come on, don't make me jump up and down and wave my arms. Heart in his throat, he willed her to look his way.

The moment she saw him, her eyes lit up like the sun rising over the horizon. And she realized her reaction and quickly tamped down the thrill, but she let the smile linger, her lower lip pulled between her teeth. Strolling through the crowd as they parted for her, she dropped onto the empty stool next to him. "This seat taken?"

"It is now."

"Ouch, did you really just say that?" She teased.

"Hey, I was just trailing your bad pick-up line."

"Mine was a simple inquiry. Yours dripped with cheap seduction."

"You'd be surprised how often those lines work. Usually gets a good laugh and breaks the ice beautifully."

Black hair standing on end, as frazzled as Rena had looked, Luke appeared with his IPA. "Hey, Aiden. You see the new menu?"

"Not yet."

Sliding a pair of menus onto the table, Luke turned to Nat. "Hey there. Natalie, right? Can I get you anything to drink?"

"I'll have what he's having," As Luke disappeared into the masses, Nat winked at Aiden again. Damn, she was... *vibrant* tonight.

"I like your hair," he blurted out like a five-year-old learning how to pay a compliment. Her gaze swept up to his, topping off the look with a sultry blink as their eyes connected, smoldering like an old movie with spotlights on their eyes and dark shadows behind them. Aiden slowly inhaled as he let the familiar zing rush through him. That damn zing he got whenever she looked at him like that, the look that had completely overtaken his fantasy life.

"Thanks."

"No, really, it looks great on you. Brings out that attitude you try to keep bottled up." And that precisely angled jawbone. And those suckable lips.

Clearing her throat, she swallowed a grin. Tilting her head with practiced defiance, she said, "Say I sat next to you at the bar. Someone you didn't know. Say I was your type, and, like tonight, you lacked female company. What line would you use?"

He smirked playfully. "Not my type, huh? You've re-defined my type." He slid his beer across the table to her and linked his feet with hers.

Taking a swig of the offered brew, Natalie swallowed the dancing thrill that rumbled in her tummy. No wonder he had such a fan club. And she hadn't even needed the easy humor to relent to a follow-up dessert with him. "Okay, I surrender. You are an encyclopedia of pick-up lines."

"What about you? What if some egotistical jerk came up, parked on the stool next to you, and told you how amazing your ass looks in those jeans?"

She slid the beer back across the narrow table. "If that was his pick-up line, I'd throw my drink in his face." Right as he brought the glass to his lips and took a drink, she added, "But as you had your hands wrapped firmly around said ass, with your tongue on my clit a few days ago, I suppose I would take it as a compliment, as you'd know from experience."

Coughing on the sip, he wiped the back of his hand over his mouth and laughed out loud, his cheeks flooding from the lack of oxygen or shock or embarrassment of all of the above. "Holy shit, Nat. Where has this side of you been?"

"I... I'm tired of hiding *me*."

A curious smile lingered on his lips, his eyes rested on hers. "I think I'm seeing that woman that let me in a year ago, for that brief moment. Tell me she's not going to hide again?"

"You're not wrong, I have a past I'd like to forget. As it's not going anywhere, well, I'd like to remember who I am."

"What spurred the change?"

I may not get to see you again? Because I'm risking everything for the chance at having a real life? "Nothing special. Best of all... my book came." Not suppressing the grin, she pulled her treasure from her backpack and slid it onto the table between them. Another beer appeared on the table, but she couldn't look away from Aiden's appreciative gaze as he studied the cover, how his breath held as he traced his fingers over the cover. As she had, he felt the contrasting texture of the title, her name.

"Nat, this looks incredible." He flipped to the first page.

"Hey, I haven't even gotten to look through it yet."

Scooting their beers out of the way, he reached around and yanked her stool next to his. Sliding the book between them, he let her take over.

"Where is this house?" he asked as they landed on her favorite page. The one he'd chosen for his bedroom. In the distance of the perspective photo, the foreground highlighting a weathered oar embedded in the sand, and her rustic cabin up the beach. She hadn't risked any other shots of the cabin that might give it away as someplace special.

"Up north."

"You should see if the owner would let you get closer. That quirky rose window in the simple structure is fascinating."

Dancing around the details, she nodded, "Next time I'm in the area, I suppose I'll ask."

Brilliantly saving the day, their dinners arrived. He'd ordered the double bacon cheeseburger on brioche that smelled amazing. Scooting the book to the edge of the table to avoid getting fingerprints on it, she snagged his burger before he could get to it. Sinking her teeth in for a massive bite, she groaned as the smoky flavor lit up her taste buds.

"Hey, that's mine."

She grinned as she chewed the massive bite. "Excellent choice," she said, her voice muffled. She offered him one of her beer-battered fish.

After biting off a quick bite of her fish straight from her hand, he snagged his burger. Flashing her a devious wink, he took a massive bite of his burger.

As they munched, they people-watched. He nodded to a guy across the bar in a pink polo, "Account manager at a bank."

"Nah. Realtor."

"Okay, what about his friend?"

"He's the banker."

Scanning the crowd, Aiden gestured to a woman in black yoga pants and a sleek black hooded sweatshirt. "Hitman."

Chills ran down her spine at his words. How many times had her brain gone immediately to thug of some sort as she scanned a crowded room? She looked over the woman. Dark eyes assessing each patron, sipping a water in the corner. Yeah, he might be right. God she hoped not. "Teacher."

Laughing out loud, he downed the last of his beer. "You're so full of shit." The server dropped off their check. Aiden swept it off the table and had his card on the tray before she could object.

"I can pay for my own—even if this was a date."

"I know. Let's call it a thank you for saving me from a lonely and boring evening—or, better yet, a congratulations on your book."

"I can't imagine Aiden McAllister ever spends an evening bored and alone."

"More than I care to admit. Besides, maybe I'm hoping I'll get lucky... enough for you to ask me out so you can treat next time."

Shaking her head, she rolled her eyes. "Damn you're good."

"You thought I was trying to buy my way into your bed." He feigned an impishly astonished look.

"Thought you'd read between the lines a little better than that." She didn't bother hiding the blush that flamed her cheeks as she tried to lay it on the line. That she... wow, she couldn't even say it to herself? How did one express their interest in a booty call? And who came up with that stupid line anyway?

His jaw dropped open, words teasing on the tip of his tongue but didn't materialize.

Turning to face him on their stools, one leg on either side of his, she wrapped her hand around the back of his neck and pulled him close. Leaning in, she parted her lips as she moved in, saying the words she couldn't articulate. A soft sigh escaped her throat as the heat of their joined mouths sent a savory tingle through her limbs.

His hands clutched her hips and slid her toward him.

She tipped her head to take him deeper.

Out of the corner of her eye, she saw the server take his credit card. Pulling away, she licked her lips and searched his sunny blue eyes for assurance that he was on board.

Like a bucket of ice water dumped over her head, her phone buzzed in her backpack. She tried to ignore it. Hating her paranoia, but accepting that she had good reason for it, she pulled out her phone. At her hesitance, Aiden politely averted his gaze, knowing she read her texts privately. No wonder women fell at his feet. Not many guys were shameless flirts and considerate.

Natalie's stomach roiled as she read the words. She should have ignored it after all.

Dawson. *He made parole. I want you off the map.*

Fighting back tears that life was just this unfair, she texted back, *Now???*

Think someone's on your trail already.

How close? She scanned the room, wondering if the hitman was truly as Aiden had guessed. Or if the banker was a cleverly disguised assassin. An hour. That's it. One hour for a fond farewell. One hour to indulge and be herself for one freaking last night in the town she loved.

Not sure yet.

Tossing her phone back in her bag, she quickly rose from the table. Blinking away the fury that risked slowing her escape, the grief that tore her to bits, she slung the backpack over her shoulder and nodded to Aiden. "Gotta run. Thanks for dinner."

"Wait." He predictably chased after her.

Stopping in the middle of the crowded bar, she shook her head and adopted a sarcastic smile. "Sorry McAllister. Looks like you're going to have to find another body to keep you warm tonight. I have to go." She tucked her hands into his waistband and tugged him close. Savoring, she trailed her hands on his skin, hating what she was about to do. Before she left, she pulled him in, thrust her tongue into his mouth and sucked down hard on his tongue, then released him just as quickly.

Parking his tongue between his teeth, glacier-blue eyes sub-zero, he crossed his arms and stood tall.

She flashed him an easy wink and strolled out the front door.

Each crack of her heel against the wood floor of the restaurant, against the concrete sidewalk, each laugh of a happy tourist, the knife in her chest twisted a little deeper.

Better this way. Things would have ended in heartache anyway. Hers, at least.

She should be thanking Dawson for interrupting before she did something stupid like letting herself fall for the playboy, on the excuse she wouldn't have to see him again.

Legs heavy, she forced a casual stroll through the crisp air of dusk setting on. Walking a block west, she looked down the darkened side street. How close were they?

After a few unpredictable jags into dark shadows, she went southwest a few blocks instead. Disappearing down the shadowy drive, she crunched over the gravel. Pulling Aiden's keys from her pocket, she let the guilt churn in her belly.

Clicking the lock, the parking lights flashed cheerfully. She should at least leave him a note. It's not like she wasn't going to return it as soon as it was safe to do so.

Sliding into the driver's seat, she smoothed her fingers over the buttery leather steering wheel. Foot on the brake, she pushed the ignition start. Purring like a lioness, the engine sounded in full support of her theft.

Getting the hell out of there, she maintained a discreet speed. Now and again, her rearview would light up with someone that would follow a bit too long, then turn away. She took an indirect route, anticipating a long, miserable night.

9

THE NEXT MORNING, AIDEN lumbered downstairs to his office. Stopping in the kitchenette tucked behind the lobby, he set the coffee pot to brew. He hadn't slept a wink last night. That phony superior look on Nat's face as she left last night shook him. He'd still been incapacitated by that kiss, by her words, her fearless attitude.

What sort of text could have spun her for a complete one-eighty? They'd been having a great time. Another half hour, and they'd have been tangled naked in his bed. Bad fucking timing.

She'd seemed so invigorated with optimism, so bright and alive. Nothing like the recluse she pretended to be. That *je ne sais quoi* wasn't a mystery anymore.

Whatever she was hiding from... what if she was in trouble? A whisper of honesty, of simply asking, and he could do something. Protect her, hide her, fight for her. Whatever she needed. Sort of what he did for a living, and if it wasn't legal help, his family was pretty spectacularly set to help someone out of a sticky situation.

As the coffee pot wakened, trickling its slothful progress, he flipped on the small TV mounted above the minifridge. Leaned back against the counter, he distracted himself with the morning news. Anything was better than the unwelcome shit bouncing around in his skull.

Stocks are up. Red Sox are on fire. A system from up north may bring drizzling rain over the next few days. *"In other news, and my favorite story to start your week: On the serene shores of the quaint fishing village of Seaview this weekend, a local artist and her boyfriend halted an armed robbery..."*

Oh shit. The video flashed to the gallery's security tapes. Freaking publicity stunt for the owner, no doubt. Nat was going to kill him. And not just for the word boyfriend.

Before he could call to shower apologies on Nat, Ev's cheerful voice call out as she closed the front door behind her. Amused smirk on her face as she entered the kitchenette, without so much as a hello, she looked him up and down. "You look like hell. Stay up too late partying last night?" Dressed like she was still working for the hot-shot firm in Boston, she looked ready to wipe the floor with the prosecutor's face today. Soon, she'd realize non-court days were much more casual around here.

No court for himself either, Aiden hadn't bothered with a suit. Crossing his arms over his button-up, no tie, blue jeans and chukkas, he leaned against the counter.

Ev's dark eyes narrowed as she looked straight through him. "Who is she?"

"What makes you think a woman did this to me?" He stopped uselessly kneading the fatigue from his eyes at her accusation.

"I know you, Aiden. You can work all day and night without getting cranky or tired. Nothing gets you down. Except for your fragile heart."

"Fine. It's a woman," he answered honestly. Sort of. Was it more that she'd ditched him once he'd turned into a puddle at her feet, or that she was probably in trouble?

"You let a woman get you down this bad?" She snorted at him. "Amateur."

"Hey, I was just being honest. It's not that she's a woman. I mean, she is a woman, and there is a fair amount of lust involved. More, she's just got this sad story that she won't tell anyone. She's scared and hiding from something, but she won't say."

"I see. A woman didn't break your heart, but your fix-everything soul." Mercifully... or maybe unmercifully, Ev gave him one of those pouty-lipped, sympathetic smiles, like he was a little kid holding an empty cone, his scoop of mint chocolate chip melting on the pavement in front of him. "When's the last time you took a vacation?"

"Uh..." He calculated. Easy math. "Never." He turned to pour his coffee.

She stilled his hand. "I only have two cases of my own and my office is absurdly well-organized. Take ten minutes to brief me, then take the week off."

As much as he felt like work might help distract him from the pity-party that was crushing his brain, he knew he was going to be useless. "You know what? I'm good with that." There were few he'd trust to take over. Ev was a little too eager for her own good, quite frankly. But today it came in handy for him. His clients deserved better than a self-pitying, blue-balled sap.

After bringing her up to speed, he accepted his spontaneous vacation. With leaden feet, he trudged up the stairs and crashed on the sofa. Tried to read a book, but the words swam around on the page. The TV just irritated him.

Hell, Nat had been so weird when she left. Taking off like the bogeyman was nipping at her heels.

Sliding his phone out of his pocket, he couldn't take it anymore and called.

Without even a ring, an obnoxious buzz and rude electronic voice informed him the number he has dialed is no longer in service.

Huh. Brows furrowing tight, he fired off a text, unsurprised when it bounced back, *failed*. Gluing his ass to the couch, he resisted the urge to track her down at work or her apartment. She'd probably just picked up a new phone and didn't feel like giving him the number. Never the one for contracts, she always had some new pay-by-the-minute phone she'd picked up on her travels.

Not even remotely hungry for a late breakfast, he curled up on the couch with his new favorite coffee table book. Nat had left her masterpiece at the restaurant in her rush to get away from him. Edgy, soothing, soulful photos of the coast. Nat had a great eye for detail. If she wanted it back, she'd have to come get it.

As the sun lowered in the sky after the laziest damn day of his life, he was still groggy with a foul fog over his brain. The massive cup of coffee he'd drained to chase it away hardly helped. Still jittery from the afternoon brew, he switched to water and tried to watch a movie. Also useless.

He sucked at vacation, apparently.

The knock on his door was a welcome distraction. Few could get all the way upstairs after business hours without his knowledge, picking the lock and getting past the alarm—a good one at that, so he didn't bother checking before opening the door.

At least Ronan waited for him to open the door this time. Looking around, he asked, "You alone?"

Scratching the five o'clock shadow he hadn't bothered to shave this morning, Aiden shrugged. "Yep."

Dropping onto the facing sofa, Ronan rested his feet on the coffee table. "I met your new partner as she was on her way out for the evening. She's nice. When did you sleep with her?"

"Why do you assume—"

Ronan gave him that look. Aiden called it the don't-lie-to-a-spy look. Might turn that clever turn-of-phrase into a children's book. A parable about honesty.

"We used to date."

Ronan gave him *the look* again.

Aiden amended, "Like were actually what some might call a 'couple.' For a few months in college."

"And you trust her enough to take over for the week?"

"Actually, yeah. She's been a good friend since, and she's a hell of a lawyer."

"What's the occasion? An entire week off work? What's up?"

"Nothing."

Again with *the look*.

Damn, sometimes he almost missed his brother's disinterest in his family. Kidding. He was still pleasantly shocked at how easily they'd found a brotherly rhythm. But his twin-siblings loved bossing their big brother around. "Okay. I'm maybe a little bit bothered about Nat, for one."

"You can't fix everything for everyone."

"It's just... if she'd just let me try to help. You don't know her like I do. Sometimes, like last night, she's so open and honest and human. Then, with zero warning, she shuts down and puts up that wall again. Whatever's bugging her, I want to help."

Ronan sighed heavily, wincing. "You didn't hear?"

"What?" Immediately, Aiden sat bolt upright, knowing his worries hadn't been unfounded.

"She's gone."

"Bullshit." He felt the color draining from his face, his lips heavy as they fell numb.

Nodding, Ronan spoke softly but frankly, "That's actually why I'm here, to check on you. She texted Payson early this morning about what to do with her things. Said she had to run; thanks for being such an amazing friend. In total denial that she's gone for good, Payson and Maddy are making arrangements to put her stuff in storage."

Scowling, Aiden let his gaze wander to his phone.

Ronan read him easily. "You going to do something about it?"

"Why would I? She made it clear she doesn't need or want my help."

"And I didn't want help when I came home. Not yours. Nor Payson's, nor Maddy's. Not Chase's, Mom's, Dad's—"

"Okay, I get it."

"You've got the week off. Go find her and see if you can get her out of whatever mess she's gotten herself into. What if we can help her? I know she doesn't seem to think we can, but if anyone could help, we'd be the ones to ask."

"Yeah, we would be. Did Payson put you up to this? What happened to 'we all have our secrets.'"

"That was before I knew she was *still* on the run. I knew she was hiding, but I didn't realize she was in active danger. I've been on the run more times than I can count, so I get it. Lawyer, retired judge, cop, spy... and Payson. Come on, who could ask for better support?"

Aiden tried to argue, to claim she was doing fine without them. For all the years he and his brother hadn't been close, which equated to their entire adult lives prior to a few months ago, Ronan could read him ridiculously well.

"When's the last time you took a day off for a pity party?"

"Never," he relented.

"You total fell for her."

"Did not."

"Did too. You won't spare most dates a second glance. The night of the beach party? You were all snuggly by the fire. Then all hyper-focused on her at breakfast the other day. I saw that look in your eyes, the very look you mocked me for a few months ago."

"Yeah, I've been spending some time with her. That doesn't mean we're picking out dishes together."

"Maddy says you're only interested in Natalie because *she* won't have *you*. Try telling me she's wrong."

"That sounds like a trap I'd fall into. Lucky me, I've fallen into enough traps to see one coming a mile away."

"Sure." Ronan eased off the couch. A little slow on position changes, thanks to his hip that still gave him trouble as a result of his attempted assassination six months back. He paced a few feet toward the kitchen but stopped in his tracks. Brow furrowed, breath held silent, he sharpened a look toward the door.

"What?" Aiden asked, thrown by his brother's intense expression.

Stalking silently toward whatever had spooked him, dodging the creaky floorboard, Ronan whipped open the door.

Grabbing the intruder by the shirt, he pulled him into the room. With a quick move, Ronan slammed him down and had him pinned on the floor before Aiden could blink.

Leaping from the couch, Aiden looked about the room for any other clues that something was up. He stayed away from the windows in case this guy wasn't alone. He moved next to Ronan.

Snickering, the intruder pulled a gleaming black gun from his jacket—with silencer.

Unimpressed, Ronan knocked the gun across the room with a flick of his wrist.

Aiden's stomach rolled at the sight. If he'd been home alone... he didn't even want to think about it.

Taking a deep breath, he relaxed his shoulders to look as calm as his brother. He leaned against the back of the couch and asked, "Who are you?"

In a clipped New York accent, the intruder spat, "Where's it at?"

"Care to be more specific?" Aiden shrugged as if the guy was an idiot, as if Aiden had tons of stuff lying around that was worth murdering for. Well, the guy was a moron if he thought Nat had shared anything important. Not that he'd even mentioned Nat, but Aiden had no doubt she was responsible for someone trying to kill him.

"The data."

"Safe," Aiden said with flat confidence, folding his arms over his chest. He had no idea what the asshole was talking about, but saying that wouldn't exactly help him to find Nat.

"Where's Natalya?"

Yep. Thanks, Nat. "Gone."

From his spot, pinned under Ronan's knee that pressed harder against his gut, the intruder's eyes were wide with fear. Yeah, he'd blown it, coming after a McAllister. Voice hoarse, he cursed, "Play it cool all you want. She told her ma that she told you too much. I saw you two on the news this morning. Tell me where the data is, and I might leave her alone." With a sharp punch to the head, Ronan stilled the creep's movements.

Whispering quietly to Aiden, Ronan didn't look away from his prey. "He came for *you*. Take my truck. There's a bag under the seat.

You know, where Dad used to hide the cigars so Mom wouldn't catch him? Take it and run. Go find Nat before anyone else does."

"My car's faster." He looked to the hook by the door, but didn't see his keys where they should be.

"Fuck, you're cute. Your car's not here. I'm going to guess Nat took it? It's a hell of a lot faster and more reliable than hers."

Visions from that night at the beach, Nat stealing and hacking into his phone without his notice, flashed forward to last night. She hadn't kissed him goodbye to rub it in, she'd snatched his damn keys, and he'd been too fucking heartbroken to notice. "Dammit, she stole my car. She stole my fucking car."

Ronan smirked in admiration, but shook his head. "Go get her."

Reassured that Ronan and Maddy were on top of things at home, he didn't hesitate. And, he really didn't want to be on the receiving end of that gnarly looking gun, or any others that may be trained on him if he didn't run. Fucking shit.

If nothing else, she *really* owed him some answers now. Throwing some basics in a backpack, he tore out the door.

Within sixty seconds, Aiden was flying out of Seaview with the rumbling engine of the old truck red lined. Checking his rearview as much as the road ahead, he took creative turns until he was sure no one was following him. Still, he drove south for an hour before turning east. Never backtracking. Never predictable.

Long after the sun had set, as clouds spread over the moonless night, he pulled into a truck stop. The motel across the street looked shady, it's neon red light indicating "v_ can_y." He assumed that meant there were rooms available.

He stretched his legs after the long day, rubbing the road fatigue from his eyes. Stuffing Ronan's bag in his backpack, he grabbed a wad of cash from his wallet and locked the truck up tight. Although, he suspected he could leave the keys in the ignition and find it as he'd left it by morning, as no one would bother breaking into the unassuming old truck.

As bright and welcoming as the grungy motel, the owner sneered with a careless nod, the overhead fluorescents accenting the creases in his gray skin. "Hour or night?"

"Uh," Aiden had to think that one over. "Night," he managed to utter, swallowing the vomit that burned the back of his throat. He suppressed the urge to ask if his anticipated six-hour stay was cheaper by the hour, but he really, really didn't want to know.

At least the place took cash and didn't ask for ID. Accepting the faded bronze key with faded *#5* keychain, he opened the door with his elbow.

Room *5* was as appealing as it sounded. Stale cigarette stench. Faded argyle sheets. A boxy tv that took up most of the rickety dresser that no one in their right mind would actually store something in. The closet-sized bathroom was even better, with hair in the drain and an empty toilet paper roll next to the sink. The rat trap behind the toilet really sealed the deal. At least it was empty. Like the soap dispenser.

This motel was not designed for human use. Well, not decent humans. He should have slept in the truck.

He plopped onto the bed and bruised his ass for the lack of cushion. Were there springs in this bed or just plywood? Whatever.

Score. Ronan's bag was a trove of covert treasure. His brother still had some serious issues, despite appearing to be settled and unafraid of being found. Fake passport with credit card under the name Kevin Olsen—good thing he and Ronan looked a lot alike. Big-ass wad of cash. Prepaid, likely untraceable phone. And, a fake passport and credit card for Paula Olsen, with Payson's picture on it. Paranoid spy *and* a romantic, apparently. Was he going to make one for the baby, too?

Aiden didn't fear being found in the sordid motel he'd chosen for the night, but the germophobe in him wasn't thrilled. Forgoing the shower, as he figured he'd feel grosser after, he used the slightly less disgusting sink for a quick refresh.

Another sleepless night.

From the motel phone, he gambled. Dialing Nat's number, again, he was unsurprised the number was still reporting as disconnected. Where the hell was she?

The sun had yet to cast more than a taunting blue glow in the distance, but he couldn't stand another minute in the infested room. He grabbed his gear, didn't bother smoothing his rumpled t-shirt and dropped the motel key in the drop box. Climbing in the truck, he pulled out a paper map of the state he'd found in the glove box.

She could be anywhere. Out of the state by now. Out of the damn country.

Trying to tap into her brain, he traced his finger along the highway out of Seaview, along the coast.

Pounding his finger onto the map, he nearly growled in gleeful satisfaction. "Gotta be it," he whooped to no one but himself. Wow, he wasn't an alone sort of guy, apparently. Barely twelve hours of complete solitude and he was already talking to himself.

10

PULLING DOWN THE LONG, overgrown drive, grass brushing the bottom of the pretty car's chassis, Natalie's replayed every step in her mind again and again. How had they found her? More, *who* had found her?

R and L would have taken off indefinitely, as soon as the magnifying glass had come down on their dealings with Peterson. If it was L that had gone after Dawson, where was R?

And what chump had granted parole to Peterson? No doubt he'd threatened enough people, maintained enough power, even from prison, to manipulate the decision.

She would probably be in prison for burglary by now, so really, she ought to thank him. Ha.

For now, she had her cabin to hide in. Regroup. She needed to test out the program, map out her route, get it exactly right before going after the data. Before Peterson roamed free.

Her favorite place in the world came into view as the windblown trees opened to the meadow overlooking the sea. Settled like it had been there since the dawn of time, the weathered cabin sat perched above the beach. Pink and blue wildflowers danced in the breeze. The same moody gray as the house, the morning clouds and misty air encased the place in solitude.

Gravel crunched under the tires as she parked Aiden's car at the side of the house. The wind nearly blew the car door out of her hands as she opened it, but she'd anticipated the gust and held firm. Looking out over the Atlantic, she inhaled deeply and scanned the horizon. Not a soul in sight.

That look on Aiden's face as she'd left. His lips parted as she pulled away, his brow scrunched as he realized she'd played him.

What must he think of her? She'd had every intention of spending the night with him. Now, she'd led him on, dropped him like a bad penny, then stolen his car. And his only crime had been in being her friend. With benefit potential.

Shaking away the foolish laments, she grabbed the bags of groceries from the trunk. Unlocking the industrial deadbolt, she pushed against the heavy wooden door that had attempted to lock in place from too many years of minimal use.

She coughed away the dust that filled her nose and lungs and quickly punched in the alarm code. Her phone buzzed in her pocket, announcing someone had entered the cabin. Sighing in relief, she was grateful her system was still working.

She'd last risked the trip up here for her book. Foolish to have included anything from the area, she knew, but she'd been sure to not draw any extra attention to it. With its cheerful rose window offsetting the weathered siding, the structure settled in like it had bravely grown from seed in midst of the harsh landscape. It would have made a perfect cover for the book.

Even placed subtly in the background, in a random photograph, Aiden had recognized the place as special.

After checking the basics, turning the water back on, she adjusted the heater to "home" mode. Dusty sheets covered the furniture, the plush sofa and chairs pristine underneath. Despite the cool morning, she opened every window to breathe in the briny air.

Maybe she'd just hide here forever. Well, after getting the data, passing it off to Dawson, then never thinking about it again. She'd tried not to touch her savings, not wanting to draw attention to herself or her illegally obtained funds. With her investments, she could live well enough in this spartan home for the rest of her life.

She pulled out her latest phone. Before shutting off her old phone, she'd fired off a text to Payson, not wanting any of her friends to worry and call out a search party. Then she'd wiped and dumped the phone.

As she settled on the sofa, she called Dawson. He answered on the first ring. "Please tell me you're hidden."

"I am. Can you please explain what's going on? I thought he was in prison for life."

"Parole. Good behavior, all that bullshit. They were supposed to give me more warning, but the hearing was last minute. Somebody's wallet just got a lot fatter, that's for damn sure."

Cringing, her stomach filled with lead.

"Peterson's not even out yet, but word is, he's already made some calls to shady folks and moved a lot of money around."

"I may be jumping to conclusions here, but are you thinking hit-man? For little old me?"

"You're the one who put him behind bars, so, yeah, you're pretty high on his list. And if he knows you have that data? We have no idea who that was in my apartment, she could have been one of his, or, fuck I hope not, but there may be others looking for it."

"Tell me about her."

"Pretty, maybe late fifties, dark eyebrows, heavy New York accent."

"Tall? Thin? A line between those eyebrows you want to flick?"

"Who is she?"

"L. My old boss."

"Shit. Makes sense, I guess. Either the buyer is still interested, or she's going to sell it back to Peterson. If she's stupid enough to try to blackmail the ultimate blackmailer."

"She might be. I know they paid me a fraction of what they took in, and I was set to make a fortune that night."

"I don't doubt it. Trust me, if it weren't for Huong negotiating your record clean in exchange for your testimony, you'd be behind bars alongside Peterson."

She pulled a wool blanket from the cedar trunk she used for a coffee table, a parting gift from Payson after her last day at Flotsam Antiques. "I know you guys put your necks on the line for me and I am eternally grateful. I should have said something before, but with Peterson in prison for life, I figured he was already paying for whatever crimes he'd committed. How could I have guessed life didn't mean squat to whoever he paid off?"

"Didn't you stop and think about who the data might have affected? Ever think about *why* we were following him that night?"

Her lips pursed tight, eyes drawing closed as she realized what a fool she'd been.

"You know what, don't answer that. I'm sorry. You've been through enough on Peterson's account. I won't add to it."

"No, I should have thought of it. I was thinking it was safer to keep it secret. He was behind bars anyway. What do you think is on it?" Her stomach churned. How could she have been so naïve?

"Not sure. We'd been closing in on an international smuggling ring. Chances were, Peterson used his role to move property internationally."

"Smuggling?" A ball of shattered glass formed in the pit of Natalie's gut. "I should have given you the damn data."

"You were a stupid kid."

"And you were a rookie."

"I told Huong we should have forced you into witness protection. You were too damn stubborn, and he'd seen to damn much to wish that life on you. Old fool had a soft spot for you, said it was because of the way you gave up everything to make things right, leaving your family, risking prison yourself. And he knew Peterson would find you if there was any trail through the department, no matter how deep we buried it."

"Who all knows about me?"

"Just me. Huong's living it up in some off-the-map town in Hawaii."

When they'd dropped her at the airport with her first fake ID after the trial, Dawson and Huong had made her a promise. No one else would know about her. On one condition. That she checked in at least once a month or he'd haul her back in for mandatory witness protection. If anyone pulled Dawson's phone records, she was an old friend.

"From the start, Huong feared Peterson had a few feds on the payroll." They usually danced around this conversation. She'd been so lucky Huong and Dawson had found her, neither giving a shit about orders when it came to keeping her safe. There had been three other witnesses. The housekeeper, his chauffer, and another guest from the party that had seen Peterson threatening the victim. Not one of them lived to testify.

"I know. Why go to all this work for little old me? By this point, you must have dozens of stupid ex-burglars you talk to every month."

"Hell no. As much as I don't want to see you get hurt, you're still the biggest lead I've got on Peterson, and he wasn't staying in prison forever."

She rested her feet on the trunk and settled into the couch. Despite her guilt and Dawson's irritation with her, it was really good to hear his voice. Aside from untraceable calls to her mother and re-routed emails to her brother, Dawson had been the only constant the past eight years. "And here I thought it was because you liked my spunk."

"Ha. Huong was the sucker." He chuckled on the other line.

"Dawson?" She paused, not wanting to ask.

"Yeah?" He yawned, his voice cracking with fatigue.

"No offense or anything, but shouldn't you be at work, tracking Peterson rather than pestering me?"

His voice smiled through another yawn. "You're not wrong. I'm seeing you're safely out of the way, then I've got to figure out a way to discreetly keep an eye on him until I get that damn data. Where is it, so I can go get it and you can get back to that guy you were making eyes at?"

"How did you—"

"Hey, my secrets are my own."

Vision blurred from too many nights of absolutely no sleep, Aiden wasn't sure he'd found the right place. The driveway was completely overgrown and unmarked. Finding it had taken all damn day, but he'd narrowed down the location, the landmarks she'd photographed in her travels. He'd gotten damn lucky at the ZippyMart. Not wanting to leave a trail leading to Nat, he hadn't been able to ask about her, nor had he wanted to bring attention to the cabin. After a lengthy conversation about the area, its history, inquiring about interesting architecture, the old man at the register had remembered the cabin fondly.

Somehow, he didn't think Nat would be thrilled to see him. Too bad.

The place was even more serene then her photo had captured. Looked like the architect—no, more like whimsical carpenter from a century ago—had constructed the place from only locally sourced materials and designed the home around the land, rather than the other way around.

And... there was his car parked at the side of the house. Fucking shit, Nat. Really? Who's side was she on anyway, the bad guys or the good guys? She didn't strike him as a bad guy... no, wait, wait, okay, he could picture it.

As he stepped out of his borrowed truck, much less comfortable and way less fun to drive than his Audi, he whistled a happy tune and tucked his hands into his pockets, already looking forward to seeing her face when she saw him. Trotting onto the front porch, he turned the knob and found it locked. He knocked politely.

No response.

His knuckles vibrated down his wrist as he pounded his fist on the door like an unwelcome guest.

Nothing.

Walking around the house, he saw her through the sliding glass door. Sound asleep. Scoping the windows, he smirked at his good fortune and jimmied the lock free. Lifting as he slid the door open, he held his breath.

Part of him wanted to be furious her secrecy had nearly gotten him killed. The furrow between her eyebrows, troubled even in sleep, told him she was so much more scared than she'd let on.

He suspected neither had slept a wink the last few nights. In that nasty motel, wondering when and why he might get shot for something entirely not his doing, he'd awoken feeling less rested than when he'd closed his eyes a few hours before. It hadn't helped, worrying over what filthy creature might crawl over his face in the night. Eyelids heavy, legs already wobbly in anticipation of the impending adrenaline crash, his stolen car outside, and that his life was turned upside down by sleeping beauty... he was pissed off as she lie hidden in her secret getaway in the middle of nowhere, bundled in a cozy wool blanket.

Taking a seat on the cedar trunk in front of her, he cleared his throat and folded his arms over his chest. "Honey, I'm home," he announced in a melodious tune.

Jerking awake, she sat bolt upright. Eyes wide, hair wild, she didn't look pleased to see him. "Aiden. I, whuh, how?" Her eyes flashed to the house alarm, realizing she'd left herself vulnerable.

Smug grin pasted in place, he raised an eyebrow and continued his chipper tone, "Don't act so surprised, Natalya."

Her face turned ghost white. Like a terrified rabbit on the run, her breathing accelerated to panic level.

Taking pity on her, he reached to still her knee, but she swiftly pulled away and stood. "Nat, wait. It's okay. Just me." He opened his arms wide to show he wasn't armed or looking for trouble. For the last ten hours, he'd planned out all the terrible things he was going to say, mostly along the lines of furious accusations and the legal action he could take. Her genuine terror sure snuffed out that fire quickly.

Her eyebrows pulled together in concern. "Then what are you doing here? How do you know that name?"

"Hitman came to see me. Not so friendly of a fellow. Stalky and solid and thick New York accent. I think he came to kill me, but that may have just been his sneaky entrance and the silencer on his gun."

"What?" She paced to the windows and back, hand clutched in her hair as she processed his words, his very presence.

"Not twenty-four hours after you kissed my brains out and left me hanging before stealing my car. He asked me where the data is." He watched for her reaction. Priceless.

Jaw firmly set, she brushed her hair out of her face and lowered back onto the couch, gaze boring right into him, their knees not quite touching. "Tell me exactly what happened."

He described the brief, but intense interaction, leaving out Ronan's involvement, as his ex-spy's past identity remained secret to all but family. Just to rub it in, he described his awful motel room with the rat that had run a tiny marathon in the wall behind his head all night. "Whatever secrets you've been hiding from, they nearly got me killed. Thanks for that, by the way."

"I'm so sorry. Really. I'm so sorry. Dammit." She wrapped her arms around her middle and glared out the window. "This is exactly why, as you said, I don't let anyone in. Why I shouldn't have let you get so close. This is my problem. I'll fix it." Wheels turning fast, her eyes shifted as she calculated a way out of this one.

Aiden rested his palms on her knees to calm the vibration. At the steady connection, he felt more like he was the one being soothed, despite his intention to calm her. "It's okay to let others help you now and again. Not that it matters now anyway. My cart is now irreversibly attached to your wagon."

She leaned back on the couch, her knees remained still under his hands. "No one else knows where you are?"

"No. I had a hell of a time finding this place."

"How did you find me?"

The corner of his mouth quirked up as he thought back to their dinner. Her giddiness over her book. How relaxed, how open she'd been. "Something about the photo of this place."

"It was so stupid of me to photograph this place."

"Coming here was a gigantic leap of faith on my part. I'm not sure anyone else would make the connection. There were a lot of pictures in that book, the gallery. Despite your best efforts, I know you better than you think."

She breathed easier and leaned back into the couch. "I'm a criminal, Aiden. You need to get away from here. Tell them you don't know anything."

"I got my car back, so I'll hold off on pressing any charges. I do know some good criminal attorneys."

"It's not like that. I mean, yeah, sort of, but... *my* crimes aren't the issue. But I'm in a lot of trouble. It's the stupid data card. I should never have kept it secret."

"What's on it?"

"I'm not sure."

Aiden chuckled ruthlessly. "You mean you're on the run because of a data card you don't know the contents of?"

Taking a deep breath, she looked him in the eye. "I'm a burglar. Very specialized. Hired for my acrobatic and tech skills... and my egotistical naïveté. I worked for some shady sorts that went by codenames R and L. They dealt in information and paid me to obtain data direct from the source for them. It was generally safer for all parties if I didn't learn the contents of anything I stole. Unfortunately for me, the owner of the data in question murdered someone as I was leaving. And, bad fucking luck, I saw the whole thing."

"Wait a minute. Let me get this straight. Not only are you a thief but a witness to a murder?"

Cringing, she sealed her eyes shut. "Yeah."

"Please tell me you contacted the authorities?" His head was about to explode as he struggled to imagine just how much trouble she was in.

She laughed at his desperate questions. "Of course. I'm in unofficial witness protection."

"Unofficial?"

"As in, the asshole went to trial. I had some fantastic, disobedient agents protecting me, so I testified, and they helped me to hide without official witness protection. I've been checking in regularly with Agent Dawson ever since."

"Why the hell would the FBI let you go like that? Why would you let them? Witness protection is there for a good reason."

"Because Peterson had his fingers in a lot of pots and has a whole lot of money. Because the other witnesses all met untimely deaths."

He wracked his brain for a minute. "Shit, wait. Peterson? Former Secretary of State Peterson? That was arrested for murder eight years ago? The only surviving witness provided a classified video deposition out of legitimate fear of retribution."

"Yep."

Leaping off the trunk, he clenched his fists at his sides. "Shit, Nat. I was in law school at the time. That case is half the reason I *didn't* go into big-shot criminal law. A damn cluster of a case, and as slimy of a defense as I've seen." He muttered under his breath, pacing so violently the entire cabin threatened to crumble down around them. "Does he know what you were doing in there in the first place?"

"Oh, I'm sure he figured it out."

"What about the FBI?"

"They were so desperate to put him behind bars, they didn't care about my crimes and buried my record, with my promise that I'd keep my nose clean for the rest of my life."

He raised his eyebrow with doubt.

"I'm not saying it was legit on their part, but I was small fries compared to Peterson."

He plopped back down onto the trunk and braced his hands on her knees. "Where's the data?"

Looking him in the eye, her expression was as dead serious as he'd ever seen. "Safe. I'm going to get it. Once I figure out the nuances of the retrieval."

"Call this Dawson guy, have him go get it."

"He can't just stroll into the place it's hidden."

11

Natalie was furious to see him.

Vulnerable.

Thrilled.

Nudging her knee with his, he asked, "And I thought my vacation was going to be boring. Should have known nothing would be as expected with you involved. Well, what's for dinner, dear?" Eyes twinkling like the sun setting over a tropical sea, his greatly appreciated subject change chipped away at the fear that had frozen into her marrow.

"What is for dinner. Dear?" she fired back, unable to prevent the playful eyebrow raise.

And there was that ridiculously sexy smile. The corners of his mouth quirked up, his eyes squinting as he gave a subtle nod. "I grabbed a few groceries for my vacation. I'll run grab them." He hopped off the couch and disappeared outside, reappearing in under a minute with frozen pizzas, microwave popcorn, and beer.

"Oh boy. What are we, twelve?"

"This is my first vacation since before law school. You get to eat whatever you want when you travel, right?" Turning on the oven, he made himself at home. He grabbed a rag from the drawer, dampened it, and wiped down the dust-encrusted countertops.

She pulled up a stool and watched him work. Quite the bartender, he popped the top off a beer and slid it across the glossy green tile to her, then flipped a fresh towel over his shoulder.

"Tell me about this guy that tried to kill you," she asked, realizing his adorableness was far riskier of a focus than the people chasing them.

"No." Popping the top off his own beer, he took a gulp before tossing the pizza in the oven.

"If we're going to get you home again—"

Shaking his head as he swallowed, he effectively ended that line of conversation. Taking her hand, he dragged her back to the couch. "Not tonight. I'm fucking exhausted. Thanks to you, I haven't slept in a while. It's your fault I'm spending my time off in hiding, when I should be relaxing on a tropical beach with a strawberry margarita."

Now that he mentioned it, she saw the cavernous dark circles under his eyes. She'd ruined enough people's lives. "Well, I can offer you a beach and beer," she offered, nodding with a silly grin on her face.

"I don't even see a TV. Entertainment? I'd hate to be bored on my first vacation since my parents took us to Maui when we were in high school."

"I have a deck of cards."

"Strip poker?" He waggled his eyebrows comically suggestively.

"No," she chuckled, shaking her head at his ridiculous flirt.

"I'll let you win the first three hands."

So she could watch him sitting around naked? Not wise. But oh-so-tempting. "What makes you think I wouldn't win on my own?"

"Strike my last comment. I will ensure that I lose at least the first three hands even if I am dealt a royal flush. Plus, you can add some layers if you'd like. You have a wicked poker face, so I have little hope of winning as it is."

"So I get to sit here, bundled up in my scarf and coat, while you are entirely naked. I'm not really sure who's winning versus losing there."

His smug grin nearly convinced her to give it a try.

Sounding obnoxiously from the kitchen, the oven timer announced the pizza should be removed immediately. Fire alarms sounded less critical. Motioning to Aiden to stay put, Natalie headed into the kitchen and removed the nearly-charred pizza. Perhaps the oven wasn't wrong in declaring the emergency.

Slicing the pizza precariously with the paring knife, and only sharp utensil in the cabin, she dished up a few piping hot pieces for each and carried them out to the coffee table trunk. By the time she reached him, Aiden's head was tipped back on the couch and his eyes were peacefully closed, mouth slightly parted. Out cold.

Sighing a long breath of relief, she let him sleep. He wasn't kidding about being tired.

Silent as the cat burglar she used to be, Natalie closed up the house for the night and engaged the alarm. She tidied the kitchen and covered his plate, storing it in the fridge in case he awoke hungry. Snagging a pillow from the bedroom and draping the wool blanket over him, she made the couch as comfy as possible.

Carrying her dinner back to the bedroom, she grabbed one of the books she'd bought on the drive north and ate in solitude, her stomach full, her skin warm and heavy, before letting sleep take her as well. What the holy hell was she going to do with him?

Blinking as the sunrise blazed into his foggy vision, Aiden held his breath, taking in the foreign blanket draped over him, the unfamiliar beige pillowcase under his head. Crisp summer morning outside, reedy grass leading to tumultuous ocean waves, cushy sofa under him, the lingering scent of last night's burnt pizza. Bolting upright, he searched for Nat.

The gurgling, sputtering sound of bacon being laid out on a hot frying pan sizzled from the kitchen. She stood with a simple black apron tied around her distressed jeans and pink cotton t-shirt, neatly laying out more bacon onto the pan. She was whipping up a hell of an apology breakfast in the dim light. While she was distracted, he snuck into the bathroom.

Twisting the handheld showerhead to massage, his neck started to soften under the beating spray. Didn't matter how hot the water, how clean he scrubbed, Aiden couldn't make himself leave the bathroom. When the water ran cold, he flipped off the faucet and dried off with a plush white towel that was still warm from the dryer.

Leaned against the bathroom door, towel slung low over his hips, he folded his arms across his chest before facing Nat. What the hell had he gotten himself into? First woman in years that stuck in his head more than a few hours, and, because of her, he was on the run, with multiple parties out to kill them both.

This wasn't his thing. Maddy was the cop. Ronan was the spy. Yeah, he'd been the adolescent that reveled in dancing the line around danger, but he'd rather liked the routine he'd developed over the last few years.

He could just make out the sounds of Nat sliding their breakfast plates onto the small wooden table that overlooked the ocean. Bracing himself, he turned and twisted the bronze doorknob. Legs heavy, eyes still gritty from sleep he had yet to fully catch up on, he trudged down the hall.

Walking out of the kitchen with a pair of coffee cups in hand, Nat stopped short, causing a few drips to slosh from each cup. Her eyes brushed up and down at the sight of him in the towel. She inhaled slowly before trapping the air in her lungs, then turned her head, and focused on her task. Off kilter as he was, apparently, her reaction was greatly appreciated.

He snatched his keys from hook by the front door and dashed outside, returning moments later with his backpack. Within a few minutes, he was dressed and sitting at a spectacularly plated breakfast table.

"This looks amazing," he said.

Nat smiled politely but otherwise masked her reaction.

"Seriously, I was expecting toaster waffles and paper plates. You've made this cabin incredibly cozy." He wiped the corner of his mouth with a white cotton napkin before returning to eat another bite of bacon from the hand-painted stoneware dish, finally raising the hammered-copper fork to tear into the eggs.

"I, uh, despite my sparse apartment back in Seaview and this dusty old place, charming as it may be, I prefer to have a few nice things rather than a lot of mediocre things. She paused, staring at her uneaten bite of fried egg before continuing. "My taste is a bit eclectic, anyway. I suffered a lot of dinner parties as a kid. My dad was an uppity businessman, my mother the entertaining wife, and we were the perfect children; athletic and scholarly."

The corner of his mouth turned up at her openness. He knew it hadn't come easily. Too many years of holding back. "We?"

She set down the fork and looked out at the ocean. "My little brother and me."

"I guess I didn't realize you had family. Despite your best efforts at staying aloof, you fit in great with mine."

She shrugged and smiled shyly. What was up with her? Was it because she was trying out this newfangled honesty thing, or that she had gotten him into this mess, that was breaking down that wall between them?

"You must miss them."

"I really do. Don't get me wrong, my dad was hardly around due to his job and my mom was the ultimate yes-woman, but I love them. Xander, my brother, is in college. He was just a kid when I left."

Aiden didn't want to push, but the lawyer in him needed the details. No case was indefensible. "Why didn't you just hand over the data to protect yourself?"

"A lot of reasons. First, I couldn't have said for sure why the FBI was at my door. Being caught red-handed wasn't appealing. Second, security. In case I needed to up my ante. I'd just stolen from a very powerful, very prominent man, and if that wasn't enough to piss him off, I'd watched him kill a woman in cold blood. I wasn't sure what all Peterson knew. I didn't leave much of a trail, but even the best hacks aren't invisible. If it came down to threats against my family? I'd have the upper hand. The FBI, Dawson anyway, now know that I have the data, and they need it to put this guy back in prison."

"So who came to my door?"

"Maybe one of his goons. In the beginning, a few of his goons managed to track me down. But more likely, it was R."

"R?"

"One of my old bosses. The other went after Dawson, so it makes sense. They're hot on the trail, either still trying to close the deal, or, more likely, knowing their preference for weaseling their way out, they're trying to get the data to keep Peterson from hurting them. Or, if they're really stupid, they're hoping to blackmail him, or sell it to the highest bidder."

"Well, R is in jail now, for trying to kill me. Who was the buyer?"

"No idea. Part of my paycheck included shut-up-and-don't-ask fees."

"Shit. This is... really bad. How do you know the buyer isn't after you as much as Peterson?" He leaned back in the wooden dining chair and ran his hand over his face.

"It's a possibility. But as far as anyone knows, unless Peterson caught on and let it out, I didn't actually take anything, so I have nothing they want." Nat stared out the window, equally disturbed.

Aiden's teeth were clenched so tight he feared breaking a molar. "Your former bosses know."

"Or, they're working on the possibility that I might have it. Which lends credence to the they're-working-for-Peterson theory. You said R told you that he heard me telling my mother that I had told you too much? Shit. She always uses the secure phones I sent, but if they're getting desperate, they might have bugged the house. She'd easily fall for some ploy, like a 'repair guy' checking the water pressure or some scam to get in the house." She ran a frustrated hand through her hair. "My mom, she's not exactly a criminal mastermind. More sweet and dopey and aims to please."

"Did you just compare your mother to a dog?"

Chuckling, she snorted as she caught herself. "Not what I meant. I guess, well, she's adorable and loveable but... there's an air of lights-are-on-but-no-one's-home-ness to her. Somehow, she still thinks I should try to lead a normal life, and, uh... she keeps asking when I'm getting married and having babies. I threw her a bone one day and mentioned we were, uh, dating."

"You've really got to slow down on the dog references, lest you let it slip in front of her sometime."

"I think she'd actually take it as a compliment. She shows corgis when she isn't entertaining my dad's business associates. Anyway, she asked if you knew the truth about me, and I said I'd told you more than I should have."

"Thanks for that." He tried to keep it light, as she was still clearly a bit sensitive over his near murder on her behalf. "So, they must be watching your parents closely. I'm no spy or criminal mastermind, but could they have tracked your cell phone?"

"Not easily. I saw to that." To pull off half the damn jobs she'd implied, she must be a hell of a hacker.

"Do your parents know about this place?"

"No one does."

"Except me."

"See why I don't let anyone get close?" She nudged him with her foot under the table.

Nodding, he'd already figured out why she'd pushed her friends away. "Hey, maybe you could compliment me on my cleverness in finding you."

"Congratulations." She nodded with the utmost feigned sincerity.

"Thanks. Did anyone know you were in Seaview?"

"I knew it was stupid keeping in touch with my mom, but I... I don't know. She knew I was somewhere on a coast, but she didn't know what coast or even what country. I've emailed her a few photos over the years, but certainly none of Seaview, and not of this place. I suppose if she'd shared some of the photos, if her phone had been bugged, I suppose someone could have narrowed it down enough. I said I was dating a lawyer. She had known I was in a small town. But it still doesn't seem like enough for us to not have seen someone poking around Seaview."

Clearing his throat, he leaned back in his chair. "Shit. I know what it was. We, uh, we made the news."

"What?"

"Footage tapes of the robbery. Brought in some great business for the gallery."

"Dammit Harlen." She pulled her cheeks strained tight in helpless fury.

"We can't stay here forever. How hard will it be to get the data?"

Grimacing, she clearly didn't like the answer.

"Nat? Where is it?"

"Safe."

"But you're not saying."

"Nope."

"Can't blame you. Eventually, if we're going to get to the bottom of this, you'll need to tell me. Everything."

"No. *You* are staying here until *I* can make this all go away." She shook her head with eyes wide.

"Haven't you figured it out yet? One, I'm in this as much as you are now. Two, I might actually be able to help you get out of this."

"I don't need a lawyer."

"And I wouldn't be your lawyer if you asked. I'm too close and couldn't distance myself. But you could use a friend."

"I know. I've been in this alone a long time. Accepting help isn't easy." Scooting back in her chair, she stacked their plates, fisting the silverware before setting it on top. "You were already nearly killed because of me."

She wasn't ready to bring him fully up to speed yet. He got that. He really did. But it was going to be damn hard to get them out of this without knowing all of the details. It was clear she trusted him more than she'd allowed herself to trust anyone else, so there was hope.

He'd only found this place because he knew her, probably better than anyone else. It would be pretty damn impressive, and ridiculously lucky, if anyone else found it. Nat felt safe here. Hopefully safe enough to actually let him help.

Without a word, he joined her in the kitchen and dried the dishes she'd washed, wiped down the counters.

Her lips were pursed tight, as if she were debating whether to speak or not. Finally, she dried her hands brusquely and leaned against the counter, letting the words out in a single breath. "I'm not ruining your career because of my adolescent stupidity."

Reaching above her, he returned the clean coffee cups to the cupboard. She didn't duck away, didn't stiffen at the light brush of his torso against hers. Looking up at him, her eyes searched his in a quiet plea.

"Do you know why I'm a lawyer?" Letting his hands rest on the counter on either side of her, he gave her an inch, but couldn't seem to pull away further.

She relaxed against the counter in front of him. As he suspected, she was tired of pushing, and maybe, just maybe, she craved the connection as much as he did. She looked up at him defiantly. "Because your mother is."

With a subtle shake of his head, he disagreed. "Because I was a stupid kid." He nudged her with his knee and added, "Not as stupid as you, but close."

Fortunately, she never seemed put off by his dumb humor and glared at him, diminished in severity by her mischievous eyeroll.

"Difference is, I grew up in a small town with a lot of support. At fifteen, Chase and I were breaking into the liquor store rather than the candy store. Stole a few cars, but always returned them after a joyride or a quickie with some chick from school in the backseat." He brushed a stray hair from her forehead, then returned his hands to the countertop around her. "If it hadn't been for my parents, for the town, Chase and Maddy, I'd have been irretrievably lost. In prison or worse. Now, I'm on the side of the law that can help those who don't have the support that I did."

Her eyebrows drew together in regret. "So it's not the forbidden fruit thing, but the helpless creature thing. Thanks, but no thanks. I can take care of myself." She pushed at his arm to get away. He didn't resist.

As she walked away, he added, "Not going to lie, there's probably a little of both involved." That stopped her. Arms folded across her chest, she stood in the middle of the hall. "There's also the way you look at me, like you are now, like I'm totally nuts. How you work your cheek between your teeth when you're worried. And your eyes are never the same color twice; today they're almost gray."

She visibly softened, cheek still between her teeth, but there was a lightness in her posture.

Afraid to startle her, he didn't move past his post. Instead, he leaned against the open doorframe and crossed one foot over the other, gaze sweeping over her and locking on to those eyes-of-many-colors. "You're a total perfectionist, but you pretend you're not, and you don't let it rule you. It breaks your heart that you can't share yourself with your friends, and that your family doesn't understand you. Not to mention..." The corner of his mouth turned up in a slow smile. "You're hot as hell. Badass attitude with athletic curves. Topped off with a wicked smile that tells me you think I'm irresistible."

There it was. That restrained laugh that danced lyrically through the air. "And you are crazy." She shook her head at him, but the smile told him everything.

"I am that. Let's go for a walk." He nodded his head toward the door.

"Okay," she nodded.

12

SALTY AIR GUSTED THROUGH her hair as she stepped outside. She pulled her knit cardigan over her shoulders and inhaled the unsettled wind.

Aiden followed close behind. "Holy mother of... shit it's cold out here. What happened to July?" Wearing what she had discovered to be his favorite artfully distressed jeans and crisp white tee, he dove back inside. Moments later, he returned with his lightweight puffer jacket. She kept her grin to herself, noting that this was indeed the lightweight one, and that his heavier jacket was likely neatly stored until fall.

Natalie locked up the house behind him, watching him stroll straight down to the middle of the sand and pause. Hands tucked in his pockets, he turned back to her and nodded his head down the beach.

She rolled her eyes at him but picked up the pace.

What the hell had that been all about after breakfast? Why her? She'd watched him since the day he'd swaggered into Seaview. Not in that creepy way, of course. She had *noticed* him, because every time she saw or even heard about him, her heart leapt into her throat, her pulse raced hot through her veins, and her tongue tied in a snug bowline knot.

It had felt so good to pretend she was normal for a few stolen hours with him now and again, when both would lower their walls, to pretend she was safe and he wasn't worrying over whether or not he'd given more of himself than he'd meant to share with a dreaded female that would claw her way into his heart forever if he didn't protect himself.

Before, once again, Peterson had ruined her life.

Aiden had poured over every photograph in the coffee table book with her. That hungry expression he'd worn, watching her lips as he hung on every word... when he took her mouth and the blaze would detonate.

"Nat?" he asked, interrupting her inner reminiscing, watching her distant expression as they strolled down the windy beach.

Shaking off the delicious image, she answered, "Yeah?"

"I'm enjoying my vacation so far. How about you?" That slow smile shot an arrow straight into her chest.

She shrugged as she caught up to him. "This is my dream vacation, of course. A few hitmen after me and the man I naively implied might be important, selfishly to get my mother off my back. The man who hates me more than anyone on the planet is getting out of prison soon. And, I get to spend this relaxing weekend planning one of the toughest break-ins of my career."

He strolled alongside her down the beach. "What is your dream vacation?"

She stared out at the ocean, the whitecapped waves telling of the incoming foul weather pattern. "You first."

"Sunshine, aqua-blue ocean all around... you lying on the beach in a skimpy bikini."

"You answered that way too quickly."

"Not the first time I've thought about it. Your fault. You always smell like a tropical getaway."

"It's my coconut lime shampoo."

Inhaling deeply, he grinned. "Damn, that's why I want to devour you all the time. It's more than the shampoo, though." He grinned and stepped closer, tipping his head back in a subtle nod for her to continue. "Come on. What's yours?"

"Paris. London. Museum after museum of art and history. Maybe some good food along the way." Embarrassed by her own nerdiness, she found her cheek wedged in between her teeth. Huh, she hadn't realized she did that. Yet Aiden had noticed.

He grinned at her. "That does sound pretty awesome. Anything in particular you're dying to see?"

"Musée D'Orsay. I once saw a picture of this room behind the clocks of the old train station. Wood floors, natural light, worn leather couches, and one of my favorite impressionist collections on the planet."

Rather than responding, he stood there, just staring. Not in a creepy way. More of that fascinated way like he had from the kitchen this morning. Then the smile he'd worn morphed into a scowl.

He glanced her way and smiled politely, then turned back toward the house. "I hope you get to see it one day."

Through the textured window, she could just make out the sun setting in the distance. Another frozen pizza, pepperoni and sausage judging by the meaty scent, wafted toward her. Her stomach growled, anticipating the comfort food. She'd like to see his vacation diet if they were in the tropics, on his ideal vacation.

Wrapping the single remaining towel around her, much too short, she looked around and realized she hadn't brought a change of clothes into the bathroom. Cautiously opening the door, she attempted a quick dash to the bedroom.

"Nice ass," she heard from the living room, but nothing more.

Grinning at the absurd compliment, she shut the bedroom door behind her and tried to shake off the odd emotions that vibrated through her. Didn't seem to matter what they were doing, where they were, Aiden was freaking upbeat. Even when he must be upset, he ensured *she* was okay.

And she was getting way too caught up in the ultimate no-win relationship.

She pulled on a light sweater and jeans, leaving her feet bare, more out of laziness than a desire to feel the cold floor on her feet. As soon as she stepped down the hall, her toes were pleasantly surprised to find the floor was almost warm. Crackling in the grate, a cozy fire warmed the room beyond the temperature.

Stretched out across the couch, feet up, arms folded behind his head, Aiden shifted his gaze from the fire to watch her enter the room. "Hey," he said, a sleepy edge laced in his voice.

Neatly plated pizza and salad was set on the coffee table. Not bad. "Hey. Thanks for making dinner."

"Gourmet frozen pizza. With bagged salad on the side, therefore it's healthy. And, in front of the fire, so it's cozy."

Her grin grew wider. "You've got it all figured out, don't you?"

"I wish." He rose to his feet, his eyes searching her, and strolled closer. Stopping just close enough she could feel the electricity pinging between them, but far enough out of reach to torment her, he crossed his arms over his chest. "Did I mention yet how much I like your hair?"

She ran a self-conscious hand through her short hair, still damp and unruly from the shower. "Thanks."

"No, really, it's fucking hot." He rocked back on his heels and glanced toward the coffee table. "Let's eat."

She downed most of the pizza and all of the salad before she dared say anything. This is exactly what she had warned herself about. "I'll be honest with you, Aiden. I haven't been with a lot of guys. Nothing prudish, it's just that hooking up is a risky choice while living on the run."

"I can imagine."

"So I'm not adept at this whole thing. The night I left, I was looking to see what seconds might taste like."

"That's what I'd thought at first. But imagine my disappointment when I discovered that instead of inviting me back to your place, you stole my car."

"Before Dawson interrupted, I'd been hoping you'd invite me back to your place," she confessed. "I knew it was time to move on, but I thought another few hours wouldn't hurt."

He swallowed a final bite of pizza and winked at her. Leaning back against the couch opposite her, he stretched his legs out next to her. "I was considering seconds for the first time in years, and I don't make that exception. A risky part of maintaining steadfast singlehood." He paused, wiping his hands on the napkin. "Another few minutes, and I was planning to invite you up to my place. And trust me, that also doesn't happen often."

"As in, you don't normally invite women over?"

"To my man cave? Hell no. Their place? I get to leave on my own terms. No pancake breakfast. Although, if you're still interested, I'm not sure if I mentioned this yet, but my ideal vacation involves a lot of sex." He nudged her thigh with his foot, an eyebrow raising in wicked invitation. "Just saying."

Shaking her head, Natalie smiled at the absurdity. She'd started off trying to explain herself, yet somehow came off sounding like she was looking for a booty call. Again. Man, she must sound desperate. "Okay. Okay. I'm going to back-peddle a bit here. I'm not actually asking to move on to seconds. Not now, anyway."

He folded his arms over his chest, shaking his head with an almost shy grin. "All the other restaurants are closed for the duration. If either of us wants to avoid starvation—"

"And I'm done with the metaphors." Her brain was about to explode. Not to mention her sex drive. "What started out as my attempt to inform you of my lack of experience and reassurance that my motive that night was not to steal your car. Yet somehow, thanks Freud, it came out as a request for you to have sex with me. Not my intent. I'm good with fasting."

"Thought you were done with metaphors?"

Exasperated, she stacked their plates and headed for the kitchen. Carelessly letting the plates clunk together, scrubbing despite the lack of debris, she glared at the sink. What was she trying to say? Was she being exactly what she had warned herself about? Expecting Aiden McAllister to suddenly decide he wasn't a commitment-phobe because she was different? Or that she wasn't another giggling ditz that clung to the foolish hope that he'd sweep her off her feet?

Appearing behind her, he stalked closer and pressed his body against her backside. Reaching around, he shut off the water. Leaning down, he placed a savoring kiss on her neck. "I think we've crossed a few lines neither of us had ever intended to cross. Your one-woman-run-and-hide mission is now a two-person operation. And as you're not willing to talk about it, I'm good with defaulting to talking about sex. But we can do more than just talk about it. If you're game." He trailed kisses up her neck and nipped at her ear. "Thanks to you, I'm only allowed to look at one woman, for fear of death if I venture out."

Rolling her eyes, she whacked him in the gut with her elbow. Not roughly, just enough to let him know she shouldn't appreciate the joke.

"Yeah, I deserved that." With one arm on either side, he pinned her against the kitchen counter.

She turned in his arms and looked up, trying to tell if he was joking, seducing, or cross-examining. "You're sleeping on the couch again."

Natalie ducked under his arm and snuck off to her bedroom until she was certain he was asleep. She checked that her backpack was ready to go, adding some extra cash from her lockbox, another ID. The night sky was pitch black. The only light in the cabin was the lingering fire he'd built for their cozy dinner.

He was going to flip out. That trust they'd been slowly building? Yeah, that was going to be erased.

His life had already been turned upside down because of her. Driving him into the heart of suburban New York, to a location Peterson was undoubtedly watching closely, was so much worse than he deserved. Yeah, she'd already recognized he dealt with anything thrown his way. Bar fights, armed robberies, attempts on his life, and finding her when no one else would have seen the subtle clue.

And what about after all of this? A little adventure together, and he was going to want to go on the run with her?

Creeping open her bedroom door, she listened.

No snoring, but he didn't snore. No movements.

Tiptoeing closer, she saw him lying on the couch, adjusting his feet under the blanket, wrapping his arms around a pillow, flipping from one side to the other.

Great. He couldn't sleep. She still had hours of driving before she could even stop off for a break.

Tucking her backpack into the bedroom, she slid off her clothes and went for the gold. Knock him out so he'd sleep safe and sound the only way she could come up with.

Like whacking his skull against a brick wall over and over. Every time he thought Nat might open up, she shut back off again. He was willing to let her sidestep the conversation and attempt to distract him with talk of sex or a walk or dinner or whatever she could come up with.

Okay, she was on the run. Multiple parties out to kill her because she'd been the key witness in a high-profile murder and bearer of data that was likely worth killing for. If they were going to get out of this, he needed a hell of a lot more to go on.

Lying on the couch, staring up at the dancing lights from the waning fire cast onto the plank wood ceiling, he played it out again in his head, compiling the bits of information she'd left like breadcrumbs in their conversations. No case was unwinnable if you could find the right angle. Piecing together the case to date, he wracked his brain.

Feeling like he was almost there, his tongue tapping against the roof of his mouth as he calculated... he was interrupted by the sound of

Nat's bedroom door creaking open. Lifting his head to see, she came strolling down the hall, naked and delicious and sultry and... Holy shit she was hot.

He flipped back the blanket and sat up, breath caught in his throat, any useful or coherent thought rushing south at breakneck speed. She glanced to the fire, back to him, that fearlessness taunting him.

While he sat stumped like a moron on the couch, she stalked closer and straddled him.

Breath whooshing from his lungs, hands afraid to touch her, fearing she was a dream and he actually had fallen asleep, he stared up at her. Penetrating eyes locked onto his, she slid her hands up and gripped the back of his neck, lips teasing his open and sweeping her tongue over his. Awakening a desperate part of him, her throaty moan as she leaned into him reminded him of every fantasy his imagination had conjured up involving Nat doing exactly this.

Hands trailing up her hips, encircling her waist, grasping over her breasts, he trailed his lips along her clavicle, her shoulder.

Taking her breast in his mouth, suckling, teasing, he let himself drift away in the fantasy.

She gasped, pressing closer. Reaching down, she gripped the hem of his shirt and tugged it over his head. Her hands trailed down his middle, her fingers unclasping the button and sliding down the zipper.

Molten lava pumping through his veins, his groin, he groaned as she teased her fingers along the waistband of his pants.

Wincing, he closed his eyes and stilled his movements. Where the hell the rational thought came from, he couldn't say. And he sure as hell wished that stupid conscience had waited twenty more minutes. Hell, five at this rate. Or even one.

Either way, she was totally going to ditch him. Knock him out with some goodbye sex, then hop in his car and take off again. His dick was furious with the change in plan, but his brain and his heart couldn't let her down.

Stilling her hand, he linked their fingers. "Not tonight."

She scowled. "What, so you're allowed to make a move, but not me?"

Pissed, he wanted to scream and rage and declare this was fucking unfair. "No. Nat, I want you so damn bad, but not like this. Yeah, I've practically been begging, but, well, I'm feeling a little used right now."

"McAllister, you're trying to tell me you don't want a woman taking advantage of you?"

"Pretty much. I wouldn't ever want to take advantage of you. When we indulge in seconds, it's not going to be because we're running for our lives and you're trying to distract me with some sort of farewell fuck."

Stealing his shirt, she pulled it over her own head and rose to her feet. "There won't be a next time."

She stalked out of the room.

Way to go McAllister. When did he get a conscience? His chest ached with guilt. And something else he didn't care to acknowledge.

But she wasn't going to be alone.

13

NOT A PEEP FROM the living room. Finally. She'd tried to get some rest waiting for Aiden to fall asleep but hadn't been able to catch a wink.

Alone, the sun a few hours from rising, Natalie slipped out of the smooth cotton sheets. Aiden would follow her right into the crosshairs, even after learning the seriousness of the situation.

In the dwindling firelight, his features were shadowed with secretive accents, making that deliciously dark side of him stand out. Even in peaceful sleep, there was nothing innocent about Aiden. The thick wool blanket only covered his lower half, tormenting her again with the desire she'd tried to snuff out a few hours ago.

Dammit, Aiden. Since when did Aiden McAllister turn down a naked woman that was actively trying to seduce him? What, it had to be his idea? She was still fuming and aroused and furious and... Okay. This was a big part of why she needed to leave. Alone.

With one last glance, she ensured he was asleep. Good thing the prick had turned her down. It was way easier to leave now. Huffy and horny was way better than bruised hearted.

Easing open the front door, she slipped out into the gusty night. Tossing her backpack on the passenger seat, she dropped into the driver's seat and pushed the start button.

Nothing.

What? Brake pedal down, keys in the car, start button not engaging.

Her head thudded against the headrest. Dammit. Glancing over, she saw Ronan's truck parked on the other side of the driveway.

If at first you don't succeed… she hauled her backpack out of the car and quietly closed the car door behind her. In the darkness, she headed for the truck.

Illuminating the drive, the front door eased open. Glowing light at his back, Aiden stood in nothing but his boxer briefs, arms crossed, and leaned casually against the doorframe. Smirking, he shook his head at her. "Did I not mention how often I used to sneak out of my parent's house?"

"You disabled the truck, too, didn't you?"

"Hell yeah. I trust you to not get me killed, but I don't trust you to not leave me behind." He crossed one foot over the other and raised an eyebrow at her. "Come on, I'd like a decent night's sleep. Then in the morning, you can fill me in on the plan."

Rolling her eyes, she shouldered her backpack and strolled back into the house. Aiden held the door open wide while she brushed past him, then closed and locked it behind her. She punched in the alarm code as he waited and stalked back to the bedroom.

Stripping back down to her cami and panties, she slid back into bed for another few hours of restless sleep. Rather than reclaiming his spot on the couch, Aiden followed right behind.

As if he belonged there, he climbed in behind her. Reaching back, he flipped off the lamp and wrapped his arms around her. She settled in against him and indulged.

Sliding into the cracked red-vinyl seat of the highway diner, Aiden grabbed the sticky menu from behind the napkin holder. Rubbing his eyes, he tried to clear the morning nap from his foggy brain. "I still can't believe you turned down frozen pizza for breakfast."

"I confess, I was too antsy to eat this morning."

His stomach grumbled painfully as he perused the carb-heavy menu. The nap hadn't just been in anticipation of a late night, but a poor attempt to fool his stomach into thinking it wasn't time to eat. "So you decided I ought to starve until nearly lunchtime?"

"You were asleep anyway."

Nat grabbed the other menu and flipped over their coffee cups as the server arrived. In her faded blue polo, the server offered a sweet smile as she poured their coffees. "Decide yet?"

Nodding, Nat hardly glanced at the menu. "Denver omelet for me, thanks."

Not caring at this point, as his stomach was desperate, he ordered the biggest hash bowl on the menu. As the waitress strolled behind the counter and passed their order to the cook, Aiden gulped down the bitter coffee.

Nat poured in a splash of creamer. He shook his head. "You are so weird."

"I know." She shrugged. "I won't risk it with ice cream, but I can't live without the little cream in my coffee."

"It's terrible coffee anyway. I'm not bothering."

"And the cream will make it not so terrible." She raised a mischievous eyebrow over her coffee and settled into the booth.

Oddly enough, she seemed more relaxed today. Rather counterintuitive in light of their increasingly perilous situation. Itching to get on the road, she'd outlined their plan to the detail as the sun rose. Lit up, sipping coffee in bed, shoulder-to-shoulder together this morning, she brought him up to speed. Finally. He could see the thrill of it, but they were both terribly out of practice when it came to breaking and entering, and the stakes were so much higher this time.

As the restaurant was nearly empty, the waitress returned within a few minutes, balancing piping plates of deliciousness. Pausing only to douse the hash with half a bottle of tabasco, Aiden risked a serious burn, shoveling in a steamy bite. Before he even swallowed, his stomach was cheering at its victory.

He'd downed most of the food in a few breaths, then glanced up to find Nat staring at him. Grin wide, her nose was scrunched in curiosity. Shaking her head, she took a cautious bite of her omelet.

Flashing her an easy wink, he downed the rest of his breakfast. Easing back into the bench seat, Nat finished off her omelet at her own pace. The waitress stopped by with a warm-up.

As he digested, he leaned back in the booth and watched the news. Hung over the bar, a TV was muted while the daily news played. For the most part, the world was miraculously boring. Stock market on a slight uptick. The Patriots were set to have a great season.

The next story burned worse than the tabasco and acidic coffee quarrelling in his chest. Nat's picture dominated the screen. The photograph looked to have been taken a few weeks ago. Was that the night of the beach party? At his panicked look, Nat followed his gaze and her horror sucked all the oxygen from the room.

Scrolling beneath, the caption read, *Wanted for information regarding a human trafficking ring involving former Secretary of State and convicted murderer Peterson...*

As the screen shifted to the next story, Nat collected her jacket and backpack. They dropped a wad of cash on the table and slid out of the booth. Was it his imagination, or were the staff and few diner patrons watching their departure?

Had they made the connection between Nat and the news story? What about the gas station attendant or others fueling up this morning? Would they have recognized her?

Stealing the driver's seat again, Nat took the wheel. Aiden had seen the frantic look in her eye, the need to find a sense of control. Not to mention, she looked damn good driving his car.

She casually pulled out of the parking lot and took a few unpredictable turns before turning onto the expressway. Glancing in the rearview mirror, she finally relaxed her grip.

"FBI, your old bosses, or the buyer? I'm guessing Peterson doesn't want to further incriminate himself on national television. I can't think of anyone else who would know what you took."

She fisted her hand in her hair. "The FBI knows where I am, well, Dawson anyway. His partner now knows about me, although not my location. R is already in custody, so I'm willing to bet L fled the country. I'm going with the buyer. Whoever wants that information clearly isn't in it for the money."

"I'm thinking they want Peterson to fry."

"Agreed. Not a peep for years, and as soon as he's out, everyone's going straight for the data. Like me, they want him behind bars."

"We can only hope they are the understanding sort of vigilante and won't kill the messenger."

Checking behind them again, Aiden tried to reassure himself they weren't being followed. Undeniably, he was more than a little frustrated that Nat hadn't trusted him sooner. Yeah, he got why, but this would have been a hell of a lot easier with Peterson still behind bars.

A few miles past, then a few more. Ever on alert, her eyes scanned the road ahead and behind.

"South Carolina," he announced.

"What?"

"License plate game."

"What?" she asked again, eyebrows raised as she gave him that look like he was from a different planet.

"You never played the license plate game? How did your parents keep you entertained on long car trips?"

"We flew."

"No road trips?"

Her grip on the wheel loosened. "Nope."

"Camping?"

"Nope," she shook her head.

"What sort of childhood did you have?"

She snorted. "Excellent question. Not a kid-friendly one. Private school and educational summer camps and gymnastics competitions. Dad was always working. It all left little time for family vacations."

"I'm sorry. How are you enjoying this road trip?"

She eased into a smile, the last traces of stiffness fading from her shoulders. Not that she didn't let up on the wheel. "It's been interesting."

14

AIDEN RELAXED BACK IN his seat, hands rested behind his head, his long legs stretched out. Natalie was still surprised he'd let her do so much of the driving. Most guys would have puffed up their chests and insisted it was their car and they were the man and they were better drivers.

"I can't live without you," he grumbled.

Cringing, she glanced over at him, quickly returning her eyes to the road as she scrunched up her nose in disgust. "That's the worst. Not that I've heard that one before, but, come on, if you really love someone that much, of course you can live without them. And should. I wouldn't want to love someone who couldn't exist without me. Awfully pressuring."

Grinning, he nodded. "Exactly. Love is a selfish obsession, that much I understand and can even accept. But excessive codependency is bad for all parties involved. I've got to admit, watching my siblings fall flat on their faces for some pretty fantastic people in the last year and a half has eased my mind a bit. They don't seem to be suffocating with their significant others."

Something in his words triggered a fluttering hope deep in her belly that she refused to acknowledge... nor could she. Even if she found a way out of this mess, she'd never be safe. She could never be normal.

More, she couldn't let that hope blossom for either of them. For both of them, she played it safe. "How about that guy that goes with his girlfriend to her pap smear?"

"Too weird. I'm good with dicks going in, babies coming out, cancer screenings, but watching some doctor going in to scope things out when it's a routine screening thing? Okay, I mean, I guess if I was worried something was wrong. That crosses the line for anything I am willing to be party to." He grimaced, stretching his legs out in front of him in the narrow space. "Asking for permission to hang out with your own friends."

"Totally. First, I'd hope we share friends. But that isn't always realistic. Second, it's only polite to check in if you live together and won't be home for dinner, but *permission* is creepy." The late afternoon sun burned low in the sky, a big ball of fire right in front of her. Natalie lowered the visor to block the blinding rays.

"Faking a pregnancy," he added, his voice barely above a whisper.

"Ouch, Aiden, I'm sorry. Someone did that to you?"

Nodding, his mouth turned down in a pained grimace. "All of the above, actually. The pap smear had insisted her vaginal health was both of our responsibility, and she needed me there to hold her hand. Oddly, she hadn't needed me to hold her hand when our economics professor put his chlamydia-infected dick in there."

"Cheating, faked babies, codependency, overbearing. No wonder you're a little gun-shy."

"You missed premature proposals and trying to get me to fight the ex-boyfriend."

Wincing, Natalie ran a hand through her short blond hair and laughed out loud, slapping the steering wheel as the outburst was uncontainable.

"Hey, I'm serious." His chuckle belied his irritation.

Her eyes softened as her laugh gradually receded, but the smile remained. "If it helps, I haven't even been close to any of that. First an athlete that had little time for boys. Then, well, as a criminal mastermind, anything more than a hello-goodbye was risky. On the run? Life-threatening for both parties involved. As you learned firsthand, when I even implied that we were dating in one brief mention, it's for a partner's safety as much as mine."

Aiden reached across and rested his hand on her knee, the warmth of his touch spreading well beyond the physical contact. "About time you let someone in enough to break you out of your rut. It's been way too long since I had any excitement in my life."

"Not the sort of excitement most people are looking for."

"You don't know the McAllisters very well then."

She snorted. Aiden had the least exciting life of the bunch, and she didn't think she'd seen him sit still for more than an hour at a time, if that. Family gatherings must have some interesting tales shared. Maddy and her time in vice with the Seattle PD, Chase a former deep-sea diver after his youth as a juvenile delinquent. Although Payson was a sweet antique shop owner, Ronan and her little European adventure last February had not been the sedate romantic getaway they claimed. Ronan was clearly more than the former computer programmer he claimed to be.

"If this is your idea of fun, I think you need psychiatric help."

"I've been stuck in a rut. Worse than a sex-less rut, although that's been painfully true the last few months. More of an all-work-and-no-play rut. Think I forgot who I was before law school." The corner of his mouth turned up in a mirthless smile. "And here I was, giving Ronan shit for being so hyper-focused on his career. All the while, I'm doing the same damn thing."

"I'm so glad I could help you find some entertainment," she uttered dryly.

"You know that's not what I meant. How is this not fun? I got my sandy beach, I slept with a gorgeous woman, ate plenty of pizza. Now, road trip with a sexy blond at the wheel."

"Ignoring the fact that you didn't get sex with said woman, the pizza was the frozen variety, the beach was cold, and the blond bullied you into letting her drive *your* car. Oh yeah, don't forget the hitman, that you may never be able to go home again, and we're on our way to break into the scariest, most dangerous fortress I've ever broken into."

"C'est la vie. Nothing ever goes the way you think it should." He reached across and brushed her short hair behind her ear. "I really do like watching you drive my car. I can't explain it, maybe it's how you handle my stick, but it's fucking hot" He grinned and raised his eyebrows suggestively.

She rolled her eyes. Did anything ever get him down? "How long was this sex rut you mentioned?"

"Too long."

She traced her thumb over the top of the gear shifter. As anticipated, he groaned and bit down on his thumb. A chuckle bubbled up from her throat. She shook her head and gave it a squeeze just to see his reaction.

Glancing back in the rearview, the mood died abruptly when Natalie saw a dark SUV changing lanes and slowing as the car directly behind her turned off the highway. They ought to be taking the other car's place, not slowing down.

Too late to sneak off the highway at the last second.

Maybe they shouldn't have taken Aiden's car. Too high profile. But damn fun to drive.

She felt Aiden tensing beside her, his fists balling up at his sides and adjusting his posture as he looked in the passenger-side mirror. "Company?" he asked, his voice clipped.

Discreetly, she nodded, keeping an eye on the rearview.

As the next exit approached, she moved into the far-left lane, leaving a nice window of space on the right. Their tail changed lanes shortly after she did, unobtrusively two cars behind. She adjusted her speed so there was a car blocking him in the left lane.

As the exit neared, Aiden looked at her. "Plan?"

Concentrating, hands firm on the wheel, she didn't dare glance away to respond.

Almost there. Breath controlled, in and out, she counted it down.

Checking the road one last time, three, two, one. She cranked the wheel and aimed at the offramp.

Their tail couldn't pass the line of cars she'd lined up between them and the exit.

Roaring with the abrupt change in direction and RPMs, the engine didn't hesitate. Sticking to the road, the tires didn't even squeal.

The tail slammed on their brakes, moving to the middle lane, but couldn't make it to the exit in time.

Her heart pounded in her throat as they pulled off the freeway, their tail disappearing in the distance.

"Nicely done," Aiden whispered hoarsely, his hands gripped on the oh-shit handle, feet pressed tight against the floorboard as he air-braked for her.

Breath still shallow as she was afraid to finish exhaling, Natalie nodded. "I like your car. But it doesn't blend in well."

"Let's get some distance, then let's rent a car."

She turned toward town, scanning the road ahead and behind. While she took a few creative turns on the off chance another tail had snuck in behind the other, Aiden searched.

"It's just so pretty." Aiden grinned at the BMW.

Shaking her head, Natalie reached for the keys. "Not anymore subtle than yours. But at least they won't recognize it. Come on *Kevin*. I'm driving."

"Oh, sorry. The car's in my name. You don't look enough like Payson to get to drive it."

Shoulders slouching forward, she dropped into the passenger seat next to him. "Are you going to explain why Ronan keeps a cache of runaway goodies?"

"Nope. I'll leave that one for Ronan to throw some lame excuse at you. I'll just say, be glad he and I look a lot alike." Still grinning from ear to ear, Aiden fired up the engine. It hummed like a satisfied tiger. "Nearly as fun as mine." He tried *not* to think of his car all alone, hidden in the storage unit a mile back.

Natalie pouted audibly. Although she had plenty of fake IDs, he didn't trust any of them right now. At least she was on board with staying off the grid, thanks to that awful news report, and not knowing who all had been watching her and for how long. They needed to get their hands on that data and get it to the FBI and the run like hell. Fast.

He pulled onto the highway and headed south again. After ensuring they didn't have a tail, Nat closed her eyes. It was going to be a long night, and he knew she hadn't gotten a wink of sleep last night.

After another few hours on the road, Aiden flipped the rearview to reduce the glare from the headlights of the car behind them. Full dark had settled, and there weren't many other cars left on the expressway.

Still, he couldn't shake the anxiety over their plans for the rest of the night.

What if the owners of the house woke up? Maybe not the most treacherous of break-ins, but it held the highest stakes, for so many reasons.

Unable to give a heads up on their arrival, her surprise visit to her childhood home was going to be more than a little awkward if she got caught. How was she going to explain sneaking into her old bedroom after years away, snagging the data card from its hiding place, then leaving quickly and quietly? No doubt, her parent's house was under close observation by more than one party right now.

Blond hair tousled rebelliously over her face, Nat was out cold. Good. He'd gotten a decent nap that morning, but she'd resisted. Maybe she was finally starting to trust him.

On closing his eyes as they had left her cabin that morning, his subconscious had given him a break from worry, from the danger surrounding them and flashed to images of last night. Of waking up with Nat seducing him. Of her waking draped over him like a human blanket. A sexy throw blanket, really.

He wasn't about to push or even make a move right now. Doesn't mean he couldn't let his imagination run wild. Of what could have happened last night. Or the night they'd been so rudely interrupted at Goldie's when Nat had been so bold. Shifting in his seat, he attempted to ease the pressure that was building in his groin.

Following the directions from Nat, he'd taken an indirect path toward her parent's home. Blinking away the bright lights that were an unpleasant change from the dark highways, he headed into civilization.

"Nat? Time to wake up." Resting his hand on her leg, he softly nudged until she started to stir.

Scowling, she rubbed the fatigue from her eyes and adjusted to the unnatural light of suburbia. A frog in her throat, she croaked, "You've got another mile or so on this road, then once the houses start getting bigger, follow the curve and head up the hill."

"Great directions."

Smiling, she sat up in her seat and watched the road. "As long as they haven't changed street names, we'll be good."

Scanning each street sign, each building, and each night owl taking a midnight stroll, Nat's brow drooped. Her heavy sigh wasn't as subtle as she clearly had hoped for.

"Nervous?"

"Hell yeah. It's been years."

"But we'll be sneaky, so they won't know we're there. Besides, do they have a clue as to the real reason you were out that night?"

She ran a hand through her hair and stared out the window, the fatigue rapidly fading from her expression. "I hope not. They thought I was just at loose ends, not tired because of so many late nights working. You know, of all the places I've snuck into, my parent's home was always the most challenging. But as long as Dad's gone, we're good."

"Do you think he'll be gone?"

"Well, we can hope. But I'm not that lucky, and we don't have time to sit and watch the house until he leaves."

"So let's plan on him being there, and consider ourselves lucky if he's not? How good is security at the house?"

She shrugged. "I think my dad designed their entire security system around me, actually. He caught me sneaking in my bedroom window once, so he sealed it shut. I've got a few tricks up my sleeve, but the entire place is booby trapped."

Not reassuring. "You have a strange relationship with your parents. I was just assigned a frightening volume of chores, whenever I got caught sneaking back into the house."

"I admit, a huge part of me wants them to catch us. The last time they saw me, I was being escorted out by the FBI."

"I'm sorry." How awful, being ripped away from your home in the middle of the night after seeing something so awful, not being able to talk to family about it. They must have been terrified. "At least you're bringing home your boyfriend rather than the FBI this time," he teased.

A subtle smile flashed across her face as quickly as the passing streetlight and disappeared from sight just as quickly. "My mom was thrilled when I said I was dating a lawyer."

"What about if anyone else is watching the house?" Or multiple parties.

"We'll be sneaky." She winked at him before returning her gaze to the dark streets.

"Seriously."

She motioned for him to turn at the next right. "We'll be fast."

"What about Dawson? Where is he? Shouldn't he be protecting his star witness?"

"I don't exist, and with his experience with Peterson, he's been assigned to lead the investigation against him."

"No way he is okay with you going after the data like this."

"He's not. But I didn't exactly give him a choice, or explain my plan. And he can't risk leading anyone back to me."

"Do you trust him?"

"Yeah. He could have—and probably should have—arrested me back then. Agent Huong, his partner, told me they needed my testimony more than a stupid kid behind bars. Dawson couldn't have been with the bureau six months and went along with it. And, he's looked out for me ever since."

"Come on, Nat. You're in a hell of a mess. Why didn't you just give them the data to begin with?"

"I was a stupid kid, remember? I had already pissed off Peterson, witnessing him shooting a woman. Stealing from him wasn't exactly going to endear me to him. He hadn't gone after my family, miraculously, so I didn't want to give him a reason."

"So you pretended you never got it? How safe did that keep you?"

"Not as well as I'd hoped. But my family has been safe."

As the road narrowed and turned up the hill, the houses increased in size substantially. Aiden pulled to the side, parking under the shadow of a tree. A few cars came and went, but overall, the road was mercifully empty under the amber streetlamps.

Nat turned in her seat and looked out the back window, her pulse visibly beating in her neck. "Dawson and Huong, that night, they told my dad that I wasn't in any trouble, that they just needed my help with a case they were working on. Dad was livid when they took me with them."

"Back to their office?"

"Just for a drive at first. When I described what I'd seen, the murder, they were clearly torn between driving me back home and making me promise I hadn't seen anything versus cheering at their big break. They offered me the choice. After what I'd seen... he needed to go to prison for what he did."

Again, she paused, turning in her seat and looking Aiden right in the eye. "How was I to know who to trust? I wasn't about to hand over the data, not knowing who would come after me and why. Peterson, my employer, the buyer, the FBI. I was safer pretending I didn't have it. Whatever was on that disk, it couldn't be as important as the woman who had lost her life, or the lives of my family, and if it came down to it, I needed the bargaining chip. Lucky for me, Peterson was going behind bars anyway."

She scowled, deep creases forming between her eyebrows as she worked it out. "I was foolish to think I could hide forever. Dawson hopes it's related to the rumors about Peterson's involvement in smuggling. After that news report, I... I think it's worse, that it is about smuggling *people*. I assumed it was something like tax evasion and wouldn't hurt anyone directly, that's most of the sort of information I stole. If I'd known what could be on it... how many people have been hurt because of my selfishness?"

"It's not your fault. They dug into every file on that guy. They would have searched his computer and found anything critical."

"Not this." She looked so miserable, leaning her forehead into her hands as they sat in the dark.

"You think you were a better hacker than the FBI?"

Shaking her head, she scowled. "Of course not, even my ego isn't that massive. This time, it wasn't just about taking the data, but erasing his hard drive to cover my tracks and remove his access."

"You never heard any whisper of who the buyer might be?"

"I genuinely don't know. Now... now I'm afraid it's either someone as cruel as Peterson and doesn't mind trampling over others to get what they want, or it's someone closely tied to the information on that card."

His gut threatened to toss the fast food cheeseburger he'd choked down for dinner as he realized how deep she was buried in this, the chances of getting her out were looking increasingly insurmountable. "Well, Nat. You really know how to get yourself in some serious trouble." Not a car in sight, he pulled back into traffic.

"Right on Adams." Natalie pointed ahead.

Winding through the fancy neighborhood, Natalie directed him to a narrow alley. They pulled into an overgrown grassy spot between houses. Grabbing their backpacks, they crept down the long, graveled alley.

No sign of life. No motors running in the distance. No other footsteps.

Nat stopped at a seven-foot high concrete wall with a wrought-iron leafy patterned fence at the top.

"Give you a leg up?"

After flashing him a lip-biting grin, she walked away, disappearing almost into the darkness before turning back, then she took off at a sprint. Leaping off of one foot, she parkoured off of a tree and caught the lower edge of the iron in one hand. Pulling herself up like she was about to spin over the bar, she stood atop the concrete fence and raised a challenging eyebrow.

Shaking his head, he grinned. Crouching down next to the fence, he thrusted upwards in a vertical leap and caught the edge of the fence with one hand. Ignoring the rough stones embedded into the fence, he swung his other hand up and pulled himself to the top.

Hardly waiting, Nat dropped silently over the fence.

The meticulously landscaped yard was at least an acre of sharply edged grass, tidy flagstone pavers, and shrubs carved into ornate topiaries. The house was equally pristine, with stark white paint that glowed in the dim patio lights. Three stories, latticed windows, black shutters. Not exactly a friendly place to grow up.

15

NATALIE STOLE ACROSS THE darkened yard, keeping to the shadows. She scanned the windows as they approached the house. No signs of life. Just after midnight, her parents should be sound asleep.

Aiden followed a few steps behind, not a stray movement or noise. It didn't matter how many times, what strategies she'd used to keep him from following. He claimed he wasn't letting her out of his sight for anything. And he'd promised he could handle it.

He didn't disappoint. Light on his feet, eyes sharp as a hawk, he was a gifted burglar. Wrapping her fingers around the handle to the glass slider that led into the kitchen, Natalie lifted, pushed, lowered, pulled, then lifted again. Smiling, she was grateful her parents hadn't figured out the door was so easily finessed open.

Without pausing to wait for Aiden, she silently dashed down the hall to the entry closet. Swiftly, she pulled up the program she'd designed on her phone and linked it to the alarm, loading up the WiFi to bypass the initial layer.

Almost. Almost.

Bingo. Alarm disengaged.

Appearing behind her, tiptoeing adorably quietly, Aiden raised his eyebrow in a combination of irritation and admiration. Grinning, she rose to her toes and kissed him on the cheek. "Keep up," she whispered with a wink.

Heading to the back stairs, she led the way to her childhood bedroom. Aiden followed her exact footsteps, even skipping the squeaky fifth step like she did. He hadn't been kidding about his adolescent life of crime. Probably what made him a good lawyer. He didn't question the why's or how's, but the justice of it.

Pausing at the top of the stairs, she slowed her breathing and listened for signs of life.

Nothing. All quiet.

Reaching back, she felt Aiden's hand slip into hers, clearly on her same page. Her palm was undeniably sweaty, her pulse a bit quicker than she cared to admit, but this was it. Hopefully her last burglary.

She wouldn't be nearly so nervous if this was a stranger's home. Her parents were another matter entirely.

They stalked swiftly but silently down the hall. She carefully twisted the nob to her old bedroom, easing the door open to prevent the grind against the doorframe that came with the swollen wood every summer.

Exactly as she'd left it. Her poor mother, clinging to all this.

Cast aglow from the welcoming lights of the driveway, the room was well enough lit, although the shadows were long and thick. Without pause, ignoring the yearning to sit on her neatly made bed and sift through her nightstand, the framed photos, books, medals; all evidence that she was once an innocent youth. Still a teenager when she left, she'd been forced to grow up so quickly. Thanks to her unusual childhood, she'd been halfway there before her life of crime began.

Sliding open the closet door, she rose to her tiptoes and snagged the sheathed data card from above her closet door. She sensed Aiden behind her, watching the door, the street, on alert without her needing to ask.

Aiden turned to her as she slid the data card into her pocket. His eyebrows raised in question. Nodding, she exhaled the breath she'd held. He stepped toward the windows and glanced out at the empty street, gesturing it was empty.

Brightness flooded the room.

Her father stepped in, his face contorted in worry and suspicion.

Not one peep, not one missed detail, yet he caught her.

He shared her eyes, her sturdy build, but that's where the similarities ended. Don was a wide bulk of a man with an angular jaw that could crunch through a steel cable, his thighs were wider than her waist, and his smile more of a sneer. "Natalya, darling? What are you doing here?" His eyes lowered to her hand in her pocket, his distrust palpable as he bit his cheek.

"Dad. Hi. I, uh." Shit. Nothing she said now could make this all okay.

Aiden stepped forward. "Hi, Sir. So sorry to wake you. We'll be out of your hair momentarily. Then, your daughter will have this entire mystery solved so she can come for a real visit in a few weeks." Not bad Attorney McAllister. Charming, solemn, and concise, his little speech hit all the key points.

Hazel eyes bored into Aiden, ignoring the politeness of his response. "Who the hell are you to break into our home in the middle of the night? Natalya can speak for herself." His furious gaze shifted down and landed on Nat.

"I'm really, really sorry Dad. For not coming home sooner. For sneaking back in now. If I can get this to the authorities, as I should have done years ago, everything will be okay."

A soft voice called from down the hall. "Don? What are you doing up at this hour?" The sound of her mother's voice melted the last of her resolve, the sadness that she'd carried all these years trembled through her bones.

With a fierce shake, her father silenced them before she could speak. "Don't crush your mother again," he whispered. "Just pretend it's a social call. I'll get you out within two hours. You can spare that."

Nodding, Natalie couldn't have argued if she wanted to. His thinning silver hair stood on end in a wild array, his black undershirt and blue striped pajama pants almost making him look the kindly father she'd always wished for.

As she entered the room, Helene's jaw dropped, her complexion paled, and her breath came out in distressed pants. "Natalya..." Tears started streaming down her face. A pair of corgis followed at her heels.

Rushing to her mother, Natalie felt her mother's tiny body melt against hers, yet gripped her with the strength of an ox. "Hey, Mom." The corgis jumped up and down to get her attention.

"What... How?"

She could see her father giving his infamous glower, shaking his head sternly, ensuring she wouldn't question his mandate. "Honestly? I'm passing through town, hoping to wrap up this mess I got myself into. I, uh, I couldn't help but stop in for a quick visit."

Sniffling, her mother looked up at her, her red and puffy eyes searching hers. "I'm so, so happy to see you."

Helene's expression morphed into welcoming hostess as she caught sight of Aiden. Always trying to marry off her children, even in weird-ass circumstances such as this.

With an easy smile, Aiden extended his free hand and shook Helene's. "Mrs., uh..." Natalie smiled; he had no idea what her real last name was. "It's nice to finally meet you. Nat couldn't resist making the stop to see you."

Awkward didn't come close to describing the painful scene. Sitting in the formal parlor in the midst of the spontaneous midnight family reunion, Aiden only half listened, staying on alert for the inevitable. Two hours was a damn long time if the house was bugged. Watching Nat's quiet smile, he knew she needed to at least try to make the most of the time they had, but her knee vibrating against his said she wasn't willing to stay the full two hours.

Helene bustled around, offering about every drink and snack she could come up with. Finally, she settled on herbal tea to relax them all, plus a plate of homemade white chocolate macadamia nut cookies. Who kept fresh, fancy cookies on hand for no particular reason? And who ate them? There wasn't an ounce of fat on any of these three.

Breaking off a piece of a sugar cookie from a dog-bone shaped platter, Helene offered a piece to each of the bouncy pups.

When Nat reached for a human cookie, her parents both looked at her in jaw-dropping shock. Holding the cookie up, Nat frowned in an annoyed expression Aiden had never seen on her. Almost teenage for its rebellion. "I like cookies. Always have. I'm not training for anything. I can eat a damn cookie."

Holy shit, what sort of childhood did she have? Not allowed to eat a cookie, and clearly hadn't ever pushed it, judging by the astonishment on Don and Helene's faces. No wonder she'd jumped at the opportunity for a secret life of crime. Or was so afraid to let anyone close. Even those who should be supportive were judgmental despite the eight-year absence. For all she missed them, she wasn't giving up the independence she'd gained.

Pride filled Aiden's chest as he watched her stand up for herself for what looked to be the first time.

Wait—pride? That wasn't an emotion he had really acknowledged before. Especially for a woman he imagined naked at least seventy-five percent of his waking hours, and one hundred percent of those spent sleeping.

"Actually, Nat's a great chef," he fired back as they seemed silenced by their daughter's change. Turning toward her, he tried to tell if her confused look at him was happy or irritated. "She doesn't advertise it, but she makes a mean strawberry cheesecake."

Helene's attitude flipped right around. Polite hostess again, she offered him another cookie. "Our girl is a wonder. She's never brought a man home, so I assume you two are... close?"

Was it hot in here? Matchmaking mother. Worse than a pap smear.

Natalie must have caught his pasty complexion. Was she smiling? Now she was enjoying herself? At his expense? "Mom, he's just a friend. It was all a mistake that he got caught in my awful business."

"Oh. Of course. Did Agent Dawson ever find you? Now that's a sweet man. Just this afternoon, he came for a visit. I hadn't seen him in at least a few years. He's a handsome man, but he still hasn't gotten married. He needs a good woman to slow him down a bit. He had a number of questions about where you were and what you were up to and who all has been asking after you."

Clever. Aiden was beginning to like this Dawson. If she told the FBI all about her daughter, what might she have told a charming stranger with apparently good intentions? And what might she have revealed to Dawson about anyone who'd been looking for Nat?

Stiffening, Don pupils narrowed. He cleared his throat and asked with a guarded gruffness. "What did you tell him?"

Smiling, Helene missed her husband's displeasure as she sat up like a show dog craving a treat. Aiden swallowed the chuckle threatening to surface, remembering Natalie's canine comparisons. She wasn't wrong.

Helene responded, "Nothing, of course. You said don't say anything about our girl to anyone. Pretend she's in Europe. So, that's all I told him."

Don's nostrils flared as he assessed his wife's statement. Finally, accepting Helene's retelling of what was likely a much more informative interaction for Dawson, he turned his attention back to Nat. She'd been watching out the window, and her eyes didn't stray from the darkened backyard. Their exit.

"Natalya, dear. Why don't you tell us what you've been up to? Your mother tells me you have been working as a photographer?" His eyes softened, but his jaw kept ticking. Had Nat been talking to her mother these past few years, but not her father?

Nat's knee ticked faster than her father's jaw. "Yeah. I really can't stay. This has been great, getting to see you both. I'll call as soon as I can."

Watching Helene, then back to Nat, Don's smile widened, but the pleasantness didn't reach his eyes. "Surely you can stay another few minutes."

Aiden stretched and said, "I'm really sorry we can't stay longer, but we have a pretty tight timeline." They didn't, but he wanted to get this data card as far away as possible. Felt like a damn bomb in the house for all the power it carried. He rose to stand.

Don stood next to him, a few inches shorter but a solid sixty pounds of bulk wider. "Don't cut short Natalya and her mother's reunion."

Nat rose and stood next to Aiden. "We really, really need to go."

Shaking his head, Don stepped to the side, between them and the exit. "Not just yet."

Darkening in her demeanor, Nat uttered in a grave tone, "Dad? Are you keeping us here?"

"Natalya, darling. As usual, you're in way over your head. Just give me the data card, and they'll forget everything."

She stiffened, her eyes darting around the room like a cornered rabbit. Grabbing Aiden's free hand, Nat took off toward the kitchen. Stalking down the hall, she led them to the door they'd come in through.

Behind them, Don pleaded without rushing, "Natalya, don't do this. These people... They're ruthless. As long as that remains hidden, you're safe. If you go public with that, you risk all of our safety."

Something shifted in Natalie's brain, like the last puzzle piece she'd given up as lost. "Who do you really work for?" All those long stretches of travel. Marrying her ditz of a highborn mother, dainty and blond and submissive. A perfect trophy wife. Pushing his children to the max in all things. Making up her alibi for the FBI before he'd even been asked for it.

"That's not important. What's important is that you hand over the data."

"I can't do that."

"We will be nothing if that gets free. I will be blamed for my daughter's insolence. I couldn't save you after you testified, but I could protect your mother and your brother."

Her gut churned as she realized just how ruthless her father was. "I'm leaving, Dad. You can't stop me anymore than you could before."

A brutal laugh erupted from his barrel chest. "I didn't try to stop you before. I'd actually considered putting you on the payroll. With your skills, you could have obtained a lot of helpful information about our adversaries. You always were a talented athlete and academic alike."

"You work for Peterson, don't you?"

"Unofficially of course. Contractor for convicted murderer and former Secretary of State under suspicion of international crimes isn't good for my image."

Some might think it a tough choice, betraying her father versus withholding critical information that might potentially unravel the web of a complex human trafficking ring, if Dawson's suspicion about smuggling was correct, plus the news report from this morning? How many could find some sort of peace or retribution from the information she carried? The more heat that stirred around it, the more she knew she had to get this into the right hands.

Don and she had never agreed politically, and now his position was so far off the mark, it was literally criminal. She'd always been disgusted by his greed, but his deceit was more than she could handle. Natalie was a burglar. Her father must be so, so much worse.

Her mother wouldn't take it well, but Natalie wasn't ever living for their acceptance again. Not when so much hung in the balance.

Backing up, she felt Aiden standing strong behind her. Sliding open the door, she let Aiden lead the way while she watched their backs, and kept her focus on her father.

Standing furiously in the doorway, her father pulled a slick black handgun from nowhere and aimed it straight at her face.

Eyes wide with the pain of irrevocable betrayal, Natalie believed her father's ruthlessness more deeply than ever. "Dad?"

"Keep backing up, darling girl. This is for him." He nodded toward Aiden.

Aiden stiffened at her side. Breath slow and steady, he shifted his gaze between two men moving out from behind the far topiaries, aiming matching handguns at them.

Panic churning out from her gut, etching into her bones, trickling into her toes, Natalie fought the numbing panic.

Feeling Natalie halting behind him, Aiden pulled his eyes off the vicious duo that crept ever closer and followed her gaze. Dear old Don had a shiny pistol aimed right at his chest.

Fuck. Fuck fuck fuck. This vacation just got better and better.

With each passing second, the furious trio of dogmatically dirty thugs were closing in. Nat's father was as devious as they came.

Her hand slipped into his, their fingers linking tight.

No way back to the rental car, and if they made it that far? Who was to say these goons hadn't already tampered with it? As much as Don didn't seem keen to actually murder his daughter, he didn't appear to have any qualms about others doing the deed for him.

Like an instant, artificial sunrise, brilliant lights illuminated the yard. Flashing rapidly, the lights strobed on and off. The pair of corgis bounded into the yard, yapping and nipping at whatever ankles they could reach.

As a unit, without hesitation, Nat and Aiden sprinted toward the door to the garage. All other exits were blocked. Shots fired all around them, all off target in the chaos as they dashed in an erratic exit run.

Ducking into the garage, Nat flicked on the lights as Aiden pushed over a steel tool cabinet to block the door. The crash was deafening.

A dozen more thugs could be surrounding the house, the garage only bought them a few seconds.

"Come on." Nat disappeared into the next garage bay.

As he reached her, she was tearing a cloth cover off of a 1972 Corvette Stingray.

"Do you see any keys?" she asked frantically.

Without stopping, he ragged as he dove into the driver's seat. "You didn't nip any this time? Must be getting rusty."

She tossed in her backpack and dropped in the passenger seat. She feverishly pulled open the glove box, the visor, searching for keys that weren't appearing.

"Some of us might not be fancy hackers..." He jammed the steering box and twisted what he hoped were the right wires in the dim light. "But I've stolen my fair share of cars."

Rolling her eyes, she clicked the garage door opener she'd found in her search for the keys.

"Duck," he yelled. Flooring it in reverse, he narrowly missed one of dear-old-dad's henchmen that stood in the driveway, the gunman diving out of the way to save his own hide.

Tires squealing, Aiden kept his head low and spun the wheel as he maneuvered down the driveway in reverse.

Don thundered after them, gun aimed straight between Aiden's eyes. Another one to add to the books of the unpleasant turns one of his relationships ventured down.

Spinning the wheel as they reached the road, Aiden shifted and took off.

Crack. The back window shattered. Ducking, he veered around the corner, narrowly missing the bumper of a parked car.

Worse than a pap smear. He'd now been shot at by a woman's father.

Breath rushing from his lungs, he sat up enough to check the rearview. Foot to the ground, he forced his next breath in, the last of her neighborhood shrinking into the distance.

Nat pulled her phone out of her bag when he began to dial back on the speed as they neared the shopping centers, the freeway coming into view. The back window was a hell of a pock mark on their subtle getaway, but police intervention actually wouldn't be a terrible idea about now.

"Dawson? It's my father." Nat's voice was strained as the line connected.

He couldn't make out Agent Dawson's puzzled response on the other end thanks to the road noise, but he got the idea.

"He's working for Peterson. I've got the data, but, I, he shot at us."

He listened as she filled him in on the attack on Aiden in Seaview, the news report, which, apparently, Dawson was already well aware of and had been trying to reach Nat all day, and then their visit to her parents.

No destination, Aiden drove far and fast to gain as much distance tonight as they could.

"No, we're safe for the moment... Okay... We'll hide out tonight, then get you the data in the morning."

After a bit more arguing, she hung up.

He waited patiently. And waited. "Uh, Nat? Plan?"

"Oh, sorry. I'm distracted. Let's find a hotel for the night, ditch the car, and Dawson will pick us up in the morning."

"That, I can live with."

He parked the 'Vette in the hospital parking lot across the street from a generic looking motel off the highway. Nat stayed out of sight while Laurence McAvoy, another of Ronan's identities, paid for the room.

Slightly more classy of a joint than the one he'd stayed in for his first night of vacation. This one actually had an electronic key and required credit cards and *didn't* ask if they preferred the hourly rate.

16

DROPPING HER BACKPACK ON the rock-hard motel room bed, Natalie headed straight for the bathroom. Turning, she realized she should check on Aiden. After all, her father had tried to kill him a few short hours ago.

At her weary look, he quit rubbing his eyes and flashed her a sleepy grin. "Go ahead, I'll just fall asleep for the next hundred years."

"Alright, sleeping beauty. We'll chat in the morning."

He dropped to the edge of the bed and nodded with heavy lids.

She cranked the water to hot, only to find it scalding. Trimming it back a bit, she froze as ice water poured over her skin. Delicately nudging it to the fine middle ground, she found a tolerable sub-boiling temperature.

Surprisingly fancy for an open-late motel, she found a single-bottle shampoo-conditioner combo and paper-thin bar of soap. As she worked her hair into a lather, she heard the unmistakable sound of a man peeing on the other side of the white polka-dot shower curtain.

Shaking her head, she smiled. Not many other travelling partners would be so... easygoing, with what had started as an awful situation, and continued to worsen with each new development. She heard him brushing his teeth with the supplies he'd bought from the vending machine outside, then head back out of the bathroom again.

It was well after two in the morning by the time she was out of the shower, teeth brushed, feeling almost human. Despite his declaration of his intent to fall asleep right away, Aiden was still in jeans and a t-shirt, stretched out on the bed. He rubbed his eyes and rolled out of bed.

As he brushed past her, he seemed to notice she wore nothing but a tiny towel, and nearly ran into the wall next to the bathroom in his bleary appreciation. Flashing her a sleepy wink, he shrugged and closed the bathroom door behind him.

The shower flipped on a few seconds later. His yelp was telling that he'd found the boiling setting, followed immediately by the freezing spray, as she had.

Still grinning from his sleepy check-out, topped off with his heavy-eyed politeness, she slipped into the only bed in the room. As she only had the few necessities she kept in her backpack, she pulled on fresh panties and a cami she'd had tucked away in her backpack. She was nearly asleep by the time the bathroom door opened again.

Too tired to think, her eyes refused to lift as Aiden climbed in behind her, pulling her tight against him, without a scrap of clothing. Her voice heavy with need for a hundred-year sleep herself, she muttered, "Don't tell me the only available room was a single queen bed?"

His breath warm against her neck, he trailed sleepy kisses along her shoulder. "No. They had a room with two full sized beds." She felt his grin against her shoulder.

"You're so full of shit." Her delirious giggle jiggled them both.

"I'm too tired to get it up anyway, so you're safe for tonight. No promises about the morning. Just being honest." Nuzzling into her neck, she felt him drift off over the course of three breaths.

As promised, he didn't make a move all night. Nor did he move all night.

Her phone chirped on its charger on the bedside table shortly after sunrise. *You awake?*

Sitting up, Nat rubbed her hand through her hair, flipping it out of her face in an effort to wake up. She clicked dial rather than responding.

Rather than *hello*, Dawson was frank. "Peterson got out last night."

"Shit." Although her brain was too groggy to respond, she scanned the room. Panicked adrenaline pumped through her veins like before a competition. Didn't parole take time? How many pockets had Peterson filled?

She nudged Aiden. Sealing his eyes tighter, he groaned.

She nudged him again.

"Whuh?" He jerked up and stilled when he saw her on the phone.

Dawson continued, "I need that data. Are you safe where you're at?"

"We're safe for now," she said. "I can pull the data and send it out within the hour."

"Send it to me and my supervisor, plus Senator Blankenship. I want you far away from this. You send that data, then run like hell, got it?"

"Got it."

"And, Natalya?"

"Yeah?"

"We've got your father and his buddies. Your mom called the cops and locked herself in the bathroom."

Heat welled behind her eyes, imagining what her mother had gone through. How they wouldn't have made it out of there without her help. Helene did not do danger or adventure or anything outside of her perfect bubble. "You'll keep her safe? And my brother?"

"Already on it. I've got local police in Cambridge looking for your brother as we speak. As soon as we find him, I'll personally make sure your mom and your brother are safe."

"Thanks." She disconnected and tossed the phone to the foot of the bed. She didn't have the time or the energy to dwell on her epically terrible relationship with her father, but that little light of hope fluttered in her chest at her mother's bravery.

Heart pounding in her chest, brain fuzzy, she jumped out of bed and threw on her jeans from last night. Tossing back the blanket, she searched for her socks.

Not missing a thing, Aiden did the same. "Talk to me," he said.

"Get ready to go. We pull that data, send it out, then hide. Again."

Nodding, he pulled on his shoes and socks, disappearing into the bathroom. Natalie checked out the window. A young couple held hands, grinning as they piled into their car and left the parking lot. A few sedans, a family van. Nothing suspicious. Hopefully.

She tossed her laptop on the bed.

Aiden came out of the bathroom, sleep washed from his face, his cheeks drawn tight. Nodding, he gestured that the bathroom was free.

Wordlessly, she slipped in and got ready to go.

When she returned, Aiden sat on the foot of the bed, arranging his IDs, counting cash. "We can rent another car, then get off the grid."

"Ronan really has some explaining to do."

Snorting, Aiden smiled. "After the interesting vacation you've brought me on? You're the one with explaining to do when we get home."

Home. Wouldn't that be a dream, to get to go back to Seaview? She didn't have the heart to say it, but there was a slim chance that either of them would be able to return. And wouldn't that be a bitch, if she got stuck with a man that not only considered settling down the worst sort of punishment, but forcibly tied to her indefinitely? Her heart shattered as she imagined him never getting to see his family again, because of her.

Not responding, Natalie plugged in the laptop. She pulled up her files and double checked that her own work was saved to the cloud.

Aiden brewed a coffee for each from the small motel pot, adding a few drips from the creamer packet in hers, dumping the rest into his.

Letting her breath escape her lungs, not realizing she'd been withholding it since turning on the laptop, she hit the final button. System erased. Painful, trusting all of her hard work to a cloud, but she really, really didn't want to risk anything tracing back to her.

If she'd had half of the programs she'd written back in the day, this would be so much easier. She was too rusty and didn't have the time to create a rootkit to outsmart what she already knew to be a complex program.

She snagged her coffee from Aiden, sipping it down by half while she mustered her courage. Unless she was really, really lucky, the data was laced with code that would lead its creators right to her. "Ready?" She whispered to Aiden.

Nodding, he handed her the data card.

Inhale. Exhale. One, two, three. She plugged it into the laptop.

Click. Open.

Scanning the files, she selected the most relevant.

Her eyes widened as she saw a glimpse of the information she'd pretended didn't exist for so long. Encrypted, no logic to the pattern, as if none of the information aligned.

Copying as much as she could, she blasted out as many files as fast as she could to Dawson and the email addresses he'd sent her.

"Six minutes." Aiden chugged the last of his coffee. He zipped up her backpack and slung it over his shoulder.

Nodding, she didn't look away from the screen. "One sec."

Pulling a few lines of code out of the depths of her memory, stuff she'd suppressed years ago, she tried to hack through the thinly coated security.

"Ten. Gotta go," he urged.

Fail.

Shit, wait, that wasn't it.

Clicking away, she grinned as her old hacks flooded to the surface, her fingers working from muscle memory.

Load file.

Nailed it.

Names. Dates. Locations.

Sending off the unencrypted data in a second batch of emails, she felt a rush zip through her veins as the secrets that had haunted her for so long came to life.

Flipping closed the laptop, she leapt up from the bed.

Aiden was watching out the window, hand on the doorknob. "That car. They've driven around the block three times now. They're pulling into the lot across the street."

"I attached to the hospital's guest WiFi. Slow, but hopefully has them sniffing in the wrong place."

"Nice," he nodded. Pausing, he held his breath, his head nodding as he counted down. "Come on."

Gripping the laptop in one hand, she slipped her other into his. Holding firm, he slowed her pace. Tempted to sprint out of the area, she realized he was right. Running would give them away from an easy, distant glance. Sauntering down the walkway as contented lovers wouldn't attract any more attention than the other motel guests that had departed that morning.

"Maybe we should have rented a getaway vehicle first."

"You know what? I say we search my dad's car for trackers, then keep it."

"You want to risk our lives for a pretty car? And you think I'm shallow for refusing to park mine on Beachside?"

She chuckled. "I never said you were shallow. I like your car. It's not the car as much as pissing off that asshole."

"I think we're both going to need some serious therapy when this is done."

"Or a nice tropical vacation." She winked, pulling him along behind her.

He grinned and said, "Or put better things in our brains and tour the art and history museums of Paris."

As they passed a rusted-out dumpster, she held her laptop over her head. Aiden flinched as if she was about to whack him over the head with it. With a shrug, she slammed it into the ground.

Shattering into a few dozen pieces, the laptop was toast. She tossed the big chunks into the dumpster, saving out the hard drive.

No sign of the car, they crossed the street to the hospital parking lot. Weaving through a tightly packed lot, they reached her father's car. "Doesn't exactly blend in," Aiden stopped and looked back at her.

"No. But he loves this thing more than my mother. I'm enjoying taking it out of spite. He never even let me ride in it. He bought this when I was in high school. I remember something about Lojack."

Chuckling, Aiden got down under the car. As he studied the bottom of the car, she heard the smug lilt in his voice. "Now you're talking my specialty." After a few moments of silence, he slid out and hopped to his feet, his brow furrowed in concentration, he flipped open the trunk. With a few twists, he unbolted the spare tire. "There she is." Pulling a few wires, twisting, he removed a small device.

Ensuring it was still active, he dropped the device in the truck bed next to them. They hopped into the car and checked the parking lot around them.

"Duck," he said as he slunk down in the driver's seat.

In the distance, the car they'd seen from the motel before drove past the end of the row. Despite the fact that there was no way they could hear, she whispered, "Think they're tracking us from the data or the car?"

"No fucking clue." Giving it a minute, he sat up and looked around. "Stay down."

Crouched down on the floorboard, squishing herself into the cramped space, she grumbled, "Next time, you get to hide while I drive."

"They know your face a hell of a lot better than mine."

After another minute, he eased out of the parking spot. Crawling past the rows of parked cars, his breath held, he snuck out onto the main road. Checking the rearview as much as the road ahead, finally, he said, "Okay, buckle up."

Glaring at him, she climbed into the seat. "Because we're being followed or because we're in the clear?"

"The latter. Hopefully."

17

The drive back north took twice as long as it could have. Taking turns behind the wheel, they wove in and out, zigzagging in an indirect path, stopping only for food and gas. The cabin was risky, but it was familiar. They could find another motel for the night, but who knew how long they'd be holed up, and they would have to lay low enough to avoid being seen.

Aiden exhaled a long sigh of relief as a big blue sign welcomed him home to Maine. At his side, Nat's legs were curled up in the passenger seat, her head leaned against his shoulder. Holding still as he passed a painfully slow dump truck, he tried to not jostle her.

Nat's phone buzzed. Waking from her well-deserved nap, the sun setting behind them, Nat sat up. His arm cold where she'd been snuggled against him, he shook his hand to wake the tingle that had started. Her voice was surprisingly alert for how mussed her hair was. "Any news?"

He could hear Dawson on the other end. Never met the guy, but he was already relieved to hear his voice. "Yeah. You hit paydirt with that data. If Peterson was pissed about you testifying against him for murder, he's going to explode when he finds out you released this. Lay low until I can get this sorted out and get him back behind bars. Nicely done on the decryption, by the way. Way faster than any of our guys would have gotten it done. My superior's trying to convince me to recruit you."

She chuckled under her breath. "Hell no."

"That's what I figured. Anyway, it'll take some digging, but it does look like the cargo he refers to is human."

At his side, he felt the grief weighing heavy on Nat. He reached across and rested his hand on her thigh. Voice flat, she asked, "If I had handed this over eight years ago, how many could have been found in time?"

"Don't do that to yourself. We have it now. A lot of this actually refers to a huge bust by Interpol nine years ago, folks already recovered but we never found the brains of the operation. This data pulls it all together, and I suspect Peterson compiled all this because of that bust. Maybe blackmail, his own safety net, who knows."

"Is it enough to put Peterson away?"

"Oh yeah. This is probably why he killed her that night."

Nat breathed slow and steady for a minute, her chest rising and falling before she spoke again. "What about my father?"

"Nothing so far. If we can find an alias on him, something to tie him to this... maybe. From what Rogers has found, your father's role was more tertiary. More of the financial side of things. No doubt he was involved in some shady shit, but I don't think he even knows the full extent of it. Not that he's getting out anytime soon. Attempted murder will hold him long enough for us to dig up more dirt."

"Thanks. I... I don't know. Any idea how my mother is holding up?"

"She doesn't seem to know a thing about your father's business interactions. We've got her in protective custody."

"Is that safe?"

"It's what we've got. She's not you. You know as well as I do, she'd be found in a day on her own. But she's got good people looking after her."

"What about my brother?"

"I'm sorry, but we haven't been able to track him down yet." Dawson's voice was almost hollow as he delivered the bad news.

Nat's shoulders slumped and she bit her lips tight together as she struggled to keep it together. "You'll keep looking?"

"Nonstop until we find him. You stay off the grid. We've got all eyes looking out for Peterson. As soon as we've got him, we'll go wide and bring in the other names in here. For now, not that you're going to tell anyone anyway, but keep it quiet. Got it?"

"Yeah. You'll tell me as soon as you find my brother and when you have Peterson in custody?"

"Of course. Stay safe."

"Thanks again. I'm going to owe you a freaking lifetime of thank yous."

"Probably. I'd love to say, 'just doing my job,' but I've known you almost as long as I've been a fed. Who will I call when I get bored on the weekends and need someone to check on?"

Expression lightening, Nat laughed. "Maybe you'll find a girlfriend. A social life in general?"

"Ha. We'll see about that. I'll be in touch."

She clicked off the phone. Staring out the window, Nat didn't say a word. Her cheeks were pulled tight.

They drove in silence for the next few hours. Nat didn't fall back asleep, but spent most of the drive checking behind them, reading the news on her phone, anything but making conversation or attempting to sleep again. The story about Nat withholding information was everywhere, her photo plastered all over the news. A few about Peterson's unexpected release, some support for him from some channels, but mostly a resurgence of conspiracy theories about his criminal history beyond murder. The BBC was the only one that seemed to be linking the two, but others would catch on soon enough.

The sky around them long since darkened, the cabin within half an hour, she exhaled sharply, finally speaking. "As much as I'm enjoying stealing my father's car, I don't want to risk bringing it back to the cabin in case it's recognized or has another tracker we didn't find. There's a state park about a mile north of the cabin. Let's stop there and walk home."

"Now you're worried about that?"

"I have been, but part of me wanted to bring on the fight. Now? I'm a little extra paranoid with Xander missing."

"We'll find him if they don't. Let's see what the feds can come up with. In the meantime, you and I can do what we can remotely. He's your brother. Think your mom tipped him off or, I hate to ask, but do you think he might have been aware of your dad's activities?"

She nodded, slipping her hand into his across the center console. "Mom may have gotten word to him, in which case, he'd be smart enough to get out of sight. He's a good guy. At least, I've always thought so."

"Then he's probably already off the grid and will lay low until this blows over."

Adjusting in her seat, she leaned her head against his shoulder. He rested his cheek on her head and took a long, savoring inhale of her tropical scent.

"Did you just sniff me?" she teased, not moving.

He smiled against the top of her head, "Couldn't help it." Planting a lingering kiss on the top of her head, he settled against her as long as the road cooperated.

Nearly midnight, and Aiden was toast by the time they pulled into the empty parking lot. His eyes ached, his ass was numb, but he didn't dare rub his eyes or readjust in his seat again. Nat needed a rock right now, not a worn-out partner.

A whitewashed stone lighthouse stood on the edge of the point beyond. In the distance, he could see its contemporary replacement. Tucked back in the trees, a venerable village of tents and RVs were lined up in the campground, the muffled voices of folks enjoying the fair weather around their campfires.

Slinging her backpack over her shoulder, Nat climbed out of the car ahead of him and paid the park fee in the drop box. Swaying with each sleepy step, she took his hand and led him down the short path to the beach. Low tide, the beach was wide with sand, the waves glowing white in the dim light of the moon.

Linking his hand with hers, Aiden said, "A midnight stroll on the beach? What could be more romantic?" He kissed the back of her hand and flashed her a wink, hoping to bring that light inside her back.

Better yet, she giggled with a beyond-tired, slap-happy enthusiasm. "You're such a dork." She bumped his arm with her shoulder.

They crawled over a rocky jetty, across a grassy field, then back to another long stretch of sand. The only sounds of the night were the waves receding then crashing, the wind rustling through the long grass.

Any other night, any other reason for being here, he'd have considered the walk to the isolated cabin exactly the romantic getaway he'd teased Nat about. "My parents used to make us play this game," he said. "Well, that's what they called it, to try to convince us it was fun.

On the way home from every trip, we'd have to tell our favorite part. No smartass responses like, 'being stuck in the car all day,' or 'when Dad got us lost,' but something that we wouldn't forget. What's yours so far?"

Leaning into him, she giggled again, then she looked up him with that *you're nuts* look he had figured out actually meant, *I adore you*. Well, he liked to think so anyway. "Shall we go with my father shooting at us? Or how about having my name splashed all over the news for being a horrible human being? I've been on the news too many times in my life, and not once was it something flattering. Failed gymnast has a tantrum at finals. Murder witness with a blurred-out face. You get the idea."

"I believe that classifies as a snarky answer and it doesn't count. I'll go first. Watching you drive my car like a stunt driver when you shook our tail on the way south."

Shaking her head, she smiled. "Fine. Discovering that Aiden McAllister loves to snuggle."

Spinning her in his arms, he pulled her close and brushed his lips along the angle of her jaw. "Tell anyone else, and it's all over. I'll tell everyone who'll listen that you keep coming after me for booty calls."

She scoffed and twirled out of his arms but didn't drop his hand. "I confess, I have been guilty of that at least twice now. Lucky thing the FBI called and told me hitmen were out to get me, or I would have ended up another notch on your bedpost." Her tone was light, but he could hear the insecurity she rarely let anyone see.

"You know, it may take weeks, even months before we can come out of hiding. Like people in prison mark their tallies, we can mark up the bedframe in the cabin."

"And you accuse me of my smartass answer? You're a walking bundle of the stuff."

The moon reflected off the rose window of the cabin in the distance like a beacon welcoming them home. Nat was hanging in there, but he was running out of distraction topics. His brain was mush after the fricking marathon they'd been through.

He'd been avoiding using the drop phone from Ronan's secret stash, but he needed to check in with home. Let them know they were okay, but that he didn't have a clue when they'd be back. If ever. Looks like Ev would be taking over his practice, not joining it. A lifetime on a tropical beach somewhere no one would find them. Appealing as it sounded, he missed his family already.

Running a hand through his hair, he tried to not let his frustration show. As glad as he was that Nat wasn't alone, this was not what he signed on for.

What had he signed on for? He'd been hoping for a mutually satisfying—brief—fling with a woman that had been haunting his dreams for longer than he'd cared to admit. And his waking hours. Had pretty much been taking over his entire fantasy life.

Bit by bit, the more the mystery around her grew, the more she'd flirted back... yeah, they would have had a great time.

Fucking eh, he was a sucker for a hopeless case, and Nat was that in spades. If he'd known what messing around with Nat would lead to... No sense dwelling. Whatever shit she'd gotten them into, he was caught between a rock and a hard place and a minefield.

Nat's chest was near bursting, her heart pounding so loud she could hardly hear her own thoughts as they approached the cabin. She checked the windows and doors, the dirt around the side of the house.

If anyone had breached her sanctuary...

Nothing. Untouched.

Relief washed over her. This place had been her one constant the last few years. She'd bought this place before she'd even come to Seaview.

Aiden dropped her hand and checked out Ronan's truck. Just as they'd left it.

She unlocked the front door and punched in the alarm. Another inspection inside, just to be sure.

Safe. Burning in her eyes, tears threatened to spill down her cheeks at the fear that held her in its clutches. She about broke down, imagining one of Peterson's guys... her father's... waiting to jump out and tear apart her fragile sense of security.

As she turned around after setting the alarm, she found Aiden stripped to the skin. "Uh..." she trailed off, completely speechless.

He flashed her a sleepy wink in the dim light of the moon. "Laundry. My stuff's still in the rental car, remember? I'd like something to wear tomorrow."

Blushing ridiculously obviously as she tried to not stare, she swallowed and backed down the hall while he headed toward the laundry. "Great. Yeah. Go for it. I'll, uh, I'll just, just go to sleep." As if she was going to get a lick of sleep now.

Every sane part of her brain wanted to remind him that he got the couch. The words were right there on the tip of her tongue, but she couldn't make herself say it. After freshening up and dumping her own clothes in the laundry bin to deal with later, she slipped into the Egyptian cotton sheets, pulling the down comforter around her shoulders.

Sand pouring over her exhausted limbs, she felt herself drifting. So many reasons to not sleep. So many nightmares that could haunt her. Squeezing her eyes shut, she refused to let the negative thoughts in, knowing the worry could wait until tomorrow.

Instead, she used her favorite insomnia treatment take over. Playing the image of naked Aiden in her mind, of the confident version of herself acting on the moment, him actually taking her up on the booty call request from the night before they'd left the cabin, she succumbed to her first decent night's rest in too long.

As the sun rose over the horizon, daylight coated her skin that tingled with arousal as the layers of sleep washed away, Aiden's bare skin against hers warm and smooth, his arm wrapped snuggly around her.

Indulging, she traced her fingers along the contours of his forearm, migrating up his bicep until she reached his shoulder. Turning in his arms, she grazed her thumb over the curve of his stubbled jaw before brushing her lips over his, teasing him to awaken.

Flinching, his eyes moved as if he sensed a change, but he didn't wake.

Pressing her breasts up against his chest, the contact shot a thrill deep in her belly. Her fingers trailed along his shoulder, goosebumps forming in their wake.

Eyes closed, he didn't question his intimate wake-up. Deliciously, soothingly warm, his sleepy lips found hers, testing, tasting. One arm reached under her and pulled her tight against him, the other cradled her cheek as he deepened the kiss.

Each kiss, each second of raw, sweet intimacy, held time in the balance as they ran their hands over each other's every curve, lips never parting.

Deep in her core, Natalie felt the pressure building within her, a furnace threatening to boil over. She traced her fingers down his abdomen, along his hip, then settled and gripped his rock-hard shaft.

Gasping at the sudden change in intensity, he groaned, "Nat, I want you so bad."

Smiling against his mouth, she teased, "That's just my hand on your cock talking." She gripped tighter, and he moaned hungrily against her mouth.

"Let's speculate after. Right now, shut up," he teased.

Even as he flipped her underneath him, her giggle rumbled through her. "So now you take me up on the booty call?"

"Thought I said to shut it." He chuckled louder than she did as she wrapped her legs around him, her head thrown back in delight.

Shifting his grip, he took her breasts in his hands and caressed, teased, driving her out of her mind with a craving for more that she couldn't remember ever feeling so fully. Anticipating her every ravenous thought, he lowered and closed his mouth over her breast and pulled deeply, suckling until she panted in pure pleasure. Electrical currents ran sizzling through her veins, sending heat licking down to her core.

Overwhelmed with sensation, Natalie cried out in voiceless gasps.

Normally easygoing, relaxed about everything, Aiden showed her a surprising, tender side of him she couldn't have anticipated. Kissing along her breasts, her jaw, his every movement was thoughtful, savoring. Tense, focused, he was throbbing with emotion as he pulled back, his dark lashes fluttering open, his ocean eyes boiling.

He reached to the bedstand and snagged a condom he must have set out last night. She raised a single eyebrow. He shrugged. She rolled it over his thick cock, gliding her fingers over his shaft as she did, until he closed his eyes and his breath came faster.

Impatience building, he slipped inside, the pressure combusting every nerve from her core to her fingers and toes. His long fingers gripped the headboard behind her, her hands clutching his hips and they moved together, accelerating beyond control.

Electric blue eyes sparked as he held her gaze.

On a victorious, breathless cry, she soared on a wave of frenzied bliss. Seconds behind, he followed her release with a shuddering moan.

18

THE HOMEY SCENT OF coffee tickled his nose, the stimulus teasing his eyes open. He'd been so sure Nat would run during the night, he hadn't slept a wink. She accused him of being snuggly, but how else could he be sure she wouldn't ditch him, thinking herself a martyr for going it alone?

Ha, nice try, McAllister. Okay, so he did enjoy inhaling her tropical scent, finding that beneath was pure earthy, like the durable bark of a palm tree. And, well, she fit so nicely, like a perfect scoop of gelato in his spoon.

As the world came into focus, he watched the sun rising high over the ocean beyond. Beautiful day. See? Exactly the beach vacation he needed.

Nat appeared in the doorway wearing nothing but his shirt, fresh from the dryer, and a pair of steaming mugs of joe in her hands. "About time you woke up."

"This hot chick wore me out in the wee hours of the morning. Freaking wildcat. I had trouble keeping up."

Flashing a wink at him, she sat on the side of the bed and handed him a cup with a healthy dollop of cream, much paler than her own pitiful splash. "One of the biggest problems with living in fear of discovery by hitmen? The lack of sex. Honestly, as I see no near end to my isolation, I should have jumped you sooner."

"Hey, you jumped me a year ago, then accused me of refusing seconds."

"As my avoiding you didn't keep you safe anyway, I should either have gone with it sooner or resisted better."

"Aw, so you only ignored my flirting to protect me? I'm touched." He grinned over the rim of the mug, earning himself a sharp whack on the arm. "Ow."

"I wasn't kidding about the bedpost notch issue. I already made one. Does the second time merit another notch or does each notch represent a different woman?"

"If it helps, as I don't usually entertain at my place, any notches being carved are not on my bed."

"Of course. You couldn't bail in the middle of the night from your place."

"Hey, of the two of us, which one has attempted the midnight hightail more? And last time, I held on for sunrise sex."

"Touché." She sipped her coffee, granting him a light smile.

He sat up higher in the bed, the sheets barely covering the good bits.

Nat's eyes lingered on his torso before rapidly shifting back to her coffee.

"We're equally stuck in seclusion. May as well enjoy our beach vacation together."

Her phone buzzed on the bedside table, building to an ear-piercing ringing. Picking it up, she said, "Please say you found Xander."

"No, but I have news," Dawson answered on the other end.

Nat's face morphed between disappointed and interested, tangled in indecision as flummoxing as this entire fucked-up situation.

"Your face all over the news? We tracked that down to a reporter at the BBC who released the initial story. No one seems to be able to tell where she got ahold of it."

"Great. So we have an antagonistic informant out there?"

"Actually, no." Long pause. "The reporter is the informant. We think anyway. Lillian Hemingway. No history prior to about a decade ago. Carries a trace of Albanian accent. I've got a friend over there, pulled her file. Good chance she was the victim of human trafficking herself. If word got out that you have information with the intent to make a profit? She fought back, no holds barred."

Nat visibly tightened at his side, her eyes glossy, jaw clenched tight. "Good for her. Let's finish this. It's gone on long enough. For her, for everyone else I was too late to save."

"Not your job. But you're making a difference anyway."

"Thanks for letting me know."

"Stay safe." Dawson's voice was as hoarse as Nat's.

"You too," she said, and hung up.

Staring at the phone, Nat held it out in her hands, motionless. Taking the phone, Aiden set it back on the bedside table and wrapped his arms around her. Letting it go, breaking down like he'd never seen, she sobbed against him.

Dammit, this is why he stuck to small town law. The world was a shitty place sometimes. To have something so major put in the hands of the jaded nineteen-year-old kid, only to have her discover her mistake as the beat-down adult, had been was so unfair. For one person to carry such a weight, so many lives in the balance.

Neither said a word. There was nothing to say. Nothing to make it okay. She needed to grieve; she'd held all this bottled up, alone, for so long.

As her shudders slowed against him, he rubbed his thumb over her cheek, drying away the last of the tears. "Come on," he said. "I'll make breakfast. Frozen pizza?"

She chuckled softly. "Sounds perfect."

"Shower first."

She never ceased to amaze him. She deserved that beach vacation more than he did. Or the Musée D'Orsay, as she preferred. He'd make it happen.

Fucking eh, McAllister. What are you doing?

Being a human, dammit.

Whichever way he mapped things out in his mind, he couldn't map out the next steps. There was this spunky blond with a heart of gold and an airtight soul that haunted his every waking thought.

And it terrified him. Soothed him. Tore him in half.

He turned on the shower to exactly the right balance of hot and cold and climbed inside. Following behind, Nat reached around his middle and added a degree of heat.

"I liked it that temperature," he muttered against the top of her head, refusing to let go.

"And I like it this temperature."

"You know? You're a total pain in my ass," he chuckled, holding her tight against him.

Sputtering as the water sprayed into her face, she shifted them, so the water puddled into the basin they'd made with their joined bodies. "I know."

A hot lump wedged in his throat as he tried to swallow.

Curled up on the couch, the slider open to the evening breeze, Natalie watched the fire dancing from the last of the embers in the oversized fireplace. It wasn't unbearably cold out, but if this was a vacation, as Aiden kept calling it, she was indulging on ambience. The man in question lie sprawled across the couch, head on the pillow, reading a J.A. Jance he'd found on her overburdened bookshelf.

Lying on the sofa opposite, with no brain for even light fiction from her library, Natalie's legs were tucked against his side while she read a cookbook. She'd never been a creative cook, but she'd always wanted to try. The cheesecake she'd made for Payson's birthday was pretty great. And Aiden had remembered. These didn't look too difficult. Maybe it was a result of living on frozen pizza for the last few days, but even that grilled asparagus wrapped in prosciutto looked amazing.

She kept intending to run. To separate the bullseye on her forehead from Aiden. Alone, he was less likely to be targeted. She'd make sure it was clear that he knew nothing. Somehow.

Yet, here she was. For now. Cuddled up with Aiden for the third night in a row. For a diehard commitment-phobe, he was a remarkably agreeable housemate. They took turns cooking, cleaning, laundry.

Not to mention, round the clock sex. That was a first for her. It had never been safe.

Aiden was insatiable. And she wasn't complaining. She had a lifetime of not-enough sex to catch up on.

After breakfast that morning, the strap to her tank top had slid off her shoulder. That's it. Nothing intentional, nothing major. His eyes had lingered on the teasing strap, finally glancing up and meeting her gaze.

In a blink, he'd closed the distance between them, and his hand cradling the back of her neck as he met her halfway. Skipping right past the testing kiss she had expected, his supple lips took hers. Equally hungry, despite the prior night of record-breaking sex, her mouth had opened for him. The velvety smooth heat of his tongue caressed hers with a knee-trembling passion.

Dizzy like she'd landed a perfect vault, elation buzzed every nerve in her body. Everywhere, she felt him, his hand gripping around her waist, his other sliding her jeans out of the way.

So, kitchen sex was a thing. She'd figured it was doable and potentially fun, but the physics of it had always haunted her. Well, now she knew it was a mind-blowing, orgasm-screaming adventure in creative positioning.

Now, snuggled on the couch, more relaxed than she'd ever allowed herself, she wanted him again.

Like the ice water splash she needed, her phone buzzed next to her. *Unknown number.*

Maybe it was a telemarketer? Scam?

She wasn't that lucky.

Holding her breath, she accepted the call. "Yes?"

"You're quite the photographer," a scratchy baritone gnawed through the airwaves. "Page fifteen. Lovely little lighthouse."

Aiden bolted up and moved close enough to hear.

Prickles crawled over her skin like a dozen spiders coating her with webs. *Peterson.* She'd heard him through the window that night and from various news reports detailing his career. Never had he been permitted to speak directly to her.

"What do you want?"

"Revenge. My life back. Your pretty blond head on a pike. Your mangled limbs scattered across the eastern seaboard. I'm sure you're familiar with the saying, 'you want something done, do it yourself?' You're a slippery one, and I'm sick of paying incompetents to find you." Prison hadn't improved his character. The impatience, the wet sneer she heard in his voice, was the result of a desperate man. "So you're going to come to me. The lighthouse. Six hours from... right... now."

"I already know you're crazy, but you're off your creepy-ass rocker if you think I'm coming to you. But I'll be happy to notify the authorities, though."

"Oh my, you are still the naïve child that stole from me all those years ago. You're not going to call anyone. You'll come alone. Unarmed. Or your brother is going to take a nasty spill."

Pulsating thunder pounded through her veins, a shrill ringing vibrating her ears until she could barely hear herself think. Her father had been right. With him out of the way, her family had become unprotected targets. It had been a flimsy hope that Xander had gone to ground. She hadn't dared let herself consider that Peterson already had him.

She didn't bother demanding her brother's safety, begging for his freedom, or pleading that he was innocent in this. "I need to know you haven't already hurt him."

"My bargaining chip? Of course not. Xander, say hello to your big sissy."

"Nattie?" Xander's voice was so different from when she'd seen him last, all those years ago. All grown up. Despite her efforts to stay away, exchanging nothing more than untraceable emails, she'd endangered him all the same. Harsh, the rumbling man's voice he'd grown into, he yelled into the phone, "Run. Don't trust him. Don't come—"

Peterson was back on the line. "As foolish as you. None so objectionable as dear old dad though. Showed his hand a wee bit early. Anyway, I digress. Come alone. Your life for his. Not to worry, we'll make it fun. Oh, and ditch the boyfriend, or he won't even make it out of the car."

The line went dead. Natalie stared at the blank screen, unsure of her next move. So many mistakes.

Cradling her jaw with both hands, Aiden wordlessly brought her gaze to his. "We can do this. Let's call Dawson. He'll back us up."

Shaking her head, she felt the panic surging, muddling her brain. "No. He said alone. I've screwed up so many times. I can't mess this up. Not for Xander."

"Shit, Nat. You work so damn hard to protect your family." Pressing his lips to her forehead, he pulled back and snagged Ronan's goodie bag. He pulled out a phone and turned it on for the first time. "We're not attempting this alone. We both have some creative shit on our records, but compared to rescuing hostages? This is way out of both of our skillsets."

"Maybe not." She wracked her brain, imagining the lighthouse, the grounds. "He mentioned the lighthouse. Aside from the public restrooms, the campground, there really isn't much else in the area. He mentioned Xander taking a 'nasty spill;' they'll be waiting in the lighthouse. Likely up top so he can watch the area."

"And he mentioned I won't even make it out of the car. He doesn't know where we are." He wiggled the phone. "First, we call Dawson. Not even Peterson knows Dawson's been in touch with you all this time."

She pulled the phone from his grip and dialed. All in one breath, she blasted the situation at Dawson.

He laughed, actually laughed. "You've never made my life easy. Okay. Give me directions to your cabin. Rogers and I can be there in five hours."

"No. You're not coming. I just wanted to let you know what's going on."

"And I appreciate the heads up. I'm not going to let anything happen to your brother, but I've also been working my ass off to keep *you* safe for a damn long time. Not about to ease up at crunch time."

After shooting off directions to the cabin, Natalie disconnected, feeling some of the weight on her chest easing already.

Aiden snatched the phone the moment she set it down. "My turn."

19

FIVE HOURS AND TWENTY-NINE minutes later, Aiden's lungs burned from the run down the beach. Nat slowed beside him. Turning back, he saw as she put her hands on her hips and paced back and forth in the gravelly sand.

Dressed in full black, a beanie covering her bright hair, she looked the part of the burglar she'd once been. Dawson and Rogers had come prepared. Dark clothes for them, and, tucked underneath, were bulletproof vests and wires.

"Around the next bend," she whispered, even though they were still out of earshot from the park.

"Already? That seemed way closer this time."

"That's because we were running, you dork."

Grinning, Aiden winked, "Really? I thought it was because of your cheerful company."

She snorted. "Do you ever get cranky?"

"Yeah, of course. Once last year when I caught my best friend messing around with my sister. And then when my coffee pot broke a few weeks ago. And worst of all, I did a few weeks ago when this gorgeous blond kissed my brains out and left me hanging and stole my car." He snagged her hand as she tried to pass him and trailed his fingers along the curve of her jaw. "It's almost over. Let's get it done."

Her lips turned up in a half smile as she nodded.

Climbing around the jetty of slick black-rock, still damp from the outgoing tide, the retired lighthouse came into view. Heavy shadows held the tower in silence, a salty gust stirring the sand at their feet.

Keeping to the rock wall, they stayed clear of any sightlines.

Aiden checked his watch. Fifteen minutes until their guest was expecting them.

From the parking lot, a late model pick-up truck with a noisy diesel engine came thundering into the parking lot. Headlights blasting, music blaring, a giddy, "Woo," howled from the driver's window.

Taking advantage of the prearranged diversion, Aiden and Nat closed the last hundred yards to the lighthouse.

Looking up at the whitewashed stone sides, he nearly scrapped the plan then and there. Not that he was afraid of heights, but Nat was freaking nuts to consider scaling it.

As he debated breaking it to her that it wasn't happening, she was already eight feet in the air, fingers digging into the narrow space between stones, toes wedged where there weren't obvious footholds.

Okay. Never mind. He'd been rock climbing once. In one of those indoor training gyms. With ropes and spotters.

Reaching as high as his arm would extend, he hooked his fingertips over a bulging hunk of stone. Easing up stone by stone, he followed her up the side of the tower.

Feeling a hint of panic brewing under his ribs, he forced his gaze up. *Don't look down. Don't do it man, just... don't.*

After a fucking lifetime of his not-so-uplifting mantra, they neared the base of the deck. About damn time.

Peeking up, Nat scanned their destination.

Glancing down at him, she nodded.

Was the nod, *all clear*, or *they're here*? They probably should have worked out the signals beforehand.

As she slipped over the rail, he presumed now that she'd meant the former. Hopefully.

He clamored up the last of the wall and over the rail. Empty. He checked his watch. Two minutes to go.

Nat slipped in through an open window into the room with the defunct light. He climbed in behind her. She nodded toward the wide opening in the floor, the access panel. Shuffling sounds below.

Leaning, he glanced down the ladder. A lanky blond kid, maybe eighteen or nineteen, was climbing up toward them. Below, a muttering wiseass criticized each step.

A true teen, Xander sniped back, "What, you didn't hit the weights in prison? Or were you too busy being somebody's bitch?"

Peterson's crackling voice snarled, "It's going to be close, choosing between you and your sister to take a nosedive onto the rocks first. And no one has ever pissed me off as much as that bitch."

Xander laughed out loud, an undisguised amusement Aiden had heard from Nat a handful of times. "Cute. You still think you're going to win. She already put you behind bars once."

Stepping back behind the bulky apparatus that used to guide distant ships, Aiden and Nat ducked out of sight. Aiden snuck around the edge, waiting just within reach of the opening in the floor.

Arms appearing, Xander grabbed the floor and pulled himself into the chamber.

Slinging one arm around him and covering his mouth with the other, Aiden yanked Xander backwards.

Eyes wild, Xander saw Nat and immediately stilled. Good kid, he didn't even yelp. Would have scared the shit out of Aiden.

While Aiden ensured his quarry was reassured and safe, Nat went after hers. Staying out of sight while Peterson climbed up the top, a bit gaunter than his photos before prison, his arms trembled from exertion as he climbed to the top.

Nicking the gun from Peterson's rear waistband, Nat chucked it out the window. Aiden flinched, thinking it might have come in handy. Too late. Not that either of them had ever touched a gun before, but Peterson didn't know that.

Nat slid back and stayed out of sight. She shook her head, letting Aiden know there was a landing beneath, don't push him down the opening. At least they'd worked out that signal beforehand.

Still talking, finding creative insults to throw at Xander, Peterson climbed from the doorway and rose to his feet. Glancing around, he discovered the upper tier to be empty.

Aiden leapt around the other side and pummeled his foot into Peterson's chest.

Peterson staggered, falling back against the open window.

Aiden hit the ground.

A loud crack resonated through the air. Peterson grabbed his side and slumped to the ground. "I thought I said come alone," he groaned.

Nat came out from behind the long-burned out light, illuminating its hollow darkness as she pulled off her hat. "I've been alone long enough because of you."

Feet thundered in the distance as the feds entered the structure below. Dawson's voice bounced off the lighthouse interior. "Everybody okay?"

Drawing another gun from under his jacket, Peterson shook his head. "Not a peep. Hear me?" Rising to his feet, gripping his other hand over the gunshot wound, Peterson winced as he cleared his throat. He sputtered and blood dripped down his chin.

He aimed right between Nat's eyes, a snarling smirk on his face. "You ruined me. Twice."

"How was Don involved?" Aiden blurted out. Arms up, chest open wide in invitation, he inched closer until the gun was aimed at him instead. Dumbass, but he didn't know what else to do.

Dawson and his cronies wouldn't be able to safely get to them. Nat's arms were raised, hovering just in front of Xander to protect him. A survivor like his sister, Xander scanned for an exit for them both.

Yeah, she was absolutely not a damsel, still trying to protect everyone else. And despite her best efforts at aloofness, she was loved.

"Don? You're worried about that imbecile? Just my financial advisor." He glared at Aiden for his stupid question.

"How about the news leak? Before anyone even knew Nat was going for the data?"

Smirking, Peterson shook his head, his skin clammy. Dying, but not soon enough. If he was lucky enough, maybe Peterson would bleed out before they had an issue. If he could just keep him talking. "My inspiration. I bought her twenty years ago for a pretty penny. Bitch turned on me the moment I turned my back."

The gun trembled in Peterson's weakening grip.

Sneering, he aimed the gun back to Nat.

Fuck. Red hot adrenaline pumped through his veins, fueling Aiden to attack, the thin thread of logic holding him back.

"Did you know?" he asked, tamping down his ire before anyone got shot.

Startled by the odd question, Peterson flinched, yet he kept the gun aimed at Nat. His finger twitched over the trigger.

"That she'd call in reinforcements? That she'd be waiting here for you? That you were too vain to think you'd get outsmarted by a teenager back then, and again by the same woman today?"

Huffing in irritation, Peterson loosened his finger on the trigger to retort back.

He'd seen enough movies. Just have to find their weakness. Play on it. Peterson's vanity had been obvious through the trial and in the news clips. His entire career, frankly.

As Peterson loosened his grip, shifting his attention fully to Aiden, Nat leapt across and kicked the gun from his hand.

Aiden dove closer and smashed his fist into Peterson's smug-ass face.

Falling straight backwards, Peterson's head hit the ground with a resounding crack.

Crumpled on the floor, Peterson's abdominal wound blackened the ground around him as it bled freely.

"Clear up here," he hollered down the ladder to Dawson.

A moment later, Dawson's head popped up through the opening. He scanned the room. Peterson's eyes fluttered, his body limp as his pathetic excuse for a life drained away.

Dawson cleared the threshold, Rogers following right behind. He pulled out his phone and checked Peterson's pulse. "Yeah, send a crew to retrieve Peterson's body... Yeah... Thanks."

Rogers nudged up her navy-blue baseball cap and nodded to Nat. "Glad to finally meet you. Imagine my surprise when we heard of Peterson's release, and Dawson mentioned he had a lead already. Let's get you out of here. Long night, huh?"

Nodding, Nat muttered, "Long eight years."

Dawson headed down first, then Rogers brought up the rear.

At the base of the ladder, Dawson hopped down and turned to Nat as she climbed down and stepped out of the way. Aiden watched from above as he came down behind her.

She looked at Dawson and sighed. Her smile was heavy, the weight of it tugging at Aiden.

As he neared the bottom step, Aiden heard a woman's voice, thick with a New York accent, like the hitman that had come after him in Seaview—now likely facing a lengthy stint in prison—spoke from the shadows, "Thanks for cleaning that mess up for me. This one's for R."
A moonlit sheen glinted off the gun.

"L? Why?" Nat hissed.

L tsked, "Peterson was ready to pay double for the data. None of his guys could find you, but no one else would know you like we did."

As L moved to shoot, Dawson spun and dove for Nat, knocking her to the ground.

Flashing against the dark, deafening, the gun fired.

Aiden launched off the ladder and knocked the gun away.

Cracking his elbow into her nose, he felt bone crunch.

Stumbling back, she roared.

From above, Rogers fired.

L crumpled to the ground.

Nat's frantic voice shook the air around them. "Dawson? Dawson? Don't you die on, me. This has been a shitty week, don't you dare make it worse."

Groaning, Dawson gripped his arm and sat up. "I'm not dying, dammit. Son of a bitch, this hurts," he muttered as he rose to his feet.

Rogers quickly scanned every shadow and finally radioed, "Lighthouse interior clear. Going to need two body bags and EMTs for a single non-fatal GSW—Dawson's been hit but he's conscious."

Lights flashing, local police flooded the park. Paramedics rushed to Dawson. Gripping his shoulder, he nodded to wave them off. "I can walk dammit." As they argued, he hobbled toward the waiting ambulance.

Checking her brother over, Nat scanned for injuries. Xander didn't push, but smiled and said, "I'm fine. Just pissed off. Are you okay?" He pulled his sister in for a hug and rocked her back and forth. Half his size, Nat wrapped her arms around her grown-up little brother and shuddered.

Aiden's limbs grew heavy as the adrenaline tapered off. He was toast. At the far end of the parking lot, subtly isolated from the chaos, he saw a 1964 and a half mustang parked and waiting.

A rush of desperate energy flooded his limbs as he sought his escape. He dashed closer to Nat and Xander. "Hey. Want to get out of here?"

Before Nat could respond, her mouth open to speak, Rogers approached, her brow scrunched apologetically under the baseball cap. "We've got a lot to talk about before you guys can duck out of here. Come on, we'll take you back to a safehouse. Get you back to your lives once we can be sure it's safe."

Nat stood with her arm wrapped around her brother, the protective big sister, while he rested his arm around her shoulder. Aiden wanted to snatch her, and her brother, from this mess and get the hell out of there.

But to what end? Take her back to Seaview? She didn't even live there anymore, had given up her apartment already. She'd want to be with her family, to get her life back.

Hell, he needed to get *his* life back. He was due in court on Wednesday.

As he stood stupidly on the sidewalk, a voice behind him interrupted his useless indecision. "Excuse me." He backed up a step. A pair of police officers brushed past him.

Nat hesitated, keeping her arm linked around her brother. The other seemed to reach for Aiden, but she ran her fingers through her hair instead, as if that was her intent all along.

Turning to Rogers, he asked, "Can I decline the safehouse? I've got to get back to work, but I'll stay available for whatever you need. I'll have more than adequate protection while you get this wrapped up, not to worry on that end of things."

She looked around at the body bags being wheeled out with Peterson and Nat's former boss. "If that's your decision. Be safe, but I think the worst of it is over. Most of Peterson's associates are either turning on him or hiding to save their own asses. Although, I can't recommend it until we find the shooter that took down Peterson."

Finding his first genuine smile in hours, Aiden shrugged. "I'm not too worried on that one."

He stole one last look at Nat. Her expression unreadable, she smiled and held her grip on Xander's arm. They'd be okay.

Pulling his watchman's cap off, he stuffed it in his pocket as he strolled across the parking lot. Sliding into the passenger seat of the old Mustang, Aiden turned to his brother. "Nice shot," he said as he melted into the seat.

"Thanks for lining up my shot. Next time, stay down until he's dead." Ronan turned the key, the engine roaring, then calming to a soothing purr that vibrated through Aiden's jello'd limbs.

20

MONDAY CAME AND WENT. Then Tuesday. Wednesday.

Pouring himself into work, Aiden didn't dare close his eyes unless he was too tired to dream. Occasional flashbacks of being chased shattered his dreams, but, most often, visions of a sexy blond with a badass attitude and a diehard spirit occupied his thoughts, awake or asleep.

By Friday night, he was out of work to do. Even his pens were aligned by how much ink remained. Ev had denied his request to steal some of his cases back from her, claiming he looked like hell and needed a real vacation now. Bossy pest.

At ten minutes until seven, he shut off his computer and dragged himself upstairs. Kicking off his shoes, he flopped on the couch and flipped on the tv. BBC reporter Lillian Hemingway delivered a gripping story about the final connections in closing down the remains of the human trafficking ring Peterson had led. With Nat's picture once again making headlines, Hemingway relayed her gratitude toward the woman previously and mistakenly accused of aiding Peterson, hailing her as an international hero.

Good. Maybe Nat could find peace, knowing her efforts were appreciated.

A knock on his apartment door could have startled him. But he was expecting his babysitter. Ronan took most nights, but Maddy and Chase took turns as well. Honestly, he wasn't sure if they were keeping him safe from any lingering goons of Peterson's, or from himself.

Ronan tossed his backpack under the entry table and dropped onto the opposite couch. "Time to shave that beard. Trust me, you can't hide behind it."

Rubbing his hand over the rough scruff on his face, Aiden cringed. Yeah, Judge Meyers would have his hide if he came to court looking like a vagrant. "When did you start knocking?"

"Figured you'd appreciate the heads up, knowing I'm not some hitman sneaking in to kill you."

"Appreciate it. The investigation should be wrapping up soon. Dawson called me this afternoon. Says he hasn't been able to find any whisper of any threats against Nat or me. Also says his arm hurts like hell and he's leaving that bullshit job now that he doesn't have a smartass burglar to look after."

"You trying to ditch out on our sleepover? I brought homemade cookies and popcorn and thought we'd see what's on Netflix." Ronan settled into the couch and plopped his feet up on the coffee table.

"Thought maybe you missed snuggling with your wife."

"She hired a full-time employee—someone to watch the shop when the baby comes. So not to worry, I'll get quality time all day tomorrow."

"You're a sap," Aiden accused his brother, watching as he grinned to himself. Aiden still couldn't get used to his brother's easygoing attitude.

"And you're not? Try telling me you haven't thought about tracking her down." Smug-ass grin.

Groaning, Aiden hopped up from the couch and snagged a pair of beers from the fridge. Popping the tops, he passed one to Ronan and dropped back onto his couch. He picked up the remote and changed over to Netflix. "I confess, I know what's going on in my heart and my dick... for once they're on the same page, but my brain is freaking out."

"Then go after her. Tell her you're having a breakdown and need her to make you function again." Ronan took a swig of his beer and fluffed the pillow behind his head.

"What if... shit, this is going to sound lame. She didn't exactly look like she wanted me to stick around. Didn't exactly seem upset that I chose to leave."

"Wow, you are full of shit. Natalie's adept at hiding her emotions to protect herself. Her dad's been arrested, her brother nearly killed because of her, plus, from what you described, her mother doesn't know her at all and never has. A lonely childhood followed by an isolated adulthood. Now, *you* don't even have the guts to fight for her."

"Pretty low, man."

"Listen to your heart and your dick and tell your head to shut the fuck up." Ronan reached across the coffee table and stole the remote.

"Did you have to drop your classes?" Natalie leaned back on the couch and put her feet up on the ottoman, chatting with her brother over the phone, simply because they could. It had been a rough couple of weeks, talking to so damn many feds her brain hurt. When they released her, she took off straight for the cabin, needing the solitude.

High in the sky, the sun rose over the horizon, orange rays blazing into her eyes and tormenting her like a nagging mother. Not that her mother was nagging her in the least anymore. She was more of a blubbering apologetic mess.

Xander cleared his throat, and she could picture the little boy with his wild hair standing on end, but the deep voice of the man he'd grown into still threw her. She'd missed so much. "Nah. My professors were remarkably understanding about the whole abductee-hostage bit. I got an extension on all my assignments. It's just summer school, so the class sizes are small anyway."

"I'm glad to hear it. At the rate you're going, you'll have your doctorate in no time."

"Only if I keep getting that mysterious scholarship I never applied for. Amazing stuff, luck. Didn't think I had a lick of it, but, what do you know? Full ride."

"Huh. Guess it was just your turn for some good luck." Wincing, she didn't want any lies between them, but needed to do this for him.

"Nattie? You've been through too damn much. Spend it on yourself. I'll get by. With all of Dad's accounts frozen, I'll probably qualify for financial aid."

She debated denying it all, but there had been enough untruths in her family. A fresh start was exactly what they needed. "I've got plenty. Let me do this for you. Plus, I'm going to use my fifteen minutes of undeserved fame to hawk my book up and down tourist shops along the coast."

"Then I'll pay you back. Every penny."

"No you won't. I put you through enough hell."

"Cut it out. You've lived through enough hell alone. What are you doing right now? Hiding again when you don't even need to?"

"Of course not."

"Where are you?"

"In my cabin."

"What happened to that guy you were with?"

"What do you mean?" Okay, so frank honesty wasn't necessary in any family.

"The one that looked super bummed when you pretty much told him you didn't care if he stayed or left? After he'd risked his life for both of us?"

"Aiden?"

"Sure. Come on, you both looked like heartbroken little puppies when he left."

Rolling her eyes, she crossed and uncrossed her feet. "Hey, just because we get to talk regularly now does not mean you get to rag me about my love life. Mom's does that enough for an entire army."

Xander laughed out loud, clearly having heard the same pressuring relationship advice on a regular basis. "True that. Fine. I won't pester. Just... that Dawson guy seems to think you don't need to hide anymore. Try to live a little, huh?"

"Sure. Any day now." She laughed as they ended the call. Despite the eight-year age gap between them, they'd always been good buddies. Even when their communication was limited to rare emails, she'd ensured he knew she was here for him. Wherever that may be.

Hauling herself off the couch, she stepped into the morning sun. Going home to Seaview sounded amazing. She already missed the easy rhythm of the locals, the vacation-buzzed tourists, her friends that dragged her out despite her insistence that she didn't socialize… and Aiden.

Now he was a mess she didn't need.

She didn't need to hide anymore, so she could date anyone she wanted.

Aiden didn't date. He did as he chose. And who he chose. And he'd had her plenty. In Aiden's world, spending much more time with her in a sex-sense, or, dare she even consider, sharing their feelings some more, and they'd be in a dreaded *relationship*.

She wasn't used to sharing her feelings. Or her personal space. He was just… convenient.

Okay. She was an adult. He was an adult. They could coexist in the same town, with the same friends, without weirdness.

Exhaling the last of the morning air, she closed the slider and locked the door. Tossing the sheets back over the furniture, setting the thermostat and alarm to *Away*, she closed up the cabin. In the driveway, she grinned as she adjusted her backpack on her shoulder. Parked in the driveway was her brand spankin' new BMW she'd traded the Corvette in for—and used some of her savings for pure selfishness.

Hopping in the driver's seat, she started the engine, the purr sending a tingling thrill through her veins. Shifting into gear, she lowered her aviator glasses over her eyes and headed south. Home.

The shadows had grown long by the time she pulled in the drive. Town was still hopping, but only a dim glow illuminated the window in question. Blinds closed, she couldn't spy on her target.

Sauntering to the front door, she pushed down the nervousness. Her hand reached for the bell, then she changed her mind.

Slipping the lock open, she silently closed the door behind her. A soft beep indicated the alarm was set. Smart man. Things were looking safe, but it would be years before either of them should relax.

She disabled the alarm within the thirty second window. As nice of an alarm as this was, he'd need to upgrade if even a rusty burglar could so easily disengage it. Of course, it was the same code he used for his phone. Keeping her steps light, she cautiously pushed open the office door.

Eyes at half mast, his chestnut hair in wild disarray, white t-shirt as rumpled as his hair, Aiden sat scowling at his computer screen. When he noticed her, his breath caught, his brow relaxed, but his eyes hazed over like she was an apparition.

Without a word, she crossed to him.

Strutting toward him with unabashed confidence, not saying a word, Nat peeled her tank top over her head. Her jeans followed, bra, panties, all scattered across his office. He didn't dare move, fearing her a mirage, and he near-fatally dehydrated, lost in the desert.

When she reached him, she straddled him, arms loosely draped over his shoulders. She lowered her mouth to his, the savory warmth teasing his lips to open.

Without hesitation, he kissed her back, pouring everything into the moment. Wrapping his hands around her waist, grazing his fingertips over her back, he spun a trail of goosebumps over her smooth skin.

Touching every scrap of his exposed skin, his arms, his jaw, she slid her hands down and tugged up the edge of his shirt. Pulling it over his head, she threw it behind her. As she explored his torso with her hands, teasing her fingertips along the waistband of his jeans.

Kissing her again, unable to resist, his hands explored, grasping her breasts in his hands.

Breaking the silence, a soprano gasp burst from her throat at his touch.

Trailing kisses along her neck, her shoulder, her breasts, he came alive.

Her clever fingers had his zipper undone in half a second.

Warm honey over silk, she glided against him. Rock hard and ready to come on contact, he stilled her hips and looked her in the eye.

Biting her lip, her breath held. Her gaze was steady, fearless, hazel eyes mysterious but unwavering. Gripping her hips, he shifted her over him.

Lowering over his cock, she moaned as he slid inside. Smooth heat, tightening around him, she felt so fucking amazing.

Rocking atop him, hips moving in rhythm with him, she pulled him with her. Where, he couldn't say, but he was right there with her.

As they moved together, ever more frantic as the energy pulsed between them, her moans became desperate, determined. Watching her take him, boldly, he fell deeper.

At last, when each had reached their release, she rested her forehead against his. She cradled his jaw in her hand, traced her thumb over his lips. "Aiden? That was an appetizer."

From deep in his gut, laughter erupted and he wrapped his arms around her middle, kissing her long and slow. "About fucking time you showed. I was about to call the FBI to find you."

She pressed her lips to his and pulled away again. "I may have been hiding from you."

"Before you? I had this great life. Everything was exactly the way I wanted it. Great job, great family. Love my house and my hometown." He trailed kisses along her bare shoulder, wanting her again already.

"And then, here comes this mysterious woman I can't get out of my head. I thought a night with her would be enough, but it wasn't. Then I figured I'd think of her less often, but even after a year, she still ruled every fantasy in my imagination. And I realized, I was lonely. I worked my ass off to keep her out of my mind, knowing she was it for me."

His fingertips graced the line of her collarbone, trailing down between her breasts. The corner of his mouth quirked up as he met her eyes again.

"Nat, you broke something inside me that needed a major overhaul. In a good way. I…" He shook his head, surprised even by his own words. "I can live without you. But I'd rather live with you. Watch you scowl every morning as the sun shines through the blinds. See as you strut into the shower with that exceptionally fine ass. Bring me coffee in bed. Then maybe I'll make you frozen pizza for breakfast. We can put our feet up and read all day while the world buzzes around us."

Inhaling deeply, her chest rising and falling, she said, "Maybe I'll take you on a vacation first. A sunny beach with tropical fruity drinks."

"Make it the Mediterranean so we can tour a few museums while we're at it."

She pressed her lips to his, tugging his bottom lip between her teeth before releasing him again. "I will never ask you come to my pap smear, or fake a pregnancy, or—"

"Hold on a minute." He couldn't keep his hands off her skin, his hand sprawled over her back. "You already left me for another guy—"

"What?"

"Two, actually. Dawson and Xander are good guys, but you still left me. Your mother has called me twice in the last week, asking when I'm going to propose—"

"She didn't."

"Oh, she did. Your father tried to kill me. Do I need to go on?"

"No, please don't."

He grinned. "I love you. Since the moment you snubbed me at Winter's that first night we met, I was a goner. You flipped my world upside down. And I'm finding I like it better like this."

"McAllister? You're crazy."

"I know. But I'm not alone."

She kissed him, rocking atop him until he was hard again. She tugged his ear in her teeth, then whispered, "I love you too. Always have."

"Say you always will?"

"And I always will."

Grinning, he pressed his lips to hers, needing her again. All of her, whatever she was willing to share. And knew he would again tomorrow. And the next day. And all the rest.

The End

Carrie Thorne is the author of kick-ass romance novels, specializing in white-hot chemistry, healthy relationships, and a mix of action and dreamily falling in love. Whether it's a sinuous flow down a lazy river or evil bad dudes hot on heels, Carrie's stories will draw you in and ruin your sleep. Happily ever afters are for everyone, and kindness is everything.

She's also an introvert who loves people, travel, fitness, video games, food, and is a true Pacific Northwesterner who lives for rain and outdoors and trees and mountains and ocean, and... she's a total dork. At home, she's lucky to have two creative and confident kids, a witty veteran husband she fell at-first-sight for, and a tiny pup snuggled at her side. In addition to writing romance, Carrie has been a nurse practitioner, a Martian and Earthling geologist, a banker, and she is usually elbow-deep in a DIY project in which she bit off more than she could chew.

Where is she now? Depends on the weather. Cozied up by the fire with a steaming mug of black coffee, or stretched out on the hammock with a frothy IPA in the shade of her forest. Either way, she's working on the next great love story to conquer your TBR list.

www.CarrieThorne.com